LOVE IS ALL

The Scottish novelist Joan Fallon, currently lives and works in the south of Spain. She writes both literary and historical fiction, and almost all her books have a strong female protagonist. She is the author of:

HISTORICAL FICTION:
Spanish Lavender
The House on the Beach
The Only Blue Door
The al-Andalus series:
The Shining City (Book 1)
The Eye of the Falcon (Book 2)
The Ring of Flames (Book 3)

LITERARY FICTION:
Loving Harry
Santiago Tales
Palette of Secrets
The Thread That Binds Us

NON-FICTION:
Daughters of Spain

(all are available in paperback and as ebooks)

www.joanfallon.co.uk

JOAN FALLON

LOVE IS ALL

Scott Publishing

ISBN 978 0 9955834 4 3
First published in 2018
Scott Publishing
Windsor, England

LOVE IS ALL

PART 1

CHAPTER 1

The front door banged behind her, the sound reverberating through the house. By the time she reached the car she was soaked: her wet hair lay flat against her head, raindrops running off it and down her face, mingling with her tears. She pulled the car door open and got in, careless of the water dripping from her coat. She switched on the ignition and slammed the car into gear; the powerful engine pulled away instantly and bore her down the drive, through the iron gates that always stood open, the grass tall and thick around their base, and onto the main road. Without more than a cursory look for traffic—more from habit than diligence—she turned left and headed north. The rain had emptied the streets, confining people to the shelter of their homes; yellow street lamps cast regular pools of light along the deserted pavements. It was raining heavier now and the windscreen wipers struggled to cope with the torrent of water cascading down the glass. The headlights sent a stream of light onto the empty road ahead, the occasional puddles, dark, irregular shapes. Teresa was oblivious to it all. She drove like an automaton, like someone in a dream, unable to see for her own tears.

How could he have done this to her after twenty-five years of marriage? And after all they'd been through together? She couldn't believe it. The man she was married to had been deceiving her for years, and worse than that, with her best friend. A double betrayal. She'd known Michelle since she was fourteen, longer even than she'd known Mark. She was her closest friend. Until Teresa had married Mark they'd been inseparable: first school, then college, even getting their first jobs with the same company.

The junction loomed ahead of her, and without bothering to change down, she pulled across into the main stream of traffic. It was late evening and commuters were still battling their way home. She had no idea where she was going, hadn't even considered it. All she knew was that she had to get away from him and his lies. She couldn't stay in the house a moment longer, listening to Mark's confession, looking at his tears and wondering why he was telling her all this. What did he want? Forgiveness? Why now? She'd forgiven him once before—at least that was what she'd told him but her heart couldn't forget so easily. Now here he was again, saying how sorry he was, that it really wasn't his fault, that he wanted her to understand that. Once again it would be forgiveness at her expense. Once again he had turned her life upside down. She'd known nothing about their affair, suspected nothing; her life could have continued unaffected if he hadn't been troubled by a guilty conscience. She felt a surge of anger, and her foot pressed down harder on the accelerator. He had taken her son from her and now he'd taken her best friend and destroyed their marriage. What more did he expect from her? Did he think he could confess his sins and all would be forgiven? Well, he could confess all he wanted to; she was no priest and she would never forgive him. For any of it. Never.

An articulated lorry overtook her, its gigantic form obliterating her view and spraying the car with dirty water; for a moment she was blinded. Instinctively she slowed slightly, letting the lorry pull ahead and removing herself from its slipstream. The windscreen wipers were at maximum, but they still had difficulty keeping pace with the lashing rain.

Michelle? She'd never suspected it for a moment. For years they'd been such good friends. Michelle had loved the children—she was godmother to all of them. Why hadn't Teresa realised what was going on? It had all seemed so natural: Michelle staying overnight, Michelle babysitting, Michelle coming on holiday with them; they were all used to Michelle's presence. Teresa had never asked herself why Michelle hadn't married, why she didn't even have a boyfriend; she had never wondered why Michelle preferred to spend so much time with Teresa's family. Now it was becoming clearer, and the clearer it became, so the rage inside her grew until she thought it would overwhelm her. She thumped the steering wheel in her frustration and a sharp beep from the horn startled her back into the present.

The rain was a torrent now, bouncing back off the road surface under its own momentum, sparkling rods of water shooting up from the ground. The drumming sound it made on the roof was hypnotic, making it hard for her to think clearly. A large blue and white sign signalled the approaching motorway; she flicked the indicator and entered the slip road.

So now what? No husband and no Michelle. He said he didn't want to leave her; he said he didn't love Michelle. He loved *her*. It had just been a fling, he said; it hadn't meant anything. This enraged her even more. If he had been in love she might have forgiven him; after all Michelle was very easy to love. Teresa had loved her for years; her sons loved her; even Teresa's mother loved her. But he had thrown away their marriage for a stupid *fling*. And what about their sons? They'd be devastated, forced to take sides, their lives turned upside down. She couldn't believe this was happening; she wiped her eyes with the back of her sleeve; her stomach was churning with agitation and there was a burning sensation at the back of her throat. She accelerated once more, increasing the speed to ninety. They were not going to get away with it. They had treated her like a fool. Her mobile was ringing. Mark? She was going to ignore it but she felt so angry with him she picked it up and accepted the call. She would tell him it was over. She was leaving him. What was the point of going on? Their marriage had never been the same since Peter died, anyway. How could she love the man who was responsible for her son's death?

One moment the car was cutting through the night as smooth as silk, the next it was spinning and turning, aquaplaning across the wet road surface. She dropped her mobile and wrenched at the wheel with both hands, pulling it back to the left, but the force of the skid was too much for her and the steering wheel resisted her efforts. She was sliding sideways, unable to stop. She braked hard, but that only flung the car into a greater spin. She was heading for the central crash barrier. A bright light was bearing down on her, closer and closer. She could hear the discordant blare of a car-horn. Suddenly there was an enormous cracking sound and the clash of metal hitting metal. The air was filled with splintering glass. The car lifted up, defying gravity and turned over and over. She was suspended in space, an acrobat of the night. The car was turning slow motion somersaults. It was quiet now. Unreal. Time had stopped. Suddenly she was falling into the darkness. A searing pain sliced through her body as the car came to rest on top of the crash barrier. Then there was nothing.

CHAPTER 2

Mark had been stunned at her reaction. They'd been getting on so much better lately, that's why he thought it was the time to confess, to get it all off his conscience. He thought she'd understand. How badly he'd judged that. He should have known better. He should never have told her about Michelle.

It was so like Teresa to over-react. That Irish temper of hers made her fly off the handle so readily. If only she'd waited to hear him out. But no, not Teresa. He could see her again, tossing her black hair in rage, her eyes flashing green with anger. He'd tried to say he was sorry, making some feeble excuses for his unacceptable behaviour, but she hadn't wanted to listen; she'd raged like a mad woman, sweeping the supper dishes off the table, hurling her half-empty wine glass at him, screaming abuse.

After she'd run out, shouting that she never wanted to see either of them again, he'd tried ringing her mobile, but she didn't pick up. Well so much for trying to be open and honest with her. He should have known she'd take it badly. And at the back of his mind was this niggling worry that although all this rage was turned against him, she was probably more upset about Michelle betraying her than her own husband.

*

The police had contacted him at once; they'd got the address from Teresa's handbag. He had it with him now. They said he might as well look after it. He picked it up and stroked the soft leather: it was a plain black sack, with some shiny metal bits, and a fancy Italian name. He'd bought it for Teresa the year before. She took it everywhere with her. He gave a sad smile; even in her anger Teresa wouldn't leave the house without her handbag. A tear rolled down his nose and landed on the bag. The policemen had been very kind; one of them had made him a cup of tea, then the other suggested they take him to the hospital in the police car. They told him that an ambulance had taken her directly to St James Hospital, the major trauma hospital for the area.

He didn't remember very much about the journey; his mind had frozen, fixed in a state of shock at the news. The police dropped him off at the entrance to the Accident and Emergency unit and as he walked through the glass doors, he saw her. She was still on the stretcher where the paramedics had left her, strapped to a back-board and wearing a neck restraint; an oxygen mask covered her face and a saline drip hung from her arm. Someone had wrapped temporary dressings round her leg. The remains of her coat trailed below the hospital blanket that covered her; it was dirty and stained with blood. He hurried towards her but as he approached, a nurse started to wheel the stretcher away.

'Stop. Stop. That's my wife,' he cried, over-loudly. 'Where are you taking her?'

'Mr Rushton? I'm sorry, but we need to clean your wife up. She's got to have a CT scan so we can assess the damage to her head.'

'I want to stay with her.'

'I'm sorry sir, it's really not possible. Why don't you go over there,' she pointed to the A and E admissions desk, 'and give the nurse your wife's details. That would be a great help.'

Mark clutched at the stretcher in desperation; he was frightened that if he let go he would never see his wife again. He couldn't drag his eyes away from her body. It made him feel sick to see her like that and yet he couldn't bring himself to touch her. His eyes ached from staring at her; maybe if he stared hard enough it would all prove to be an illusion and they'd both wake up. They'd be back in their own home. Teresa would be making the dinner and telling him about her day and he'd be opening a bottle of her favourite wine.

He looked up. The nurse was saying something. 'Sorry?'

'Just wait here, Mr Rushton. I'll let you know how we've got on, once we have your wife stable.' She smiled at him, kindly.

She was a young woman, who, despite the fraught atmosphere in which she worked, seemed able to maintain a calm, almost serene, composure. Only the premature lines across her forehead suggested that she'd been working in A and E too long. She gently prised his fingers from the stretcher, and pushed Teresa away, towards the lifts.

'Mr Rushton.' The woman at the desk was calling him. 'Mr Rushton, would you mind giving me your wife's date of birth?'

He felt he was moving through water, every step heavy and slow; he was aware of everything around him yet nothing seemed real. He answered the woman's questions one by one, some automatic response taking control of him.

'Fine, that's all I need for now. Thank you Mr Rushton. Now if you'd like to take a seat over there, someone will come and tell you when you can go up to see your wife.'

She took the consent form he'd just signed and put it on a pile of similar papers. Mark didn't move. He watched as she turned back to her computer and began to type. She must see people like him every day. It meant nothing to her. She would continue with her mundane job while his world lay in ruins.

'There's a coffee machine down the hall, if you'd like some coffee,' she suggested, looking up at him.

'No, thank you. I'm fine,' he replied. 'I'll just sit here and wait.'

It wasn't her fault. She couldn't know the pain he was feeling. He chose a seat that gave him a clear view of the passage; he didn't want to miss Teresa when they brought her back. He leant against the wall. This was all his fault; he had done this to his wife.

A tall woman rushed into the waiting room, shaking raindrops from her umbrella as she struggled to close it. Mark didn't look up at her; he continued picking at the stuffing that protruded from a slash in the plastic covered chair.

'Mark, darling. I'm so sorry. This is awful. I just had to come to see how she was. So how is Teresa? Do you know what happened yet?' The woman stopped, waiting for him to break the awkward silence that was lengthening by the minute.

'Michelle, what are you doing here?' he asked at last. He looked anxiously around him. He didn't want anyone to know that the first thing he'd done when Teresa had stormed out of the house, was ring Michelle. She'd come straight round, just as he knew she would. She'd still been there, in the house, when the police arrived with the news, although they hadn't been aware of her.

'I've come to see how Teresa is, of course.'

'She's unconscious. But she's alive. They haven't told me anything else yet,' he replied in a monotone.

'Oh, thank goodness. My poor Darling, you look terrible,' the woman said, attempting to put her arm around his shoulders.

Mark sprang to his feet. 'Don't touch me,' he snapped.

Michelle stopped, her mouth dropped open in surprise. 'But sweetheart, I just wanted to comfort you,' she explained.

He looked at her coldly. 'Maybe you should come back later, Michelle. There's nothing you can do now. We won't know anything for ages.' He saw the tears well up in her eyes and added, more gently, 'I'll telephone you when there's some news.'

'What about Teresa's mother? Does she know?'

'Yes. It's all in hand. You go. I'll ring you later,' he repeated.

'Okay, if you're sure that's what you want.' She seemed uncertain whether to believe him.

'Yes, it is what I want.'

There was no mistaking his tone of voice this time, so she picked up the umbrella. But still she didn't leave.

She stood there, smoothing the skirt of her coat and pushing some strands of blond hair back into place.

Mark knew she wanted him to relent. He knew she was suffering as much as he was but he continued to stare at the black and white tiles at his feet.

'Well, just 'phone me if you need anything,' she said at last. 'Promise.'

'Yes, okay. Now go.'

As soon as she turned away, he slumped down in the chair and buried his head in his hands. He could hear her high heels clicking rhythmically on the hard, hospital tiles as she left.

Mark couldn't stop thinking about how angry Teresa had been when he'd tried to tell her about him and Michelle. She didn't even let him explain that it was all over, had been for months. Her rage had just wiped all reason from her mind. He should have restrained her, stopped her from taking the car; he knew how her temper could consume her, making her do things she'd later regret. But he'd done nothing to hold her back, neither by his words not his actions. He had let her go. Then, when it was far too late, he'd phoned her mobile. Was that what triggered the accident? Had that been his fault, too? The police said her mobile was open on the seat beside her. Had she reached for it and then spun out of control? He put his head in his hands. He couldn't bear any more of this.

'Mark.'

He looked up. An elderly woman, with short, white hair that lay close to her head in well cut layers, and eyes the colour of cornflowers, stood before him.

'Bridget.'

He stood up and took the woman into his arms; her frail body was shaking with sobs. He could feel her fragile bones protruding under her raincoat and he held her until the sobbing ceased, then sat her down in a chair next to his own.

'Where's Teresa? Is she alright? What happened? I don't understand. Where was she going at that time of night?'

His mother-in-law's questions poured out one after the other. He waited for her to calm down before answering, 'Teresa's unconscious; they've taken her for a scan to see if there's any brain damage.'

'Oh, my God. Oh, Jesus, Mary and Joseph. My poor baby. Oh no.' The woman's crying began again. 'No.'

'Bridget, we must try to be calm. We'll know soon how she is. At least she's alive,' he added, taking out a paper tissue and wiping his mother-in-law's face gently. Somehow caring for her made it easier to cope with his own distress.

Bridget took a deep breath and struggling to control herself, took her son-in-law's hand in her own. 'Where are the boys?' she asked.

'Well it will take them a while to get here, you know. Alex's in Brighton at a conference and Ian is working in Edinburgh at the moment. I telephoned Alex as soon as I heard and he said he would let everybody know.'

'Yes, he telephoned me right away. I'd just gone to bed. He said not to bother coming over tonight; he said come over tomorrow, when they would know more. But I knew I wouldn't sleep until I'd seen her. I just had to come. So I walked down to the corner and got a taxi. I couldn't face driving; I haven't stopped shaking since I heard.'

Mark noticed that her hands were trembling as she spoke. He stroked the back of her hand, trying to comfort her; the skin was smooth and fine, slightly brittle, like paper, and its paleness was broken by a scattering of dark stains—age spots she called them. Her nails had been carefully shaped and filed into perfect ovals and painted with a pale pink polish. She wore no adornments, only her wedding ring, now worn to a thin band with the passing of time.

'How long were you and Patrick married?' he asked, his fingers touching the ring lightly.

She looked at him in surprise. 'Fifty years,' she said, 'actually it was nearly fifty-one, when he died.'

She didn't ask him why he wanted to know; she knew he was thinking of himself and Teresa. They sat, side by side, not talking, each lost in their own thoughts. Mark looked at his watch; it was almost ten o'clock. He'd been there less than an hour and yet it seemed like days.

'I think I saw Michelle leaving just as I arrived,' Bridget said, suddenly.

'Oh, yes. Alex must have 'phoned her. I told her not to stay; I said we'd ring when there was some news.'

Bridget looked at him, her pale blue eyes swimming with tears. 'You haven't told me what happened,' she said.

'Well, I'm not sure I know for certain. The police said that when they spoke to the lorry driver he said that she skidded and went out of control; he tried to slow down and avoid her, but the car just kept coming towards him. He said it all happened so fast that there was nothing he could do; he hit the side of the car full on.'

His mother-in-law gave a low moan. 'Oh my poor Teresa.'

'Then the car turned a few somersaults and landed upside down on the central reservation.' Describing the accident aloud was painful, but he couldn't stop; he could leave out no detail. 'The fire brigade had to cut her out.' He stopped, then added, 'The police said she wasn't wearing her seat belt.'

'What? No. I don't believe that. Teresa always wore a seatbelt. She was fanatical about it. My daughter was a very conscientious driver; there's no way she would have been driving on the motorway without a seatbelt.'

'That's what they said.' Mark had found that strange, as well. Bridget was right. Teresa even buckled her seat-belt before she backed out of the garage. If she drove without one, it meant one of two things: she'd been so upset she didn't realise she hadn't put it on, or—and this he wasn't going to say out loud to anyone—he'd hurt her so much she wanted to die.

Bridget's grip on his hand had tightened with each new revelation, until now he could feel her nails cutting into his flesh. 'Was anyone else hurt?'

'Only the lorry driver; he had a broken collar bone. There wasn't actually a lot of traffic, according to the police. That's why they found it a bit strange; they think she may have been driving too fast for the wet conditions and lost control.' He didn't tell her that they'd asked if Teresa had been drinking, nor that they said they found her mobile open on the seat beside her.

'I have always thought that Teresa was a very careful driver. It would surprise me if she was driving too fast in bad weather. And with no seatbelt. No, I can't believe it. It's so out of character. Something must have upset her.'

'Well, we don't know that she was driving too fast; it's only an assumption. We'll ask her as soon as she's better,' he said in a vain attempt to sound positive.

'God willing,' she murmured.

He squeezed her hand gently.

'Have you seen her yet?' Bridget asked, her voice barely audible, as though she didn't really want to hear his reply.

'I saw her being wheeled down for her scan.' He saw his mother-in-law's pleading look. 'She didn't look too bad. She had some cuts to her leg and some minor abrasions to her face.'

'Oh, good. She's such a pretty girl; she wouldn't like her face to be scarred.' Her mother smiled sadly to herself.

*

Time seemed to pass very slowly as they sat together, their closeness giving them some combined strength to face the ordeal. In the stark neon light of the waiting room his mother-in-law's face looked old and tired; Mark thought how her outward frailty belied her inner strength. He remembered how well she had coped when his father-in-law died, only a few years previously.

'Here's the nurse coming, now,' he said. The same young woman that had wheeled Teresa away was walking along the corridor towards them. He stood up.

'Mr Rushton, you can come and see your wife now, but just for a moment,' she said. She looked tired and her face was drawn, but she smiled cheerfully at him.

'How is she? What did the scan show? Is she alright?' Mark was desperate for some kind of answer.

'We've moved her into Intensive Trauma for the night. We'll know more tomorrow when the neurologist has a look at her.'

Intensive Trauma. That sounded serious. 'Does that mean she might die?'

'She has to be under close observation until we know the full extent of the damage.'

She looked across at Bridget.

'Oh, sorry. This is my wife's mother,' Mark said, putting his hand on Bridget's shoulder.

The nurse smiled at Bridget and said, 'Well you come along as well. But I'm afraid you won't be allowed to stay very long.'

They followed the nurse along the corridor; her rubber soled shoes moved silently across the gleaming floor. Mark hated hospitals; he hated the pervading smell of antiseptic; he hated the preponderance of stainless steel vessels and cold hard surfaces; and he hated the filtered and warm air that seemed to stifle him. But today he was grateful to be there, because this hospital was going to care for Teresa, make her well and send her home to him. Then he would make it up to her; he would show her how much he really loved her.

They took the lift to the fifth floor, where the IC unit was located. The nurse indicated that they should wait outside, while she went in to check on the patient. A moment later she returned.

'Only one of you can go in at a time. Maybe you'd like to go first, Mr Rushton, then your mother-in-law can go next,' she suggested.

Bridget nodded meekly and sat by the door. Mark followed the nurse into the room. He felt unbelievably nervous; his hands trembled and he thought that he might be sick.

The IC unit was made up of a number of hexagons, each with a small room on five of its walls and a central nursing station and control centre. The nurse led him to the hexagon that was identified as Neuro ICU and into the room where Teresa lay. Despite the fact that she had an oxygen tube attached to her nose, a saline drip in her arm and numerous attachments to her body which fed back instant information to the bank of screens and monitors that formed a backdrop to her bed, she looked relatively peaceful. There was a soft humming in the room, broken by occasional bleeps. Someone had removed her stained clothes and washed her body; they had dressed her in a pale blue cotton robe and placed her arms on top of the sheet. He saw the bruises from the accident and gently traced the purple stains with his finger. This was not his Teresa; this woman was too fragile and still. He looked enquiringly at the pulsating screens.

'They're to keep a check on her blood pressure, breathing rate and pulse,' the nurse said.

Mark nodded. He leaned across the bed and stroked his wife's hand; it was cool and clammy.

'I think she's cold,' he whispered.

The nurse felt her hand. 'No, she's fine,' she said, but nevertheless pulled the thin hospital blanket over Teresa's arms.

'Has she gained consciousness yet?' he asked.

She shook her head. 'No, we're keeping her sedated to control any brain swelling.'

'Is that why she's on a ventilator?' he asked.

'Yes, it's standard practice with traumatic brain injury,' the nurse explained. 'We mustn't let the blood circulation to the brain become restricted.'

Mark remained there looking down at his motionless wife. He bent down and kissed her lightly on the forehead. He couldn't stay there any longer. He had done this to her. It was as if everyone knew it was his fault. Her motionless body was accusing him.

'Maybe her mother could come in now,' he suggested, standing up abruptly.

CHAPTER 3

By the time the taxi dropped him at the end of his drive, it had stopped raining and a pale moon cast its watery rays across the garden, making everything look unfamiliar and forbidding. Mark fumbled with his door key, eventually slipping it into the lock and opening the door. The house was dark and empty—the policeman, who'd come to give him the news—had made sure that he'd gone through the usual routine tasks before leaving: switching off the lights, locking the doors. Now he longed for some bright light, some warmth, some company, anything to alleviate this numbness that dragged at his legs and arms, that had made him incapable of thinking straight.

He went into the lounge, switching on the lights and turning on the central heating. It was only just September and, in the interests of the environment, they tried to put off for as long as possible the moment when the heating was set to automatic. He heard the boiler purr into life. Moving to the drinks cabinet he poured himself a large glass of Glenfiddich and sat on the sofa in front of the television. He picked up the remote control and began to flick through the channels: a game show, the re-run of Arsenal's match against Chelsea, the latest situation in the Brexit negotiations—something he and Teresa had argued over vehemently, now so inconsequential—a South American soap opera and a very old movie with Humphrey Bogart. Nothing that appealed. Nothing that could distract him from the thoughts whirring around in his head, nor ease his guilt. He switched it off, tossed the remote onto the sofa and selected one of his favourite CDs instead.

*

The London Philharmonic were into the last movement of Mozart's Jupiter symphony when his mobile rang.

'Hi, Dad. It's Alex.'

'Alex, where are you?'

'I'm just entering the M40 now. Where are you? Are you still at the hospital?'

'No, I'm at home.' Mark could tell from the silence that followed that his son feared the worst. 'No, it's okay; Mum's still alive. She's in Intensive Trauma. They wouldn't let us sit with her. They said it was better if we went home.'

'So how is she? Is it bad?'

'It's too soon to say. She's still unconscious. They won't know any more until tomorrow when the neurologist looks at her.'

'I'll come straight home. Be with you in about half-an-hour.'

'Drive carefully, Alex.'

'Yes, don't worry Dad. See you soon. 'Bye.'

Mark leaned back and closed his eyes; he felt comforted by the fact that his son was coming home. He knew he should be the one consoling his sons, but right now he needed someone to put their arms around him and tell him that everything would be alright. For a moment he wished his parents were still alive; they would have known what to do.

The sofa was made of soft leather; Teresa had bought it in the January sales. Most evenings, when they watched the television together, she would kick off her shoes and sprawl along its full length, leaving him to sit in the reclining chair next to her. He felt an ache at the thought of her, as if someone had reached inside him and squeezed his heart. If he'd been a religious man he'd have gone to the church and lit a candle for her— that's what Bridget would do. She was probably there now, going through the mumbo-jumbo that gave her solace. Instead he reached for the whisky and poured himself another glass.

'Oh, there you are Smokey Joe,' he said as their Burmese cat leapt up onto his lap. 'Your mistress isn't coming home tonight. You'll have to make do with me.' He stroked the cat's silky fur and began to sob. He was to blame for this.

*

Mark was woken by the sound of the door bell; the music had stopped and his empty whisky glass lay on the sofa beside him, a tiny dribble of liquid spreading across the leather surface.

'Alex, come in. God, it's good to see you.'

Mark hugged his son, burying his head into the young man's shoulder, hiding the tears that he was unable to prevent spilling down his cheeks.

'Dad. Hey, don't take on, now. It's going to be alright. She'll pull through this, you see,' his son said, patting his father's back awkwardly. 'Here, let me get you a drink.'

He pulled away gently and guided his father back into the living room. Mark collapsed onto the sofa. He hadn't wanted to break down in front of his son, but he couldn't stop the tears coming. He rubbed at his eyes angrily. Right now all he wanted to do was throw himself into bed and sleep but he couldn't leave Alex so soon. Some music might make him feel better. He selected another CD and turned the volume to low. The soothing strains of Jacqueline Du Pré's cello began to calm him.

'Thanks Alex,' he said accepting a glass of whisky. 'Have you eaten?'

'No, but I'm not hungry. Don't worry about me; I'm fine with this,' he added as his father started to get up. He swallowed greedily on the whisky. 'Now tell me what happened.'

He leaned back in the chair, never taking his eyes from his father's face, listening to him explain how his mother had run out into the night and changed their lives forever. He didn't ask why they'd been arguing; Mark wondered if he was being considerate of his feelings, or if he already knew the reason. Whichever it was, Mark didn't want to talk about it just yet. His affair with Michelle would come out eventually, but not tonight. He couldn't bear to see his son's look of disapproval when he knew that he was the cause of Teresa's accident.

'What did Ian say when you 'phoned him?'

'He asked a lot of questions that I couldn't answer. You know Ian, he wants all the details. He said he would ring the hospital himself and assess the situation and probably get a flight down tomorrow if it was warranted.'

'Warranted? Warranted? His mother's in a coma. Isn't that warranted enough?' Mark felt a wave of anger sweep over him, no doubt aided by his third glass of whisky.

'He's only being realistic, Dad. It's a long way for him to come; he just wants to know exactly what's going on first. I'm sure he'll come. I expect the company will give him compassionate leave.'

Mark didn't reply. His two sons were so different: Alex took his role of elder brother very seriously and had always looked out for Ian; Ian, had led a more sheltered, one could almost say spoilt, existence by comparison. Mark loved them both, but increasingly found himself running out of patience with his younger son. They'd been in secondary school when Peter was born —Ian had just passed his eleven-plus and Alex was in his third year, captain of the chess team and head of his year. Both Mark and Teresa were worried what their sons would make of the new arrival but they had treated baby Peter with a vague interest and some brotherly affection and carried on with their lives.

'Look, I think I'll go to bed. I want to get up early tomorrow; I'm picking your Gran up at eight to take her to the hospital,' Mark said, swallowing the last of his whisky. It was warm and comforting. He'd have liked to have sat alone and finished the bottle, drinking himself into oblivion and obliterating today's events from his memory, but his son wouldn't approve.

'I'll come with you; we'll take my car, if you like.'

'That'd be good, Alex. Thanks.'

His son picked up the empty glasses and replaced the whisky in the cabinet. 'Can I sleep in my old room?' he asked.

'Of course. Your mother always has your bed made up ready, just in case you stop by.' Tears welled up in his eyes again at the thought of Teresa. She'd found it hard to show much affection to anyone after Peter died but he knew she adored all her sons. She'd loved him too, until he let her down.

Alex put his hand on his father's shoulder. 'Have a good night's sleep Dad. I'll give you a knock about seven-thirty. Okay? And don't worry. We'll get through this, you'll see.'

Mark nodded. 'Goodnight son.'

But would they get through it? Even if Teresa survived her dreadful injuries, would their marriage survive? She had left him once before, after Peter drowned. She'd gone to her mother's and taken the boys with her. Six months she was there. It had taken her a lot to forgive him that time and he was sure she only came back for the sake of Alex and Ian—certainly not for him. They were grown men now and her responsibility to them was over. There was nothing to stop her leaving him now.

CHAPTER 4

As they sat in the corridor outside the IC unit waiting for the doctor, it seemed that they'd never been away; under those neon lights, night ran seamlessly into day. There was something about waiting in hospitals that made him feel that he was suspended in time and space, in an alien world, where he sat helpless, devoid of power, waiting for some crumb of information by which to orientate himself. He couldn't see Teresa—they'd put a screen around her bed—but he could see the shadowy figures of two people attending to her.

Alex came striding along the corridor. 'The doctor starts his rounds at nine,' he informed them.

Mark looked at his watch. 'Just about now then.'

'When will we get to speak to him?' Bridget asked. She'd applied some make-up this morning and wore a smart, blue wool suit, the colour matching her eyes.

'Nobody would say. We just have to wait until they have some news. Oh, by the way Dad, Ian telephoned again. He's catching the first available flight to Heathrow; he'll ring when he lands.'

'Good. Your Mum will be pleased to have you both here. How's he getting to the hospital?'

'I said I'd pick him up.'

Mark smiled; Alex was such a dependable lad. They sat there, three sad figures, drinking weak coffee from polystyrene cups and talking quietly, as they waited for news. At last a nurse came up to them; she wore an ICU insignia on her uniform.

'Mr Rushton, the doctor will see you now. Would you all like to follow me,' she said, turning away and leading them down the corridor, her hospital-issue shoes silent on the tiled floors.

*

Dr Stevens' office was small and crowded with furniture. His desk was swamped with yellow post-its and buff coloured folders; a computer terminal stood at one end, a geometric screen saver twisting and curling its way across the screen. The doctor rose to his feet when they came in, indicating, with a wave of his arm, the empty chairs that they should occupy. He was a youngish man, with a small, neat beard that had been tapered to a fine point, and he wore thick, rimless spectacles. His white coat hung open, revealing a reddish-brown shirt and light coloured slacks; there was a stethoscope around his neck and a pager stuck out from his top pocket. He smiled pleasantly at the group before him.

'Mr Rushton,' he said extending his hand in welcome.

'Good morning, doctor,' Mark said shaking his hand. The doctor had a warm, firm grip. It gave Mark a fleeting sensation of confidence. This was the man who would save Teresa. 'This is my son, and my mother-in-law,' he added, nodding towards his companions.

'Good morning.'

Alex and Bridget smiled, but said nothing. They waited for the doctor to begin. He leaned his elbows on the table and put his hands together, regarding them gravely.

'Well,' he said. 'Your wife has been in a very serious accident. I'm sorry to say that there is some considerable damage to her brain.'

Mark heard Bridget give an involuntary gasp.

The doctor glanced at her and continued, 'Our preliminary tests show that she received a closed head injury; as yet we don't know how severe this injury is, but it seems to be focal.' Seeing a look of puzzlement cross Mark's face, he continued, 'By that, I mean that the damage occurred when her head made violent contact with some object during the accident, but that object didn't break through the skull, and the ensuing damage is confined to only one area of the brain.' He paused, waiting to see if they had any questions.

'So is that good news?' Bridget asked, her eyes brimming with tears..

'It's impossible to say at the moment. As you will appreciate our prime concern was to ensure that your daughter's condition was stable before submitting her to too many tests.' He pulled out a large manila folder and extracted some documents. 'However, I do have the results of the CT scan we did last night. There seems to have been an intra-cranial haemorrhage, that is, some heavy bleeding in the skull.'

Mark felt he was going to be sick. He swallowed hard.

'The neurosurgeon will look at her later this morning and probably operate right away to repair the haematoma,' the doctor continued.

'Did the scan reveal anything else?' Mark asked.

'There doesn't seem to be much in the way of broken bones or fractures, which is amazing considering the force of the impact, but we'll do a MRI scan next—that will give more detail than the CT scan.'

'Has my wife regained consciousness yet?' At last Mark managed to ask the question that had dominated his mind all morning.

'No, I'm afraid not. But that's not unusual.'

'Can we go and see her?' Alex asked.

'Yes, but visiting is strictly limited while the patient is in the Intensive Trauma Unit, so please speak to the nurse first. Is there anything else I can tell you?'

'About the operation...'

'Yes?'

'When will we know if it's been a success?'

'Well, after they've operated on your wife, she'll be returned to the ICU until we're sure she's stable enough to be moved. Then we'll be in a better position to give you a prognosis.' He waited to see if they were going to ask him anything else, then stood up, saying, 'Now if you will excuse me I have to continue with my rounds. Mr Brightwell, the neurosurgeon, will contact you after the operation.'

'Thank you very much, doctor,' Mark said, shaking the man's hand.

Bridget and Alex followed suit, then filed out of the office.

They heard the doctor pick up the telephone. 'Yes, I'll be right there,' he said to the person at the other end of the line.

Alex had his arm around his grandmother's shoulders. 'Let's go and have a cup of tea, Gran. Then we'll come back and see if we can visit Mum,' he suggested.

'He didn't have much to tell us, did he,' Bridget said.

'No, maybe we'll know more later.' Mark had never felt so useless; there was nothing he could do but wait. Everyone was kind, but nobody could tell them anything.

*

The day passed slowly; there seemed to be hours of endless cups of hospital tea and aimless walks down corridors that all looked alike. He bought a newspaper in the hospital foyer, and tried to concentrate on the news: the Hollywood sex-scandal no longer dominated the headlines and once again Brexit was attracting all the media attention this week with speculations about the floundering negotiations. Mark turned to the puzzles page and began to tackle a Sudoku puzzle, but with little success. By mid-morning he decided he should telephone his secretary to explain what had happened and ask her to rearrange his schedule for the week. Then he telephoned his boss.

Mark's boss was the Director of Human Resources at Faber's Chocolates. Mark had worked at Faber's Chocolates for almost twenty-five years. He'd joined as an operator on the production line, a decision that caused his father great annoyance.

'You could do much better for yourself, my lad. You've had a good education. Why do you want to work on the shop floor when you could be a manager?' he'd said.

But Mark had needed the money; he was newly married, had one small son and another one on the way. Besides which the hourly rate at Faber's Chocolates was ten percent above the average. Mark was a hard worker and got on well with people; it didn't take his managers long to see that he had potential for a more responsible role. First they promoted him to line supervisor, then they sent him on a series of training courses and gave him a shift manager's job. He coped well with everything that was asked of him, and about ten years ago when a vacancy came up in the Human Resources Department for a day-shift personnel officer, he applied for it. Despite his lack of formal training in personnel work they gave him the job, and neither side had ever regretted the decision.

Mark's boss was very sympathetic when he heard what had happened to Teresa. 'Mark, that's terrible news. Now don't you worry about work; your place is with your wife. We can cope here just fine; I'll ask Rosemary to check your mail each day and deal with anything urgent. You just concentrate on your family, and Mark, keep me informed.'

Mark only wished he had something to keep him informed about; this lack of information was frustrating. He wandered back to the ICU and sat outside, trying once more to concentrate on his newspaper, but the print danced before his eyes and refused to make sense.

Bridget and Alex had left. Bridget had reluctantly agreed to let Alex take her home, but only after he'd promised to ring her as soon as they had any news of Teresa's progress. Then he was going on to Heathrow to collect his brother.

*

Alex was waiting for him when Ian walked through into the arrivals hall. His brother was easy to spot, standing a good head taller than those around him, his long hair flopping over his forehead.

'Hi there. Good flight?' Alex gave his younger brother a brief hug.

'Yeah, fine. I came as quickly as I could. How's Mum?'

'She's still unconscious, but her condition is stable,' Alex said, repeating the neurosurgeon's words. 'They operated this morning to stop some bleeding in her head.'

'But she's going to be okay, right?'

'We hope so. Nobody is saying anything really.'

'Bloody doctors. They treat us like kids. Why can't they tell us what's wrong with her.'

'I don't think they know yet, beyond the fact that she has some sort of brain damage. It's only been eighteen hours since the accident you know.'

'What about the police? Are they doing anything? Do they know why it happened?'

'Well I don't know what they can do. They think Mum must have been driving too fast for the weather conditions. The lorry driver said she went into a spin long before he hit her.'

'But they only have his word for it, don't they?'

'I hadn't really thought about it, Ian. I've just been so worried about Mum,' Alex said patiently. 'Come on, my car's in the carpark. I'll take you over to the hospital. Dad will be very pleased to see you.'

'I doubt that.'

'He wants us all here when Mum wakes up,' Alex said.

'You. He wants you there, you mean.'

'Don't be childish. Of course he wants us all there. What if Mum wakes up and you're not by her bedside? What will she think?'

'Do you think she'll even notice? It's not as though she's had a lot of time for either of us since Peter's death. Sometimes I think she believes she is the only one who is grieving. She may have lost a son, but we lost our baby brother,' said Ian. He was angry with his mother. She'd shut them both out after the accident and now there she was, lying in a hospital bed and he had no idea what had happened. No surprises there.

'Why did it happen? Where was she going at that time of night? It's so unlike Mum,' said Alex, echoing Ian's own thoughts.

'Maybe she was upset about something,' Ian said, as they walked towards the exit. 'You know what a temper she's got, when roused.'

'Possibly. Dad said they'd been having a row.'

'Did he say what about?'

'No. I didn't like to ask him. He was so upset last night. And he'd been drinking.'

'I bet she found out about Michelle,' Ian said.

Alex stopped and looked at him. 'Michelle? Do you think he's still screwing Michelle?'

'It's quite likely. She's always round there on some pretext or other.'

'But I thought that it was all finished, after that time we walked in on them.'

'Well, that's what they said, remember. "It's all been a mistake," they said. "Don't tell your mother, she'll be devastated," they said.' Ian couldn't keep the sarcasm from his voice. He used to like Michelle until he found out his father was screwing her. He'd even fancied her himself when he was a teenager.

'Fucking hell. I bet you're right. I bet Mum found out and went dashing out just to get away from him. It's the sort of thing she'd do.'

Ian glanced up at his brother; he didn't often swear. He was very fond of his older brother but they were very different from each other in both looks and temperament. Whilst Alex was tall and slender, with black hair like their mother's, Ian was only just five-feet-eight and there was a fleshiness about his face that suggested he might become fat in later life. He neither resembled his father, nor his mother, having inherited from his great-grandfather a shock of red hair that looked like a mown cornfield—his grandmother's description— and a ruddy complexion. Where Alex was patient and dependable, Ian knew he could be erratic and hasty; where Alex was warm and loving, Ian remained self-contained and critical; where Alex was tolerant and quick to forgive, Ian had been known to bear many a grudge.

'Look, don't say anything to Dad. He's got enough on his mind at the moment and we may be wrong, you know,' Alex said.

'Whatever you say. But what else could it be?'

They walked across the covered bridge and into the carpark. Alex had parked near the exit barrier.

'Nice car, Alex. When did you get it?' Ian asked.

'About six weeks ago. It's great, isn't it? They promoted me to Senior Sales Manager and this was part of the deal. You don't think I could afford the latest BMW otherwise?'

They drove out of the carpark and entered the traffic; soon they were leaving the airport behind them and heading for the M4.

'She really goes, look.' Alex changed down a gear and pulled out to overtake the car in front, demonstrating the car's power of acceleration.

'Yeah, pretty powerful. The company must be doing well.' There was a touch of envy in his voice.

Ian worked for Scottish Antiquities, an offshoot of Scottish Heritage. He loved the work, which entailed travelling all over Scotland researching and cataloguing national antiques—in the vain hope that they would not all be exported to the United States. He found the work both rewarding and interesting, but remunerative it was not. No company car for him.

As they sped up the motorway, the two brothers chatted comfortably about the merits and demerits of the cars they'd owned at various times in their lives. They both shared a passion for fast cars and one of the few pastimes that they still had in common was motor racing. They were still arguing over whether Lewis Hamilton would supersede Michael Schumacher as the greatest Formula One driver ever, when they arrived in the hospital carpark.

*

Mark was sitting in the same place, outside the IC unit, when they reached the fifth floor.

'Ian. I'm so pleased to see you,' he said, embracing his younger son vigorously. 'Thanks for collecting him, Alex.'

He patted Alex on the arm.

'Yeah, thanks for collecting me, Alex,' Ian said with a laugh. It was as though they were still at school.

The men sat down, one either side of their father.

'How is she, Dad?'

'Just the same. No news yet,' Mark replied.

He went over to intercept a nurse who was just leaving the ICU. 'Excuse me. Is it possible for my sons to see their mother? Teresa Rushton. She's in bed ten.'

'Teresa Rushton? I'll see.'

She went back into the ward and he could see her speaking to one of the ICU team. They both looked in Mark's direction, then she returned. 'Yes, your sons can go in, but they have to go in one at a time, and they can't stay very long.' She looked severely at the young men, as though they may have had other plans.

Alex went in first and the others returned to their seats.

'I'm so glad you could get away, Ian,' Mark said, putting his hand on his son's arm. 'When your Mum wakes up she'll be really pleased to see you both here.'

Ian nodded.

'So, how is your job going?' Mark asked.

'It's fine, Dad. I'm up in Stirling at the moment.'

'Oh, beautiful part of the world, that. Centre of the antiquities world, is it?'

'Well actually, I'm looking into some pretty interesting things at the moment.' Ian paused then continued, 'Dad what happened last night? Where was Mum going?'

'I don't know Ian. We had a row and she just leapt up and rushed out into the rain.'

'But didn't you try to stop her?'

'No.' Mark looked away. 'You know your Mum; it's very difficult to stop her from doing what she wants.'

Ian was about to continue, but at that moment, Alex returned. 'You can go in now. She's still unconscious, but maybe she can hear us. I hope so. I want her to know we're all here for her,' he said. His eyes shone with unshed tears.

'Okay. I won't be long, Dad,' Ian said, smoothing down his unruly hair as if he was going for an interview.

Alex sat down next to his father; he seemed agitated. 'Dad, I think we should try talking to Mum. What if she is able to hear us and we aren't saying anything to her.'

'Alex, she's still unconscious.'

'But maybe she's in a coma.'

'What's the difference, unconscious, in a coma; it's all the same. She can't hear us.' Mark hated to see his son so upset, but he didn't know what to say to comfort him. It was better that he faced facts.

'Are you sure? I'm know I've read somewhere, or maybe saw it on the TV, that you should talk to coma patients.'

'I don't know, Alex. I'm not a doctor,' Mark replied, burying his head in his hands. It was all too much to bear.

After a few minutes Ian came back and retook his seat beside them without speaking.

'Are you alright Ian?' Mark asked.

'Yes, I'm alright Dad. But I promise you one thing, I'm going to do everything in my power to help Mum get better. Whatever it takes. I can't believe she's survived that accident just to spend the rest of her life in a coma. She has to get better. We can't lose her as well.'

Mark put his hand on his son's shoulder. 'Don't get up your hopes, Ian. It's too soon for them to say what's going to happen. All we can do, is wait and pray.'

'I don't think they have any idea when she'll regain consciousness,' Alex said, quietly.

They sat there, in silence, staring ahead of them. Nobody wanted to give life to the thought that hung in the air between them: not when, but *if* she regained consciousness. She might never wake up.

*

Teresa could hear someone calling her. She was in a warm deep sleep, but somewhere a voice was saying her name. She was too tired to answer; later, when she had slept some more she would see who it was. Her body felt light and warm; she drifted away again.

CHAPTER 5

A man's voice broke through his reverie. 'Mr Rushton.'

Mark looked up. Dr Stevens was standing before him. 'Dr Stevens, hello. Have you any news?'

'We're going to move your wife to another ward. Maybe you'd like to wait outside my office and we'll let you know when she's settled.'

Mark felt his stomach give a jolt. 'Is that good news?'

'Well, she's been in Intensive Trauma now for ten days and we don't think it's really necessary any more. We've taken her off the ventilator and she's breathing by herself now. She'll progress just as well in a normal ward.'

Ten days. He couldn't believe that ten days had passed already.

'Maybe I'll just pop home and clean up a bit first.' He passed his hand over his face; he could feel the rough stubble where he needed a shave. He didn't bother to ask if there was any news on her condition; he already knew the answer.

'Good idea, your wife will be ready by the time you get back,' the doctor said, moving on, probably already thinking about his next case.

Mark stood up, stretching his legs; he felt stiff and tired from sitting so long in one place. His sons had left; they both had to return to work, but promised to come

and visit at the weekend. He couldn't blame them; life
had to go on.

He too would have to think about returning to work
soon; he didn't want to take advantage of the company's
generosity. After all, when Teresa did wake up, he would
need some time off to look after her.

*

Their Burmese cat, Smokey Joe, was sitting by the front
door, waiting to be let in when Mark arrived home. He
bent down and stroked him, sinking his fingers deep into
his soft fur.

'Hello there, old chap. Been a bit lonely have you?
Me too.'

He opened the door and the cat ran straight in, heading for the kitchen, leaving a trail of perfectly formed
muddy paw marks on the hall carpet. Mark looked
around him as if he'd never been in this house before;
he realised how dirty and uncared for his home had become. The sun shone through rain streaked windows,
accentuating the layer of dust that covered everything
like a fine muslin cloth. He'd hardly been at home since
Teresa's accident; barely stopping to sleep in his un-
made bed, or take a quick shower and pull a razor across
his sunken cheeks. He followed the cat to the kitchen; it
was standing by the fridge, mewing. Mark took out
some cat food and tipped it into the cat's bowl, then
pulled the hoover out from the cupboard under the stairs
and attempted to clean the carpet. The cat must have
walked across Teresa's vegetable patch, because the paw
marks were of damp earth, and resisted any attempts to
remove them. He abandoned the hoover and took a
black plastic sack from the cupboard under the sink in-

stead, and set about collecting the debris of the last ten days: old newspapers, discarded cigarette packets, beer cans, empty cat food tins, the uneaten remains of a pizza he had shared with his sons one night, and some dead flowers that he vaguely remembered bringing home a couple of weeks before. Had they been a peace offering? He couldn't remember. There had been so many rows over the last five years, followed by long silences and his feeble attempts at reconciliation. He put the sack by the back door and proceeded to tackle the dust with a can of spray polish and a cloth. He wasn't very domesticated; there had never been much need. Before Peter's death, Teresa had enjoyed being a full time housewife: she baked and cooked, cleaned and sewed, she made elegant flower arrangements and tended the garden, she bottled plums and made her own jam, she knitted jumpers for the boys and attended all the PTA meetings. She even found time to go to a watercolour class. Her life had been replete with her home and her family. But that was before. She'd still kept the house clean and cooked dinner every night, but after Peter drowned, her heart was no longer in it; she was never the same person. It was as though he'd lost both his wife and his son. Nevertheless he couldn't bear to think that her house was so neglected; he resolved to arrange for someone to come in once a week and clean it while Teresa was in hospital.

His mobile rang. It was Michelle. He switched it to silence and returned it to his pocket, then continued with his chores. He didn't want to speak to her; he didn't feel able to cope with someone else's emotions and Michelle was always a very emotional person. He took some clean linen from the linen press in the hall and went into the bedroom. He was pulling the dirty sheets off their bed when the telephone on the bedside table began to ring. At first he ignored it, but then he heard the answer machine click in.

'Hi Mark, this is Michelle. I'm so worried about Teresa. You said you'd let me know how she is, but I haven't heard from you. Please ring me and give me some news.' She emphasised the word 'please', drawing out the syllables slowly. 'I've tried 'phoning the hospital but they won't tell me anything because I'm not family. Please...'

Mark picked up the receiver. 'Hello Michelle,' he said, interrupting her message.

'Oh, Mark, thank God. What's the news? Is she going to be alright?'

'I'm sorry Michelle, they're not saying much. She's still unconscious.'

'I must see her. Can I, Mark? She's my oldest friend you know.'

He knew she'd ask this. He took a deep breath and said, 'I don't think it would be a good idea. You do realise it was because of us that all this happened.' She might as well know. Why should he carry the burden of guilt alone?

There was a brief silence then Michelle asked, 'What do you mean? How does she know? I've always been so careful. You know I never wanted to hurt her. How did she find out? Surely the boys didn't tell her?'

'No. I did.'

'You told her?' The disbelief in Michelle's voice was tangible. 'But why? It was already over between us. It has been for ages.'

'I don't know. I felt I couldn't love her like before, not with this lie between us. I wanted a clean slate, for things to be like they used to be.'

'Mark, I can't believe you did this. She'll never speak to me again.' She began to cry. 'This is awful. What have we done to her?' Her voice was rising in pitch.

He was glad she was not in the room with him; he hated to see her cry. He could picture her large, round eyes, their irises the colour of nutmeg, filling slowly with tears that would spill noisily down her cheeks.

'Look, don't cry Michelle.' His tone had softened towards her. 'Come over to the hospital this evening. If I'm not there I expect Teresa's mother will be. She'll be pleased to see you. She's been asking for you, anyway,' he added.

'Thank you Mark. I...'

He didn't hear what she was about to say; he'd hung up. How had he got into this mess in the first place? He thought back to the moment when his relationship with Michelle had changed; it had been almost five years ago.

*

It was six months after Peter died. Teresa was still living with her mother, Ian was in Edinburgh, checking out the university, Alex was in Norfolk visiting a customer and he was at home, alone, looking after Smokey Joe, when the telephone had rung.

'Hi, Mark. Teresa not back yet? Do you fancy going for a curry tonight?'

'Hi Michelle. No, she's still at her mothers. But a curry's not a bad idea; the boys are both away, so I'm all on my own. I must warn you though. I'm not very good company at the moment.'

'Life has to go on, Mark. I know how hard it is for you both, but you've got two other sons to consider. Come on. You're not going to embarrass me by turning down my offer, are you? I'm paying.'

It was a long time since he and Teresa had been out for a curry. It seemed a long time since they'd done anything together, in fact. The loneliness that he'd almost become accustomed to since Peter had died, wrapped around him once more and he felt a surge of self-pity. She didn't want him anymore; he knew that, although she'd never said as much. Teresa was not a cruel woman; she may have changed, her heart may have withered inside her, but she would continue to do her duty as a wife and mother. Duty but not love and certainly not passion. Perhaps it was time to think of himself. 'Why not. I'll come and pick you up. Say seven-thirty?'

'Perfect. We'll have a drink at my place before we leave. I've got some quite presentable Chardonnay in the fridge.'

'Sounds good.'

He still couldn't understand it; they never made it to the restaurant in the end. It was almost as if they had been hungering for each other for years without realising it. She'd opened the door, dressed in jeans and a white voile shirt, which she'd tied in a knot at the waist; she wore tan sandals and her hair hung loose over her shoulders in a cascade of golden curls. It was still Michelle; she was smiling and chattering about her day in her usual gossipy way, but somehow she seemed different. He had closed the door behind them and followed her into the kitchen, barely listening to what she was saying. He felt strangely nervous; a sensation that reminded him of when he'd been a teenager.

'I booked a table for eight-thirty, so we don't have to rush,' she said.

His mouth felt dry and he could hear his heart pounding. He watched her go to the cupboard and take out two glasses.

'Here, would you like to do the honours?' she asked, handing him a bottle and a corkscrew.

He looked at her; she was captivating. It was if he was seeing her for the first time. He took the bottle and corkscrew from her and put them down on the kitchen table, and without saying anything, took her into his arms. Except it wasn't quite like that; they had moved towards each other instinctively, unconsciously, and everything else was forgotten in the heat that flared up between them. From that first kiss their passion consumed them; they thought of nothing else except how they could meet and be together again.

CHAPTER 6

'Well, I've been looking it up on the internet. Do you know that there was a woman who was in a coma for thirty-seven years, one hundred and eleven days. She's in the Guinness Book of Records.'

'So what happened to her?'

'She died, without ever waking up.'

'Oh my God, Ian. Don't tell Gran that; she's upset enough as it is.'

'Has Dad been on to you?'

'Yes. He seems a lot better, more positive. He wants us to draw up a rota for sitting with Mum. He says we have to work as a team in order to cope with this tragedy.'

'Tragedy? Is that what he called it? Peter's death was a tragedy,' Ian snapped.

'Yes. Well this is a tragedy too, and we can't leave them to handle it on their own, can we?'

'Okay. Well I don't know how I'm going to manage it; it's a long way. I'll talk to Andrew and see what he can suggest. Maybe I could work ten days straight through, then have four days off and fly down. Look, leave it with me and I'll see what I can come up with. What about you?'

'Well it's a bit easier for me, because I only live down the road.'

'But aren't you away a lot?'

'Usually, but I can delegate a lot of the trips. Simon will like that, he's always complaining that he doesn't get out enough.'

'Does Dad realise that this could go on for a long time?'

'I don't know. What I do know is that this is as important for him as it is for Mum, so it's worth giving it a shot. Okay?'

'Yes, I'm with you, Bro. I'll email you with my schedule for the next month and we'll take it from there. Look, I must go, now. I'm meeting Jenny at seven.'

'Okay. Give her my love, will you, and keep in touch.'

Alex hung up. He didn't know why he'd said that; he didn't know Ian's latest girlfriend and probably would never get to know her. Ian's relationships were notorious for both their brevity and their anonymity. He had never once brought a girl home to meet his family. But maybe that wasn't so surprising. They were hardly a united family any more.

His mother had taken her youngest son's death very badly. As Ian had said, it had been a tragedy that sent shock waves through all their lives. It was only natural that his mother would miss him the most—she had spent most time with him—but they had all loved him; she forgot that. In her grief she had pushed them all away. She had said nothing when he told her he was getting a job instead of going to university, and yet she had been the one who had been so insistent that whatever he eventually did with his life, he should get his degree first. Now his future didn't matter to her. She hadn't even commented when Ian said he was going to stay in

Edinburgh after he qualified. Both her sons left home and she never shed a tear.

His mother had cried a lot when Peter drowned. A lot. Then one day she stopped and it was if her grief had frozen inside her. Alex couldn't remember seeing her shed another tear, not even when they all went to Granddad's funeral.

*

Teresa felt she was waking from a deep sleep, but her eyes were heavy and she couldn't raise the energy to open them. It was as though she was on a boat, drifting with the tide: she would float into consciousness for a moment, then drift away again. She couldn't control the boat; it took her where it wanted to, bringing her almost to the shore then returning her each time to the darkness. She tried, but she couldn't hold on to anything for very long; it all drifted away again.

*

When Mark arrived back at the hospital, he spotted Bridget near the lifts, looking slightly lost, and they walked together to Dr Stevens' office; the doctor was already there, talking to a young woman in a white coat. Mark knocked tentatively on the door. His stomach was churning and he felt sick. He wished he'd eaten something before he'd left home.

'Come in. Sit down, please.' Dr Stevens seemed even more harassed than usual. 'Before I take you along to the ward, my colleague and I would like to have a word with you both.'

They sat down, apprehensively. This didn't sound like good news.

'Mr Rushton, Mrs O'Sullivan,' the neurologist began. 'First of all let me introduce Miss Barnett, our neuro-radiologist.'

He waited while the small group nodded their acknowledgement of the new specialist, then continued, 'I thought it would help if we explained Mrs Rushton's condition to you.' No-one spoke. 'Your wife is in a deep coma; in terms of the Glasgow Coma Scale, she is at point five—the scale goes from 3 to 15, so you can see it is not the worst but it is severe. At the moment she doesn't respond to pain, nor light; she cannot hear; she cannot make any voluntary actions and she has no normal sleep-wake cycles.'

Mark could see his mother-in-law struggling to hold back her tears.

'So, does that mean she has no hope of recovery?' he asked, his voice cracking as he spoke.

'Not necessarily so,' the neurologist replied. 'Most comas rarely last more than five or six weeks, but the shorter the time she is in that state, the better her chances are of recovery. Of course when she wakes up we'll have a much better idea of the extent of her disability.'

'Disability?'

'Yes, it's almost certain she'll have some kind of disability. The MRI scans have shown that she's received some damage to the brain stem, that is the lower part of the brain that adjoins and is structurally continuous with the spinal cord. Unfortunately at the moment we can't tell how extensive that damage is.'

'Does that mean that when she wakes up she could be a vegetable?'

'That's a harsh way to put it, Mr Rushton. There is a possibility that she will suffer from Persistent Vegetative State, but not necessarily. However there is likely to be some damage to the motor and sensory systems of the head and neck region. Nine of our twelve cranial nerves pass through the brain stem, connecting the brain to the head and face. They control a range of functions, such as smell, taste, and eye movements. Often people who suffer a traumatic brain injury, such as your wife, also have damage to the facial nerve, causing a paralysis of the muscles in the face.'

'What about the rest of her brain?' Mark asked, his own brain having difficulty in assimilating what he was being told.

'So far we've not detected any damage to the upper brain, but as I said, we'll know more when she comes out of the coma.'

'So there is no hope of a full recovery?' Bridget asked, her voice breaking.

'I'm not saying that. There's always hope. The brain is remarkably complex and sometimes when one part is damaged, another part learns to take over the job of the damaged part. But all that takes time. I just want you both to be aware that when Mrs Rushton wakes up, she may not be the same as she was before.'

'So what do we do now?' Mark asked.

'Now all we can do is wait. Which is why we have put her in Ward...' he looked at his colleague enquiringly.

'In Ward 2D. It's a medical ward. As soon as we have a vacancy we will transfer her to Neuro Rehab.'

'Neuro Rehab? What's that?' Bridget asked.

'We have a specialist neuro rehabilitation facility attached to the hospital for traumatic brain injury patients,' she explained. 'Unfortunately there's no empty bed at the moment.'

'But what if something happens in the meantime? What if she wakes up and there's no-one around to see?' Mark was beginning to realise the significance of moving her out of the heavily monitored ICU.

'No, don't worry; it's not like that. Your wife will still be connected to a range of monitoring systems and the staff will be checking on her regularly. Look, why don't you go along and see her now.' He looked across at Miss Barnett again.

'Yes, I'll show you where she is,' the neuro-radiologist volunteered. 'I have a patient to visit there, anyway.'

'Thank you doctor,' Bridget said, wiping her nose with her handkerchief, 'for all you've done.'

'That's alright Mrs O'Sullivan. I'm sorry that the news isn't more hopeful.'

Once again they shook hands with Dr Stevens and then followed Miss Barnett to Teresa's new home.

*

Despite the specialist's gloomy prognosis, both Mark and Bridget were cheered to see Teresa in a normal hospital bed. They felt that some progress was being made at last. She was in a separate room, leading off the main ward and close to the nurses' station. The walls had been painted duck egg blue, and the window looked out over the hospital carpark and a large bank of trees beyond.

'Oh, this is much nicer,' Bridget said, smoothing the coverlet with her hand and looking around.

'Yes, it's very peaceful in here,' Mark agreed.

His wife looked lovely. She still wore her pale blue hospital shift, but her hair had been washed and combed; its black, silky tendrils fanned out across the pillows. Her face was a perfect oval and the abrasions from the accident had already healed. He tried not to look at the tubes and the monitors banked up beside the bed and concentrated instead on her skin; she had always had such beautiful, soft, white skin, and despite being almost fifty, there was hardly a wrinkle to be seen. Teresa never sunbathed; she liked to protect her face from the sun. She had a wide mouth, with full, carefully delineated lips, which he mostly remembered stretched in a smile that revealed her small, uneven teeth. He wanted to touch her lips, to press his own against hers. If only this were a fairy tale and with one kiss he could wake the beautiful princess from her hundred-year sleep. But he was no handsome prince; this waiting had taken its toll on him. His face was grey and his cheeks hollow. His hair—badly in need of a haircut—flopped across his forehead, greasy and uncombed. His trousers hung loosely from his waist and the skin on his neck had become as scraggy as a chicken's.

Teresa too had lost weight. He thought back to the days when she complained because her trousers were too tight and she would lie on the bed struggling to close the zip on her jeans. Whatever that brown liquid was that they were feeding her through a stomach tube, it was definitely low calorie.

'I'll stay with her a while, Mark. You go home and get some rest; you look all in,' Bridget said. She had pulled the visitors' chair up close to the bed, and was sitting holding Teresa's hand in her own. The rosary she'd given her daughter lay on the bedside table.

'Okay, Bridget. I'll do that. I'll come back this evening.'

He reached down and stroked Teresa's hair gently. 'Goodbye my love,' he murmured.

He stopped in the doorway and looked back; his mother-in-law sat, her head bowed, the rosary slipping bead by bead through her fingers as she prayed silently for her daughter's recovery.

*

Teresa was dreaming of her mother. They were in the big house by the sea, her grandmother's house. She must have hurt herself, because her mother was stroking her forehead and telling her everything would be alright. Now she remembered: she was eleven years old and it was the Easter holidays. She and Jimmy had been climbing on the rocks and she'd slipped and cracked her head on a stone. Jimmy had run to get Mammy, while she sat there crying and trying to staunch the blood that dripped onto her new jeans.

'Teresa, you poor wee thing, what have you been up to?' her mother had said, washing the blood from her face.

Mammy never got cross with her, not even for staining her new jeans.

*

Mark didn't go straight home; he desperately needed to get away from the hospital to have a change of scene, but he couldn't face his empty house. It was too early to go to the pub, so he decided to drive to the river and walk along the tow path.

The rain of the previous few days had made the river rise to almost flood level, and it had overflowed its banks in one or two places. As he walked under the bridge he saw that it had almost reached the high water mark of 1912. Further on, the path disappeared altogether and he had to make a detour through the adjacent meadow, picking his way carefully across the mud and cow pats, to reach dry land again.

A rowing eight were out practising; he could hear their coach shouting instructions through his megaphone as he cycled crazily along the towpath on the opposite bank. Mark's sons had made an attempt at rowing once, but neither Ian nor Alex had the physique that was required to be successful. He stopped for a moment to watch the crew go by; they pulled in unison, muscles bulging, a team united in a single goal.

A cool fresh breeze blew off the water, reviving him; for the first time in a long while he felt the tension slipping away from his neck and shoulders. He had to get a grip of himself, reorganise his life around this new state of events. The doctors were doing all they could to help Teresa, so there was nothing he could do, except hold their lives together. That was what he would do for her; he would look after her mother and he would take care of her house and her sons, and her cat, so that when she came home she would forgive him. Only in this way would he able to cope with the waiting. If the doctor was to be believed Teresa was going to need some sort of care, whatever the future had in store for her. He would be there to give her that care. He would look after her.

He breathed deeply and looked around him; it was a beautiful afternoon and the sun shone on the swirls and eddies of the river, causing him to squint involuntarily. He reached into his jacket pocket for his sunglasses. A pair of mallards battled upstream, their glossy green heads bobbing in the backwash of a passing skiff. He put his sunglasses on, turned back towards the town and began to retrace his steps. He no longer felt rudderless, drifting out of control, impotently waiting for the doctor to tell him that his life could continue. He had a plan, and having a plan, however sketchy, always made him feel better. He had a lot to see to.

CHAPTER 7

It was Ian's turn to visit his mother. He'd arrived that evening on the last flight and gone straight to the hospital. When Mark arrived he saw his younger son leaning over Teresa's bed.

'Hi, Ian. What are you doing?'

'It's okay, Dad. Don't worry. I'm just trying something I think might help Mum.'

'But what are you doing?' Mark repeated. His son was bent over the prostrate figure of his mother, attaching a set of headphones to her ears.

'Well I read in this magazine that in Germany they've had lots of success with music therapy.'

'What's the point of that? You know they said she can't hear.' His frustration made him speak sharply to his son.

'We don't know that for certain. It can't hurt to play her some of her favourite music, can it?'

'It's not going to do any good. Don't get your hopes up.'

'It's not going to do any harm, either. Let's at least give it a try. Look, I've downloaded "The Monteverdi Vespers", a selection of opera and some Elgar,' he said, plugging the headphones into an iPad. 'What should we start with?'

'Oh, I don't know. Put on Elgar's 1st Symphony, if you must; she loves Elgar.'

Ian selected the piece his father had chosen and placed the iPad by her bed.

Mark looked at his wife carefully. There was no movement: her eyes remained closed and her body motionless. Was she ever going to wake up? Somehow he doubted it.

'How do you know if it works?' he asked his son at last, his curiosity overcoming his irritation.

'Well there are hundreds of hospitals using Music Therapy. Mostly they use it with semi-conscious patients to help with their rehabilitation because it doesn't rely on language and the music can elicit an emotional response from the patient, even one in a coma.'

'So how does it work?'

'Well it works best when it's done on a one-to-one basis; the music therapist normally spends a couple of sessions a week with each patient. They use familiar music, something that the patient knows and loves: it could be a simple song or a piece of orchestral music.'

He took the earpiece from his mother's ear and listened to check that it was playing alright, then adjusted the volume slightly.

'So you think this will help your mother?'

'I don't know, Dad. But we can try. They say that it can help to stimulate sensory and motor responses, and that's what Mum needs.'

Ian was very enthusiastic about what he'd read. Despite his misgivings, Mark was impressed with his son's attempts to help his mother. He hadn't been able to come up with anything like that. All he'd thought to do was keep her house clean. What good was that when she might never even go back there?

'So why those particular pieces of music?' He knew that Teresa had a very eclectic taste in music and would listen to anything from Bach to Bartok.

'Well they say that any piece of music that the person knows will encourage a response and the better they know it, the better the response.'

'Maybe we should ask your Gran for her CD of "Danny Boy." Your Mum always used to cry when she listened to that.'

'Yes, but that was usually because it was Christmas and she'd had a few.'

The two men laughed at the shared memory. Teresa had been born and bred in the south of England, but loved to talk of her Irish roots, especially at Christmastime. She always said it didn't matter where she was born; her heart was Irish. Her temper certainly was.

*

She was on the hillside, near her grandmother's house. It was a beautiful day and the sun had appeared from behind the clouds, making the Atlantic gleam like wet slates. She stood with her arms outstretched, facing into the sun; the fields unfolded below her, tiny patchwork squares of green and brown, hemmed with dry stone walls. She could feel the warmth on her face. And there was music surging through her body, making her spin and turn, her skirt twirling outwards, a Catherine wheel of colour. Her grandmother was calling her; she could hear her name: Teresa, Teresa. It was coming from far away. It must be time to go home for tea.

*

It was exactly four weeks after Teresa's accident when Bridget told Mark that she'd noticed a change in her daughter's condition. It was when she had called in to see her on her way back from Mass.

Bridget went to Mass every Sunday without fail and always had. Mark was sure that now she sang the hymns and repeated the words of the Eucharist with greater fervour, as she tried to convince God that her only daughter merited some special attention. He knew she'd have liked him to accompany her, but he always refused. He had said to her once, 'Okay, so there could be a God, but I don't see a lot of evidence for one. And besides, I personally don't have any time for religion; it has caused too much sorrow in this world.'

She'd questioned his ability to cope with Teresa's condition when he had nothing to hang onto; she told him it was only her faith that sustained her. But then she'd let him be.

'Mark, I'm sure I saw Teresa's eyelid flicker. It was at about one o'clock.'

Mark looked at his mother-in-law; she was so desperate for some sign of recovery. 'Just once?' he asked.

She looked at him sadly. 'Yes, just once. But I'm sure I saw it. I was talking to her; I was telling her how Father O'Reilly had said a special prayer for her and how he asked everyone to remember her in their prayers each day. I told her how we lit candles for her and called for the intercession of the Blessed Virgin Mary to help her get well.'

Tears were running down her careworn cheeks, as she told him. Mark thought how much she had aged in such a short time. They all had. Even the boys had lost that youthful flippancy that used to irritate him; now he would have been grateful for any one of their inane remarks. Teresa's accident had taken over their entire lives. He moved closer to his wife's bed, his heart pounding, but he could see no change.

'You know Bridget, if she stays in this coma for much longer, it is highly unlikely that she will ever come out of it. You have to prepare yourself for the worst.' He put his arm around her shoulders and gave her a squeeze.

'There it is again. I knew I hadn't imagined it,' she cried, pulling away from him and grasping her daughter's hand. 'Teresa, Teresa. Sweetheart, can you hear me?'

There was no response. Bridget gently put her daughter's hand back on the bed, and leaning her face against it, began to sob, uncontrollably. It seemed to Mark, that the sorrows of a lifetime were surfacing and spilling themselves over that narrow hospital bed. He wanted to comfort her, but something told him she was best left alone.

CHAPTER 8

Teresa opened her eyes. Where was she? It was hard to focus; there was a bright light and something white above her. She closed them again then tried opening just one at a time. Everything was still blurred. She could hear voices somewhere, but couldn't make out what they were saying. She felt strange: as though she had no substance. Where was she? She tried hard to concentrate; she remembered something about a crash, an image of rain beating against the windscreen. Yes, that was it; it had been raining and she had lost control of the car. No sooner had the memories started to come back than they receded again; she could remember nothing more. There must have been an accident. If there'd been an accident they would have taken her to hospital. That was it. She was in hospital. She'd probably been unconscious; that would be why she felt so sleepy. Well, someone would come and tell her soon enough. She closed her eyes and let the current take her away again.

*

The nurses manoeuvred Teresa's body onto the trolley and covered her with a regulation blanket; they lifted her arms and laid them on top of the blanket.

'Well this is good news, Mr Rushton. Any slight movement is a positive sign. We'll see what the scan has to say about the activity in your wife's brain. It could be that she is about to wake up,' the doctor told him.

They were all there: Mark, Bridget, Alex and Ian. Nobody wanted to miss the moment when Teresa regained consciousness. They were all so hopeful, so full of longing for the moment that she would awake. But they weren't to know what the future had in store for them.

As it happened they all missed it, because it was when they were pulling her out of the MRI machine, that Teresa chose to open her eyes and identify her new world.

'Hello Mrs Rushton. Teresa,' the doctor said. 'Can you hear me Teresa?'

His patient was regarding him with her sad, green eyes.

*

So, she hadn't been dreaming; she was in a hospital. She wondered which one it was; probably St. James, that was the main one in their area. She'd taken Peter there when he fell off his bicycle and broke his wrist.

There was someone leaning over her; he seemed to be whispering to her. She couldn't recognise his face. The doctor, maybe? Had he been examining her? She tried to turn her head to see what was happening, but she couldn't move it. Only her eyes moved. Suddenly she realised she couldn't feel her feet, and tried to raise herself to see why. Again nothing. She mustn't panic; this was probably the drugs. Most likely they'd given her a very strong sedative so that she didn't move while they were examining her. She closed her eyes; it was probably better to sleep now. When she woke up, the sedative would have worn off and she'd be able to see how much she had actually been hurt. At least she couldn't feel any pain.

*

The doctor beamed at them. 'Yes, the results of the scan show distinct activity in certain parts of her brain. It may take a couple of days for her to regain full consciousness, but I would say she's definitely coming out of the coma, at last.' He looked very confident at his prognosis.

Alex hugged his grandmother, unable to conceal his delight. 'Oh, thank goodness. I thought these last few weeks would never end.'

Ian, ever the pragmatist, said, 'Well, remember this is only the first step. We still have to see what else has been affected when she regains consciousness.'

'Yes, but the doctor said that she looked straight at him. She could see you, couldn't she doctor?' Alex directed this last remark to the doctor, who was busy studying Teresa's chart. They were all standing around her bed.

'Yes, I'm pretty sure she could see me. I think the best thing you can do now is to keep talking to her, try to stimulate her into a reply of some sort. Let her know that you're all here.'

He made some notes on her chart and replaced it at the foot of her bed. 'Now, if you'll excuse me, I'm wanted in A and E.'

When the doctor had left, Mark turned to his family. 'Okay. What about taking it in turns for one of us to stay with her all night?' he suggested. 'Just in case she wakes up.'

'Good idea. Gran, you take the first turn, then you can get home to bed,' Alex replied.

His grandmother smiled at him and nodded.

'Right, who's next then? You Dad?' asked Ian.

'Yes, okay.'

'Right, Alex you do the next one, and I'll come in about four o'clock and do the last one.'

'In that case, Ian, shall I get back here tomorrow at eight o'clock?' Bridget asked.

'That sounds about right. It's not too early for you, is it?'

'Not at all.'

'What about playing her some more music, Ian?' Mark asked.

'Yes. Okay, Dad. Let me know if there's anything you think she'd like and I'll download it onto her iPad.' Ian subscribed to one of the numerous music companies on the internet and it was a simple task to look up music that he knew his mother enjoyed and download it. 'I might sort out some poetry as well.'

'Poetry? Mum doesn't like poetry,' Alex said.

'She might. I've read that they have poetry workshops in prisons and they help the inmates who are suffering from depression. They use them in grief counselling sessions as well. It's well documented.'

'Well, she's not in prison,' snapped Mark.

'She might as well be,' said Ian. 'Look at her. She's a prisoner of her own body.'

'Well I think it's a good idea,' said Bridget. 'Anything that can help, is worth doing.'

'But why poetry? Why not novels or the newspaper?' Alex asked.

'Apparently because a poem has less words, the listener can identify more easily with their own situation. I thought it was something we could do, read to her.'

'Well, she can't do it for herself, can she,' said Mark, grabbing his jacket and standing up. 'I think you're just grasping at straws, Ian. You should leave it to the doctors. They know what they're doing.'

'He's just trying to help, Dad,' said Alex. 'Right, we'll get off then, Gran. Ring if there is any development.'

*

Bridget sat by Teresa's bed for almost four hours, holding her hand and talking to her in her soft, sing-song voice. At first she was unsure what to say to the supine figure on the bed beside her; she didn't want to talk of the future and she couldn't bring herself to talk of Teresa's life, now so precariously on hold, so she told her about the old days when she was a small child in Kerry, the youngest of ten children.

'Your grandmother was a fine woman, Teresa; a tall woman with wide hips and a grand head of hair. The colour of golden corn, it was. She bore your grandfather twelve children, five boys and seven girls, but two were born dead, so we were really ten. Then the twins, Margaret and Siobhan died from scarlet fever when they were five; they were identical you know, and I remember seeing them wrapped in white sheets and lying side by side in the big bed. They looked so lovely; everyone cried when they came to see them, and my sister Theresa—the one I named you after— swore she would become a nurse when she grew up, so she could help poor sick babies. She never did though; she got a job in the local pub and married the man who delivered the Guinness every Friday. I expect you remember her; she always gave you a lemonade and a bag of crisps when we went to visit. Then there was Declan, the eldest. He died in the war; he was only nineteen. I cried for days when we received the news that he was missing; he was always my favourite, even though he was ten years older than me. The rest of the boys thrived, grew up and moved away to new lives in England and the North. Life was pretty hard for everyone in those days and it was testament to the good care my mother took of us all that any of us survived past childhood.

Your grandfather was a fisherman. He and the other fishermen rowed out around the islands in curraghs, traditional boats made from tarred canvas stretched over a wickerwork frame. They'd been using them for centuries and they were so light that two men could carry one. You must remember them? Once when you saw some men carrying one upside down on their backs, you laughed and said it looked like a beetle with long legs. In the winter your grandfather fished for mackerel and in the summer he set down his pots to get the lobster. Each day at daybreak your grandfather would row round to each pot, checking for a catch and replenishing the bait, then he would repeat it all again in the evening. I was always amazed that he could remember where he'd placed the lobster pots; to me the tiny coves and inlets all seemed the same. Each day the fishermen would crate up their catch of lobsters and send them off to the market; they were all bound for fancy restaurants in Dublin and Cork.

Your grandmother made sure we all did our share at home. Once school was out, each of us had our chores to do, even me, the baby of the family. I had to feed the chickens and search in the hedgerows for their eggs. I would line an old reed basket with some straw and place the brown, speckled eggs carefully in it. I loved collecting the eggs, but I didn't much like the chickens; they were bad-tempered birds and would peck at my legs if I was slow in scattering their feed.

Do you remember your grandmother's house? It was long and narrow, and dug into the hillside to shelter it from the Atlantic winds; the walls were painted white with lime that we mixed in a bucket with water, then slapped onto the stone walls with a big, horsehair brush. It was always your grandmother's job to do the painting, but sometimes she'd let us help her. In the old days the roof was covered with the same tarred canvas that they used for the curraghs, not slate tiles like today. There was one long living room, with a hearth at the west end and all the bedrooms at the east end. Of course by the time you saw the house, it had been modernised, and had electricity and a gas cooker and its own bathroom, but when I was a girl, we burnt thick slabs of black peat in the hearth and used the fire for cooking, heating our water and keeping us warm. I remember my mother hanging the mackerel in the chimney to smoke it and then we would have it for our tea with thick slices of brown bread and butter. You know I can still recall the damp, earthy smell of that peat fire today.'

She told of the day that Mikey had refused to continue with his studies for the priesthood, and how Father O'Riley had spent almost the whole day at their house talking to him and how her mother had cried for two days. She told her how one day her father didn't come home from fishing for the mackerel; how he'd been washed overboard in a storm. She talked and talked, her Kerry accent growing stronger as she reminisced about her family and her childhood, but her daughter lay motionless, her eyes closed, listening or dreaming; she knew not which.

*

Teresa was dreaming of her grandmother's house again. She knew it was a dream because Jimmy was there; they were on the beach together. Jimmy had his swimming trunks on and a red and white towel wrapped around him. She was laughing; it was far too cold for swimming and she knew he wouldn't go in the water despite what he said.

They ran along the beach together, the white sand pushing its way up between her toes with every step and setting up a fine spray for the wind to carry away. Jimmy was heading for the rocks at the end of the cove, to the point where they jutted out above the sea like row upon row of giant teeth. She followed him, hesitating a moment to watch as he climbed gingerly over them, picking his way through tangles of greenish-black seaweed, squashing the bulbous pods with a wet sounding crunch. His legs were thin and white, but she knew he was a strong boy. He would be thirteen in July.

They had reached the cliff face now; she stopped, slightly out of breath, and sat down on the rocks. Myriads of barnacles clung to their wet surface, glistening in the morning sun; minute lives suspended until the tide returned again. She dipped her feet into a rock-pool and poked her toes into bunches of tiny mussels that gently waved to and fro, open-mouthed, and watched as a startled crab scuttle sideways from his hiding place.

She began to feel cold and called to Jimmy to climb down and come home with her. He was up on the cliff now, waving his red and white towel in the wind.

*

'Mrs Rushton. Teresa. Can you hear me? Teresa.'

She opened her eyes as wide as she could. There was the doctor again. This time she could see him quite clearly.

'Good. I'm glad you're awake, Teresa. We'd like to do a few more tests,' he explained, leaning over her.

She could see tufts of nasal hair in his nostrils and a patch of dark bristles under his chin that he'd missed while shaving that morning.

'Teresa, can you hear me? Just nod if you can hear me, Teresa.'

He waited a few minutes, then peered into her eyes with a bright light that hurt them. 'I don't think she can hear me,' he added to someone she couldn't see. 'I'm not getting any response.'

A familiar voice answered him. Was that Mark? She tried to turn her head to see him, but nothing responded. God, these damned drugs were still paralysing her, didn't that stupid doctor realise that? By now the doctor had moved out of view, but she could hear him talking to someone. She strained to hear what they were saying.

'She's definitely coming out of the coma, Mr Rushton. The scans we've done show that she has developed a distinct sleep/wake pattern and there are signs of activity as though she's been dreaming, but so far we're not getting any cognitive response when she's awake. Her pupils are slightly dilated, and there's no physical movement, so I can't definitely say that she's conscious yet.'

'So what does all this mean, doctor?'

It was Mark. As if in response to her unspoken desire, he moved into her range of view and leaned over her.

'God, Mark, you can tell them. Tell them I can hear them,' she wanted to say.

'We can't be sure at the moment. We need to do more tests, but we cannot rule out the fact that she might be in a persistent vegetative state.'

'Oh, my God.'

She saw Mark's face crumple in disbelief. 'When will you know?'

'It may take some time. We've got a spare bed in the Neuro Rehabilitation ward for her. We'll probably move her across tomorrow, then we'll be able to monitor her progress more easily. Hopefully in a few weeks we'll know the extent of the damage.'

Were they talking about her? Persistent Vegetative State? That was like being a vegetable or something, wasn't it? She racked her brain to remember what she'd heard about the condition.

When she was a child they'd had a neighbour who fell off the roof of his house while trying to mend the chimney; he broke his neck. They said he was in a Persistent Vegetative State. She remembered seeing him once; his wife had made up a bed for him in their sitting room. He couldn't move, nor speak and he lay all day looking at the ceiling. She'd been afraid to go in, but her father had said that the poor man was not aware of what was happening to him. He said it was a shame; he was just a vegetable. Then the man died and everyone said it was a blessing for him and his wife.

Mark was looking at her again; there were tears trickling down his cheeks. What had happened to her? They were talking again, but she couldn't hear what they were saying; the sound came and went like waves on the shore. One moment it was roaring in her ears, like the sound of the sea when you put your ear to a seashell, the next it was totally quiet. She closed her eyes and drifted off to sleep.

*

The doctor had summoned them all to his office. They stood there, before his desk, like schoolchildren waiting for the results of their exams. Teresa had been moved to the Neuro Rehabilitation ward that morning.

'Good morning. I see we have the whole family here today,' he said looking at Teresa's mother, her husband and her two sons. 'Right, I won't keep you waiting any longer. From now on Mrs Rushton will be under the care of the Neuro Rehab team, that includes myself and one other neurologist, a speech and language therapist, a physiotherapist and an occupational therapist. The aim of this team is to help your wife recover some if not all of her faculties. I'm sure you all realise that if we are to succeed with this mammoth task, we need to enlist the help of the entire family. The therapy has to be ongoing.'

'This sounds very positive Dr Stevens. Does this mean that you think my mother has some hope of recovery?' Ian asked.

'I'm sorry I can't give you a definitive answer. I can only repeat that we must be patient and see what develops. In the meantime it's important to try to stimulate her brain into taking over some of its old functions. That's why we put so much emphasis on the therapy.'

'Can we go and see her?' Alex asked.

'Yes, of course. You're free to come and go as often as you wish in this ward. Obviously there'll be times when your mother is having some treatment or other, and you'll have to wait, but the more visitors she has the greater the stimulation and the better her chances of recovery.'

'Where exactly is the Neuro Rehabilitation ward?' Mark asked.

'On the fourth floor. Go up there right away, if you wish. She should be settled in by now.' He checked his watch as he spoke.

They trooped out of his office, unsure if they'd just received good news or bad.

'Well at least she's out of the coma,' Alex said.

'I just can't understand why it's so hard for them to give us a straight answer. They have so much sophisticated equipment, but they cannot tell exactly what has happened to her,' complained Ian.

'Maybe she's never going to recover,' said Alex. 'Maybe that's what they're not telling us.'

CHAPTER 9

Teresa could hear people approaching her bed; they were talking very quietly, as if they were frightened of disturbing someone. She lay there with her eyes open, looking at the ceiling. She'd been looking at the ceiling all morning; she knew it's white, plastered surface intimately. If she closed her eyes she could still see the patch where the paint had peeled and been retouched with a whiter shade of white, and she would still be able to trace the trajectory of the spider that had woven its web from the ceiling rose to the light shade. She knew by heart the words etched across the light bulb that told her the wattage and voltage. If only she could move and change her view before she went mad from boredom. A group of people had stopped at her bed. Ian's shock of red hair moved into her line of sight. She wanted to smile at him, to say 'Hello my darling,' to throw up her arms and give him a big hug, but she could do none of those things. She tried as hard as she could to wrench her face into a smile, but nothing moved. She prayed something of her feelings for him would show in her eyes.

'Hi, Mum. We've come to see how you're doing,' he said. His voice sounded stilted and even a little false.

Poor Ian, how frustrated he would be feeling with the situation. Well, darling, not as frustrated as I feel. Another head came into sight; it was Alex. Her beautiful, dependable Alex. He looked so sad. There were bags under his eyes and he seemed to have lost weight.

'Hello, Mum. How're you feeling?'

Why did they keep asking her questions that she couldn't answer. Who else was there? She saw Mark lean over and kiss her cheek; she could feel nothing but she could smell his after-shave and stale cigarettes. Had he started smoking again? After all these years? It had to be bad; he hadn't even returned to that old habit when Peter died. And her mother? Was her Mammy here? From the corner of her eye she could just see Bridget sitting by her side. They were all here. They were talking amongst themselves, as if she couldn't hear them. She felt invisible, a fly on the wall, witnessing her family discussing her as though she were some inanimate object.

'My poor Teresa, she looks so thin,' her mother said.

'That's normal Gran. I've been reading about trauma victims: they often develop an increase in their metabolic rate, which creates heat instead of producing the energy needed to keep the organ systems working. That means they often suffer from muscle wastage and tissue starvation,' Ian explained.

'That sounds like starving to death?'

'Well they won't let her starve to death. That's what that brown gunge is for; I'm sure it's full of all the nutrients her body needs.'

'I think Mum would prefer a big plate of spaghetti Bolognese and a glass of Chianti,' Alex said.

'Do you think she can hear us talking about her like this?' Bridget asked, tears running down her face.

'That's what we don't know Gran,' Alex said, putting his arm around his grandmother.

'She still isn't moving,' she said, desperation making her voice crack a little.

'Well she can open her eyes now. That's something,' Alex said. 'It's a first step. Remember the doctor said this could take a long time.'

Mark was listening to his family, but his attention was focused on Teresa. He reached out and stroked her hair, but she felt nothing. Why couldn't she feel his touch?

'Teresa, my darling. I'm so, so sorry,' he whispered.

She could hear him. She could hear them all. She closed her eyes; she didn't want to look at him anymore. She wanted to think about what was happening to her, about why her body was being so unresponsive. But it was impossible; her thoughts wouldn't stay in place. It was hard to concentrate. She felt desperately tired.

*

She was sitting in the living room of her grandmother's house. Someone had lit a fire in the hearth and every so often wisps of sweet smelling peat smoke would curl up over the stone mantelpiece and drift into the room. Her mother and her grandmother were dressed in black; they were seated at a table, drinking tea out of her grandmother's best tea cups. She thought that was strange; she'd never seen anyone use those cups before. Her grandmother always kept them in the glass cabinet. Her father came into the room; he was wearing his best suit and he looked very sad. He carried a bottle of Jameson's whiskey and a couple of glasses, which he put on the table next to the teapot. Teresa noticed two of her

*grandmother's friends sitting on high backed chairs
against the living room wall; one of them, Mrs O'Leary,
was wiping her eyes with a white lace handkerchief.
There was a knock on the door and the priest came in;
he was wearing a black coat over his long black robes
and carried a black hat with a wide brim in his hands.
He looked like an enormous crow, with his great beak of
a nose and his grim expression. It was Father O'Connor. She didn't like him; he scared her. The priest went
across to her mother and put his hand on her shoulder.*

*'Now, don't blame yourself Bridget. It is God's will.
And don't blame that poor wee Teresa; she's only a child
after all,' he said.*

*

When Teresa opened her eyes she couldn't tell if it was
the same day or the next one. The spider was still at his
post by the ceiling light and she could hear people moving around the ward. She tried moving her head again.
Nothing.

'Teresa. Good morning. Did you sleep well?'

From the corner of her eye she could see a young
nurse in a white uniform. As she moved closer into her
range of vision, Teresa saw that she was smiling at her.

'Just going to give you your morning bath and get
you dressed,' she continued.

A second nurse joined her and pulled a curtain
around the bed to shield them from prying eyes. Together they lifted and turned Teresa's inanimate body, ma-
nipulating it in the contorted dance that they called a bed
bath. As they struggled to redress her, Teresa watched in
horror as she realised that part of the daily ritual from

now on was to swaddle her in a giant nappy. Did nothing work?

Half an hour later they left. She was still lying on her back watching the spider, but now she smelt of carbolic and cheap talcum powder. She could hear the squeak of trolley wheels and the clatter of plates and cutlery. It was breakfast time; she could smell coffee. What she would give for a cup of strong black coffee right now. Her mouth began to salivate at the thought and she tried to swallow. It was impossible; she could feel her mouth filling up with saliva and running down her chin.

'Good morning Teresa.' It was her mother. She leant over her and kissed her.

If only she could feel her mother's lips. If only she could kiss her back. She began to cry.

'Nurse, nurse,' her mother was calling the nurse across. 'Look, she's crying,' she told her with the same sense of pride a mother has over her baby's first steps.

The nurse took a cotton swab and wiped Teresa's eyes. 'It's just the tear duct watering,' she said and took a small tube and syphoned the saliva from Teresa's mouth. 'There, that should be better now.'

'But it's not my tear duct watering; I *am* crying,' Teresa wanted to shout. 'Look at me, I'm crying.'

Her mother was searching in her bag for something. 'I've brought you some nice soap, Teresa and some body lotion and your favourite perfume. I don't know whether you can smell that awful soap they wash you with, but just in case you can, I've brought you something nicer.' She held a bottle of Dior in front of Teresa's eyes.

'You like this one, don't you?' she asked and sprayed Teresa's wrist and the spots behind her ears. 'I'll put it all here in your cupboard and I'll tell the nurse when she comes back.'

The smell of the perfume, both flowery and heady at the same time, made Teresa want to cry again. Her mother was right; it was her favourite. Mark or one of the boys always bought her a bottle for her birthday; it had become such a ritual that she felt disappointed if they failed to do so. Would she be home this year for her birthday? She was beginning to doubt it.

CHAPTER 10

It was not until she noticed the bunting hanging from the light above her bed, that she realised it was almost Christmas. She was still in the same bed, in the same position, unable to move. The sight of the streamers made her cry. Christmas used to be her favourite time of year. Unlike many of her cynical friends she enjoyed the holiday with all its traditions and did everything to make it a special time for her family.

She thought back to the Christmas before Peter died. They had the usual Christmas tree: it was always a big one and Mark had set off to buy it, armed with specific instructions as to its shape and condition, 'Make sure it hasn't started to moult, or it will never last until Twelfth Night. And try to get one where the branches are close together and don't spread out too widely.' Peter had gone with him. He'd stopped at the door and turned to her with a wide smile and said, 'Don't worry, Mummy. We'll get the best one there.'

For as long as she could remember her sons had enjoyed decorating the tree, and it was a tribute to the strength of this family ritual that it still continued even after Peter's death. In a sad way, it made them all feel closer to him. He was their own, personal ghost of Christmas past. Some of the decorations were as old as her sons. Every year since they'd been married Mark had bought Teresa a new tree decoration: one year it was a star made of Waterford crystal, another time it was a glass ball with a thousand different facades that had caught his eye in the local Chinese bric-a-brac shop, last year it had been a porcelain fairy wearing a pink tutu— Teresa could remember when she'd received each one. Each year, two or three days before Christmas Mark climbed into the loft and brought down the box of old decorations. It was usually on Christmas Eve, after everyone had arrived, that they set about decorating it, carefully removing each decoration from its tissue wrapping and taking it in turns to hang it on the tree. She cooked mince pies for them to eat while they worked and Mark opened a couple of bottles of champagne. Then she and Mark went to midnight mass at St. Clements.

The boys had stopped attending midnight mass sometime in their teens. Mark said he felt like a hypocrite, because it was the only time in the year he crossed the threshold of that church, but Teresa liked to go to hear the carols. Her mother always attended St. Joseph's Catholic Church to take Holy Communion, but Teresa wouldn't go with her. She'd stopped being a Catholic when she was thirteen. Teresa preferred St. Clements; it was a Norman church, in a small hamlet on the outskirts of the town. The vicar was a young man with a Dominican wife, and he preached to them in a strong West Indian accent. The church was always decorated with flowers and bunches of holly at Christmas, and after the service, they were served mulled wine in the vestry.

On Christmas morning Mark opened more champagne and poured them all a glass of Buck's Fizz while they opened the presents. She thought back to the Christmas morning when Ian had been seven; he'd stood before them, with his hands on his hips and demanded to know the truth.

'Billy Richards says there's no such thing as Father Christmas. He says it's just a big lie made up by our parents, so that they have an excuse if they can't buy us any presents.'

They had exploded the childhood myth as gently as possible, but there'd still been tears. Alex had been bitterly disappointed to have a part of his childhood removed so brusquely, but Ian was just annoyed that they had lied to him. She felt that something of the magic of Christmas had disappeared with that confession, and she silently cursed Billy Richards. Of course, when Peter was born, the boys joined in the pretence as wholeheartedly as ever. By then they were old enough to understand the importance of maintaining the magic as long as possible.

After they opened their presents, Teresa set about preparing the Christmas lunch. Until the "Mad Cow" scare they'd always had a large rib of roast beef as the main course, but nowadays they had turkey. Mark used to help her stuff the bird with her own recipe of sausage meat and herbs and, once it was in the oven, the whole family went for a walk along the tow path. She remembered that last walk clearly—another family ritual—it had been a beautiful bright morning, with no clouds and enough sunshine to almost warrant wearing sunglasses, but the wind was blowing from the north and it whistled along the riverbank, making them walk briskly and pull their scarves around their ears.

The memory pained her. How long had it been since she'd seen the sky, never mind the sun? What was it like to feel the wind on her face and shiver with the cold? Living in this cocoon she could experience none of this. Nobody seemed to realise that she was still alive inside this shell that used to be her body. She felt that she couldn't go on living like this any longer; it was too cruel for everyone. Every day she prayed that it would be her last. What did she have to live for? Her beautiful boy was dead. Her husband and her best friend had betrayed her, and now she was nothing more than a vegetable. She wanted to die.

*

There was a muted argument going on around her bed. She could make out the voices of her husband, and Ian and somebody else, possibly the doctor.

'Dr Stevens, I know you're the expert, but we're her family. My grandmother is convinced that my mother can hear us. Look at her eyes; she can move her eyes from left to right. She can blink. We think she knows what's going on.'

'Ian, tell them. You know me. You're right my darling, I can hear you. Please tell them. Make them help me,' she silently pleaded.

'Well, it is possible, I suppose. We'll do some more scans and see if there has been any change over the last three months. But please don't get your hopes up too much.'

'That's all we ask, Doctor. Have another look at her.'

When the doctor left, they resumed their seats.

'Dad, I'm sorry, but after Christmas I can't come down so often. Andrew has been very good so far, but he can't be expected to rearrange the department on a permanent basis just for me. From the beginning of January I'm going to have to resume my old hours. I'll try to get down one weekend a month, but more than that will be impossible.'

'That's okay Ian. None of us thought your mother would take so long to recover.'

'And it's not as if there is a time limit on it; she could continue like this for years,' Ian added.

For years. What did they mean 'for years?' She couldn't bear the thought. Why did they have to sit there talking about her in this negative fashion?

'Yes, Ian, you're right. We can't leave our lives on hold for ever.'

On hold? So what if their lives were on hold? What about her life? They could always leave. They could get up and walk down the corridor, take the lift to the ground floor and walk through the wide glass doors and out into the carpark. They could climb into their cars and drive out of the hospital grounds and never come back. They could go to bed that night and in the morning rise and shower and take the train to work. The minutiae of their lives was intact. It was her life that was on hold. She felt anger welling up inside her: anger against her son and her husband because they still had lives to discuss, anger against the hospital because it had failed to come up with a miracle cure, anger against a God that she didn't believe in, but nevertheless felt had let her down and anger against herself for being unable to die.

'I'll put some music on for her,' Ian said, taking her iPad out of the bedside locker. 'Maybe it'll help.'

Ian was right. The music soothed her. Her son was tender as he fitted the tiny plugs into her ears, and adjusted the volume so that she could hear it, but it didn't drown out all the other sounds around her. Teresa's anger abated; Ian was a good son, and after all he was only young, with all his life in front of him. It was natural that he should want his life to return to normal as soon as possible. His choice of music was excellent; she was surprised that he understood her taste so well. She closed her eyes and let the chants of Monteverdi's Vespers take her off into a Renaissance world.

*

A week later Mark and Bridget were sitting by Teresa's bed when a nurse approached them.

'Mr Rushton, Dr Stevens would like to talk to you.'

Mark rose as if to follow her, but she put out her hand and said: 'No, that's okay, he's coming up here in a few minutes.'

'Do you think he has some new results?' Bridget asked her son-in-law.

'Who knows. Even if he has, it isn't going to make an immediate difference to Teresa, is it?'

They looked at her motionless figure. Mark reached over and took the perfume spray from the cupboard and sprayed the air above his wife's bed.

'Mark, don't do that. It could be bad for her lungs.'

'Well, I can't stand the smell. Perhaps we should buy some air-freshener to keep by the bed.'

'Oh, look, her eyes are watering again.' Bridget dabbed at Teresa's eyes with a paper tissue.

*

How could Mark say something so unkind? She knew she stank, but what could she do about it. The nurse was not due to see to her for at least another hour. She sobbed and sobbed, but nobody was aware of her distress. How could she continue like this? Her life had become meaningless, replaced by an empty void that stretched ahead of her into an interminable future. Even the people she loved, and who she believed loved her, were becoming impatient of this terrible condition that was day by day turning her from a wife and mother into one of the undead.

'Mr Rushton. Mrs O'Sullivan.' The doctor extended his hand to them each in turn, then pulled up a spare chair and sat down.

'Well, I have had some lengthy discussions with my colleagues about your wife and we think we should amend our diagnosis. We have decided to rule out Persistent Vegetative State, because we are now sure that there is no damage to the upper part of the brain. We believe that Mrs Rushton has retained complete cognitive awareness.'

'So what is it then?' Bridget asked.

Teresa could just see the back of her mother's head as she turned to face the doctor.

'We think your wife has a rare neurological disorder called Cerebromedullospinal Disconnection; it is often referred to as Locked-In Syndrome.'

He paused to see if they had anything to say then continued, 'You may remember that when Mrs Rushton was first admitted, I told you that she'd suffered damage to the lower part of her brain, in particular, the brain stem. Well this is still the case.'

Teresa saw Mark nod his head. So far she hadn't heard anything very encouraging.

'So why have you changed your mind about the diagnosis?' Mark asked.

'It's very difficult to identify Locked-In Syndrome, especially in the early stages. The patient appears, to all intent and purposes, to be completely unaware of what is going on around her.'

'Can you now explain what is wrong with my daughter?' Bridget asked.

Teresa couldn't see the doctor, but he sounded grave. 'Your daughter's body is completely paralysed; she can move her eyes and, possibly with time, she will be able to move certain facial muscles. She can feel sensations throughout her body but she cannot move. She can breathe without a ventilator, but she can't produce enough breath to make her vocal chords vibrate. However she can hear and reason.'

'My God. That's awful. She's trapped inside her own body.'

'Yes, that's right. That's why it's called Locked-In Syndrome.'

'Is there a cure?'

'No, I'm afraid there's no cure. There are however a number of treatments we can use to alleviate her condition.'

'So there's no cure,' Mark repeated. He sounded stunned. For a moment Teresa felt sorry for her husband.

'No, I'm afraid not. We can try stimulating the muscles with electrodes; this has been known to have a limited success at times, but most treatment is symptomatic and supportive.'

'So she'll be like this forever?'

Teresa could imagine the doctor nodding his head gravely at them. She could hear her mother sobbing, a strange strangled cry breaking free from her throat. No cure. Was this what it was like to hear the judge pronounce one's death sentence?

The doctor continued, 'However now that we know that she can hear and understand us, we must make even more effort to provide her with external stimuli. For a start I think it is about time we tried to get her more upright. We can even get her a wheelchair so that you can take her outside occasionally.'

Teresa wanted to laugh. As far as she could see, nothing had changed. She found it hard to imagine Mark wheeling her through the park, a lifeless doll in an outsize nappy.

'Also, we will get the speech therapist to come and see her.'

'But you said she can't speak.'

'Yes, but she can learn to communicate through blinking her eyelids. It has been successful with similar patients.'

Teresa thought about the Christmas cards they bought from the charity for painters who painted with their mouths and their feet. She had always felt so sorry for them and admired their tenacity. But she wouldn't even be able to do that; all she could do was blink. Suddenly it was all too much. She wanted to scream at them. She wanted to tell them it wasn't worth the effort. Give her something to end her life, quickly and painlessly. Then her family could get on with their lives.

There would be no need for anyone to have their life on hold—not even her.

'Bridget, I'm sorry. I'm going home. I'll phone you later,' Mark said abruptly.

She heard him walk briskly away and out of the ward. If only she could do the same. If only she could walk away.

*

Mark didn't look at his wife as he left and he didn't look at the doctor. He just had to get out of the hospital as soon as he could. He had to get out before the scream that was building from somewhere deep inside him, burst and woke them all from their locked-in lives.

How he got home, he never knew: suddenly he was there, turning his key in the latch. He slammed the door behind him and going straight to the drinks cabinet, poured himself a large Scotch and sat down on the settee. Smokey Joe leaped onto his lap, purring his delight at seeing him.

The walls of the sitting room were covered with Teresa's paintings. They seemed to look at him accusingly. Teresa had been at art school before she met him and had been thinking about becoming a professional artist, but marriage and two children in quick succession had put paid to that. She never complained; she said her career was as a wife and mother and she was happy with that, but she continued to paint. Whenever she had a spare moment she took out her easel and painted, first oils and then watercolours. Until Peter died and then she stopped. The day the accident happened, she'd been painting a watercolour of Hurley Lock. It still lay in the garage, unfinished, alongside all her brushes and paints, which had remained untouched ever since.

'Oh, Smokey Joe, what are we going to do?' he asked, and burrowing his face into the cat's silky fur, burst into uncontrollable tears.

He knew now that Teresa would never come home; she was condemned to that hospital bed forever. And now, when he would have said it was impossible for the situation to be any worse, now he knew that she too was aware of her fate. Why couldn't she have been killed outright? Why couldn't she have stayed in a coma until death took her quietly away? But life was not like that; life was full of surprises; life could take you by the throat and choke the breath from your body; life could take a knife and not only plunge it in your heart, but turn the blade. One wet night, a few angry words and all their lives had been turned upside down.

He poured himself another whisky and took it into the bedroom. There was a packet of cigarettes open on the bedside table; he took one out and lit it with the usual sense of guilt. He'd better let the boys know the latest news. He dialled Alex's telephone number.

'Hi, Dad. I was just thinking of telephoning you. How's everything?'

'Hi, Alex. Look I've got some bad news.'

He told him what the doctor had explained to them, as simply as he could.

'I'll come down on Friday, straight from work,' Alex offered.

'There's no need Alex. What can you do? What can any of us do?'

'Now, come on Dad, that sounds defeatist to me.'

'But why, Alex? Why this? Haven't we all suffered enough?'

'I know it's hard Dad, but we can't give up on her yet. Maybe the doctor's right, maybe she'll improve with some treatment.'

'You weren't there. It's not like that. There is no cure. And the worst part is that she knows it.'

'Look, you hang on in there, Dad. I'll be round on Friday about seven. Maybe you can buy me a pint,' he added.

'Okay son. I'd like to see you.'

'Would you like me to ring Ian?'

'No, I prefer to tell him myself. I know he's going to take it very hard.'

In fact Ian had responded to the news in his characteristic pragmatic manner. 'All the more need to talk to her and keep her mind active,' he said. 'Look, I can't make it this weekend, but I'll be down on the twenty-third. Try to keep positive, Dad.'

Then as though he sensed his father's black mood, he chatted on about his work and the recent discoveries they'd made in the cellars of a manse in Dundee. 'There are only two other paintings by this man in all of Scotland,' he told him. 'It's quite a find, I can tell you.'

By the time Ian had rung off, Mark felt a bit more positive. It was time to reassess his own life, he decided. He looked at his reflection in the bedroom mirror; he was letting himself go. He needed a shave and a decent haircut. He took off his shirt and sniffed it; he must have been wearing it for at least three days—and he had the nerve to complain about Teresa smelling.

He picked up the telephone again; this time he dialled Michelle's number.

'Hello Michelle, it's Mark.'

'Mark. This is a nice surprise.'

She didn't sound at all annoyed with him despite the way he'd spoken to her during their last conversation. He decided to come straight to the point. 'Look, Michelle, are you busy tonight? Do you think I could come round?'

'No, I'm not busy. Of course you can come round,' she paused, 'if you're sure you want to.'

'Yes, I want to,' he said.

PART 2

*"I am fading away. Slowly but surely.
Like the sailor who watches his home shore gradually
disappear, I watch my past recede."*

*Jean-Dominique Bauby
"The Diving-Bell and the Butterfly"*

CHAPTER 11

The back of Teresa's bed had been raised to an angle of forty-five degrees, and a cage of pillows and metal bars prevented her from unbalancing and slipping off. She found this new position very uncomfortable—all her weight seemed to be channelled down onto her coc-cyx—but at least she had a better range of vision. Over recent months the sensations in her body had returned, but not the movement. To think how she had longed for the feeling to come back to her body, to be able to feel the brush of Ian's stubbly chin when he bent to kiss her goodbye, to feel the gentle touch of her mother's hand on hers. Now, when a harassed orderly knocked her knee against the bed frame as he struggled to move her, she could feel the pain but do nothing about it. Some-times they would leave her nightdress bunched up be-hind her back, the ridge of material chafing her skin, or she would experience a terrible itch on her nose and be unable to scratch it. Even before her accident her mother used to say she was like the princess in the fairy tale, The Princess and the Pea, but these small irritations were now unbearable.

Some days she would look with interest at the rest of the inmates of the Neuro Rehab ward; but at other times it made her even more depressed to see her own infirmities reflected in their twisted bodies. There was no mirror by her bed and at times, if she tried very hard, she could imagine she was unchanged, just resting motionlessly for a few minutes in a yoga relaxation position, before getting up to go out to dinner.

'Good morning Teresa.' A rather round woman in her forties stood at the foot of her bed. It was the speech therapist.

'The doctor tells me that you are getting on so well that we should have another try with the alphabet board.'

She opened her case and took out her equipment, smiling hopefully at Teresa as she did so. First she cleared away some items from the hospital trolley that stood by Teresa's bed and pushed it so that it stretched across Teresa's legs. Then she set up a perspex board that contained all twenty-six letters of the alphabet, in such a position that Teresa could see it easily. The letters were each about an inch high, and arranged in order of their most frequent use in the English language, starting with E, N, R, S and T and then finishing with Q, X and Z. She took out her notepad and pencil and sat down next to the bed.

'Okay Teresa. Now, you remember how this works; I will point to each of the letters in turn and when I point to one that you want me to write down, just blink,' she explained.

Just blink. As though there was anything else she could do. In the blink of an eye her life had changed for ever. 'Just blink,' the woman said, as though there was an alternative.

'Now is there something you would like to ask me, Teresa?'

She began to point to the letters, one by one, and Teresa dutifully blinked at the letters she wanted.

'Teresa, are you sure you meant to spell this message?' She held up her notepad so that Teresa could read it; it said, I DON'T WANT TO DO THIS.

Why did this woman persist? She didn't want to communicate with anyone; she wanted to die. She thought of the time they'd tried to get Mark to use the board. He'd become tongue-tied; he, who could communicate freely, whose tongue could move with ease and whose voice box vibrated readily whenever a word wanted to fly out of his mouth, had nothing to say. It had taken her almost twenty minutes of blinking her eyes to simply ask him if Smokey Joe was alright. Teresa closed her eyes; with her eyes closed she could block it all out.

*

Christmas fell on a weekend that year, so the holiday was even longer than usual. Ian had booked a flight on the twenty-third as he promised; his office had finished at midday on the Friday which left him with time to do some last minute Christmas shopping: a tartan shawl for his grandmother, a bottle of Scotch for his dad, a CD for

Alex and a red silk scarf for his mother. It was cold in Edinburgh and snow was forecast; people hurried along the street, hats pulled down over their ears and muffled in scarves and thick coats, anonymous shoppers intent on finishing their tasks and returning to their centrally heated homes as soon as possible. It was already growing dark and the strings of Christmas lights that stretched across the main street would soon be lit. He heard the familiar strains of canned Christmas music floating out of shop doorways, open portals that offered glimpses of more than one rotund Father Christmas issuing vague promises to expectant children. A group of Salvation Army carol singers stood on the corner of Princes' Street; the breath from their open mouths condensed in the cold air and like fine smoke, floated heavenwards with their singing. A woman in uniform waved her collection tin at him as he passed. He tossed in a coin, hearing it rattle hollowly. Instead of making him feel more festive, all these familiar rituals made him sad; they were the same sights and sounds of other Christmases, but this one was going to be different for his family.

*

It was evening when he arrived at his father's house. Everything was in darkness. He looked at his watch: it was almost seven o'clock. His father was probably still at the hospital. He reached up and felt along the top of the porch; there it was, as always: the spare key. It was a bit rusty, but slipped into the lock with ease; he turned the key and let himself in.

The house was silent and empty; even Smokey Joe wasn't there to greet him. As he opened the lounge door he could detect the musty smell of stale food and cigarette smoke and a sudden feeling of sadness overwhelmed him; he realised what it must be like for his father to come home to this empty house day after day.

'Come on Ian, snap out of it. It's Christmas. It's no time to feel sorry for yourself,' he told himself. He spoke aloud and his voice reverberated around the empty room.

He opened his case and removed the presents; this year there was no tree under which to place them, so he piled them up on the little table by the window. Then he went to the refrigerator and helped himself to a beer, sat down on the sofa and turned on the television. There was a Christmas concert being performed at the Albert Hall. He turned up the sound and leant back thinking of previous Christmases. None of them had been particularly jolly since poor little Peter died, but this one promised to be the worst of all.

His mother had been responding well to the music that he played her; she seemed more relaxed when she listened to it. More serene. Even the poetry seemed to go down well. He'd found some audio recordings of Derek Walcott's latest anthology and put them on her iPad. Perhaps he'd look for some Christmas music for her. Or was that too risky? It might bring back too many sad memories and that would be counter-productive. What he wanted was for her to become more positive, to have hope, not to be depressed.

He'd tried so many things but the music and the poetry were the only things that seemed to work. Jenny was a great one for alternative medicine, maybe she could come up with some suggestions—but he hadn't seen her in ages. What he needed was something to change his mother's mood, to give her hope. He'd tried Reiki—Fiona had said it helped her sister who was depressed after her husband left her—but it did nothing for his mother; her life force remained as low as ever. He thought of the Dr Bach Flowers, but how could he give them to her when she wasn't able to swallow. Then he bought some crystals: rose quartz, black obsidian and clear quartz. Between them they were supposed to make her feel more grounded, improve her self esteem, restore her confidence, help her emotional balance and release the anger that he knew was eating away at her. Nothing to repair her brain stem but he hoped something would give her back her interest in life.

He finished his beer and was just looking for a second one when he heard the front door open.

'Ian, is that you?'

'Hi, Dad. I'm in the kitchen.'

'Good flight?' He pointed to the beer in Ian's hand. 'Oh, pour me one as well, would you. That hospital always leaves me with a raging thirst.'

'Yeah, the flight was okay. I got here about half-an-hour ago.'

He handed his father the beer. Something looked different about him; he didn't appear quite so drawn and something of the old sparkle had returned to his eyes.

'How's Mum? Any news?' he asked.

'No, nothing. Everything is just the same. They're a bit worried about some bladder infection, but I don't think it's anything serious.'

'Poor Mum, what else can happen to her?'

'Have you heard from your brother?'

'I spoke to him in the week. He said he's busy tomorrow, but he'll come round early on Christmas Day, so we can all go to the hospital together. He offered to pick up Gran on the way.'

'Isn't she going to her sister in Dublin, like she usually does? Mark asked.

He followed Ian into the lounge.

'No, she thought she should stay with us this year.'

'I wish she would go. What's the point of us all being miserable.'

'I expect Gran will feel miserable no matter where she is. She isn't going to forget Mum, just because she's in Dublin, is she?'

'What's that?' Mark asked, pointing to the pile of presents.

'Just a few gifts. Not much really.'

'Well that's very nice of you Ian, but I haven't really been in the mood for Christmas shopping. I haven't even bought anything for our Christmas lunch.'

'Don't worry Dad, I don't think we'll feel much like celebrating. It won't be the same without Mum, anyway. Look, talking of food, I haven't eaten anything since this morning, why don't we go to that Indian place around the corner tonight?'

'The Bombay?'

'Yes, that's the one.'

'Okay, sounds good. Just let me have a quick wash and change my shirt. The stink from the hospital clings to my clothes; I can still smell it when I leave.'

*

Christmas Day was difficult for them; the brothers tried to remain cheerful for their father's sake, but the season held too many memories for them all. The hospital staff had done their best to make the wards as seasonal as possible for the patients: there was a Christmas tree at the entrance to the hospital and streamers strung around the nurses' station; there was even a Father Christmas making the rounds of the wards with small gifts of chocolates or soap for each of the patients.

When Teresa's family arrived at the hospital, her bed had already been raised to its semi-recumbent position and someone had misguidedly placed a paper hat on her head.

'Some people have no sense of propriety,' Mark said, angrily removing it and throwing it into the bin by the bed.

'Don't take on so, Dad. I expect they were just trying to include her; look everyone else has paper hats,' Alex said, pointing to the rest of the patients in the ward.

'Well, they all look pathetic,' he hissed. 'What's the point of pretending? No-one in here is going home again; at least not in the foreseeable future.'

Alex looked at Ian. They knew their father was probably right, but somehow it seemed necessary to keep the pretence going.

'I just bought a few gifts, nothing much,' Ian said, pulling out his bag of Christmas presents. 'This is for you Gran. It's pure Scottish wool.'

'Ian, it's lovely. It'll keep me warm when I'm watching the telly. My, but it's grand. Thank you, sweetheart.' She reached over and kissed her grandson.

'And this is for you Mum. It's silk and is as soft as anything.' He waited, but there was no response from his mother, so he wound it carefully around her neck and tied it loosely, so that the fringe hung across her breasts. 'It's red, Mum, to give you energy.'

'You seem to know a lot about this psychic energy thing these days, Ian,' Alex said.

'Not really, but I am learning about it.'

'Do you really believe in all this mumbo jumbo?' Mark asked.

'Well I don't believe it's mumbo jumbo, for a start. I don't know enough about it to say what works and what doesn't, but I don't want to dismiss anything, just in case it can help Mum. Look the doctors act as though she's never going to get better. I don't believe it. There has to be something that we can do to help her, even if the doctors won't.'

'Lots of people believe in alternative medicine these days,' Bridget said. 'Mary Bridges' niece went to a hypnotist to help her stop smoking.'

'So what happened? Did she stop?'

'Well she did for a few weeks, but then her husband ran off with the woman next door, so she started again.'

They all managed a laugh at that.

'Well I suppose it was understandable in the circumstances,' Alex said, unwrapping his gift. 'Thanks Bro. Just what I wanted.'

He pulled the cellophane off the CD and read the list of songs on the back. 'I've been waiting for this to be released. She's got a wonderful voice; she takes all the old songs and makes them sound fresh and new again.'

'Pretty gorgeous too,' Mark added.

'Yes, she's okay.'

'Look, guys, I was wondering if we should try to find a healer for Mum?' Ian asked, rather tentatively.

'A healer? Ian have you gone mad? This is a hospital; they aren't going to let you bring a healer in here.'

'I don't see why not. They let priests and psychiatrists in.'

'That's different.'

'Well, we don't need to announce that she's a healer; she could just be a visitor.'

'A woman is it? Well it won't do any good. Can't you understand Ian; your mother is not going to get better. It's time we all faced up to it.'

'Look, Dad, Ian, let's talk about this at home, alright?' Alex intervened.

Ian looked at his brother. 'Okay, after all it is Christmas Day,' he said.

Everyone was trying to be jolly, for Mum's sake but Ian knew that they had all become resigned to Teresa's condition; it was too hard for them to continue battling with the belief that she might one day improve. He seemed to be alone in his struggle. Even Alex, who'd always been the one to make the decisions, the sensible one, the one he'd always looked up to, was backing off in this case. Today he just sat in the uncomfortable hospital chair and looked lost.

They sat around Teresa's bed and talked to her about the wonderful Christmases they remembered, but she closed her eyes and wouldn't look at them. They told her that they had given Smokey Joe his special Christmas breakfast of tinned pilchards. They told her that this was reputed to be the warmest Christmas in the south of England on record, and that daffodils were already coming up in the London parks. They tried playing her some Christmas music, but she screwed her eyes so tightly shut that they decided that this was her way of telling them to turn it off. They lapsed into silence, but still they didn't dare leave her on this of all days, so they stayed and watched the Queen's speech on the television that hung above her bed; then they sat through an old film version of Charles Dickens' 'A Christmas Carol'. They took it in turns to slip down to the cafeteria and drink lukewarm tea made with UHT milk and eat cold mince pies.

At one point Ian and Alex decided to walk around the ward and talk to some of the other patients. There was a woman of about their mother's age who had had a massive stroke: the whole of the left side of her body had been affected and she was unable to walk unaided. Her family had been to visit her earlier, but now she sat alone, listening to the small radio by her bed. When Alex enquired after her health, she put her right hand in front of her mouth, so that he wouldn't see the lopsided way her mouth twisted when she answered him. The effort of talking to strangers obviously tired her, and after a few minutes they moved on to speak to the young man in the bed opposite Teresa, and left the woman listening to the Christmas edition of Twenty Questions.

The youth's name was Joe and he looked no more than eighteen. According to the nurse he had suffered severe brain trauma after being knocked off his bicycle at the traffic lights. Ian admired the young man's courage; he had been there almost a year and had progressed from having no movement at all to being able to move his right hand with enough dexterity to feed himself. At first he'd been unable to speak, but now he could say isolated words and augmented this sparse vocabulary with a series of signs. He also communicated through an alphabet board similar to Teresa's. As the doctor had explained, his brain was having to relearn everything it knew, and each day—even today—the youth did his exercises. If there was no physiotherapist to help him, he did some of the simpler ones himself, propped up in his bed. He was determined to get well, but then, he had all the positivity of youth. They wished the young man a happy Christmas and returned to their mother's bedside.

At eight o'clock, when they were halfway through watching a variety show that Bridget swore was a repeat, the nurse came and told them that it was time to get Teresa ready for the night. They kissed her goodnight and told her that they loved her, then like inmates released from a day's imprisonment, they hurried from the ward, the nurse's wishes of a Happy Christmas falling on deaf ears.

There was a tacit agreement between them to treat the day like any other; Alex took his grandmother home, then rejoined his father and brother at the family house. This year there was no Christmas dinner waiting for them, but as nobody was really hungry, it didn't matter. In the end they took some frozen pizzas from the freezer and heated them in the microwave. They drank beer and Scotch until they were all drunk, then Mark staggered to his room, leaving his two sons in the lounge, where they too fell asleep, thankful that the day was finally over.

*

Teresa was relieved when they went. She felt extremely sad. Christmases had always been like milestones for her: measuring her sons' journey from infancy to adolescence and then on to maturity, and now another one had been passed. She couldn't stop herself wondering how many more she would see. Would she see them journey on through their lives to become husbands and fathers? She felt the tears running down her cheeks and could do nothing to wipe them away. The ward was quiet now; the nurses had withdrawn to their stations and the rest of the patients were either asleep or, like her, awake and praying for oblivion.

CHAPTER 12

Alex lay stretched out in his king-size bed, looking at the ceiling. It was Sunday morning and time he got up and joined his usual crowd of running friends. Most of them were in training for the local marathon but that was too much of a commitment for him; he just went along for the exercise. Sitting in a car, or at his desk all week, he felt the need to do something to keep in shape —running fitted the bill perfectly. Afterwards they always went for a few pints at the Bull and Bear and a pub lunch. Every Sunday was the same. His life was prescribed and regular. As regular as clockwork. Tick-tock tick-tock. That was his life, ticking away.

Try as he might, he couldn't get the memory of that awful Christmas Day out of his mind. It wasn't just his mother, condemned to a living hell in her hospital bed, but the other poor sods as well. That young boy, Joe. His life had changed in a single moment. One minute everything was as it should be and the next— thanks to a moment of inattention by the driver of a BMW—he was fighting for his life. As quickly as that.

He swung his legs over the side of the bed and sat up. What if it was him lying there in that hospital bed; what memories would he have? He wasn't sure. Plenty of regrets, that was certain, but memories he could savour? True he had this lovely apartment, with its view across the river, and a company car. He had a safe, well-paid job but did he want to remain a car salesmen all his life? He'd taken the job when he was at a low point—Peter had just died and there didn't seem any point in going to university anymore. Life was too fragile, too short.

His original ambition had been to work in conservation or something to do with protecting the environment. And now what was he contributing to society? Nothing. Ironically, by selling cars, he was doing the opposite; he was helping people to pollute the atmosphere and add to the congestion on the roads.

He pulled on his running socks and rummaged under the bed for his trainers. True, he had lots of friends, but most of them were busy with their own lives. There were a few special people in his life, but no serious relationships; his sex life consisted of a number of one-night stands. So in the end what did it all amount to? A healthy bank balance, a secure job and a comfortable apartment. Would that be enough if his life were to change tomorrow? If he were to end up like Joe, or his mother? Was that going to be the sum of his memories? No; he didn't want that. It was as clear as day that the time had come to make a change. He was tired of being old, dependable Alex. He wanted some adventure in his life. He wanted to make a difference to the world—a small one, maybe, but a difference in some way.

*

He didn't hesitate. If he hesitated with this first step, he'd never take the second one.

'Good morning Beryl, is Reg in?'

'Yes. He's got an appointment in twenty minutes, so don't keep him too long,' the Divisional Manager's secretary replied.

'It won't take a minute. I promise.'

Alex tapped lightly on his boss's door and went in.

'Alex. Come in. How's your mother? Any change?'

'No. She's just the same. Reg, can I have a word with you?'

'Of course. Sit down. Now, what can I do for my top salesman?'

Alex ignored the compliment and said, 'I'd like to hand in my notice.'

'What?' Reg Williams had been lounging back in his chair, fiddling with one of those executive toys. Now he sat up with a look of astonishment on his face. 'You're leaving us?' The toy slipped from his fingers.

'Yes. I'd like to give a month's notice.'

'But why? You were top salesman two years running. You have a bright future here at Bettericks.' He rubbed his bald head in astonishment. 'What is it you want, Alex? More money? A promotion? Has one of our competitors offered you a better job? Now don't be hasty. I'm sure we can work something out. Just leave it with me and I'll talk to HR to find out what can be done.'

'No, Reg. It's none of those things. I'm just tired of selling cars. I want a change. I'm going to work for the VSO.' When he saw Reg's puzzled expression he added, 'Voluntary Service Overseas.'

'Oh. Teaching African kids? Something like that?'

'Yes, something like that. I start the beginning of next month. I thought that would give you time to get a replacement for me.'

His boss looked bewildered. 'Well I never expected to hear that. I had you marked down as a lifer. I thought you'd be stepping into my shoes one day.'

'That's what was worrying me,' said Alex with a smile.

The door to the Divisional Manager's office opened and Beryl said, 'Your meeting is in five minutes, Mr Williams.'

'Thank you Beryl.' He closed his laptop and looked at Alex. 'Well, I'm very sorry to hear your news. I wish there was something I could say to change your mind but maybe this is what you need.'

'It is,' said Alex, standing up.

'Just remember, when you get tired of VSO work, and you fancy a bit of the good life again, your job will always be here for you.' The Divisional Manager stood up and stretched out his hand to Alex.

'Thank you, Reg. That's very good of you,' Alex replied returning Reg's rather flaccid handshake.

It was done. The first step was taken. All he had to do was ring the VSO and confirm that he was available and then he'd be on his way. He felt a sensation half-way between fear and excitement. He was finally breaking free. Now the only thing left for him to do was to tell his family. Perhaps now was the time to reveal his secret, the one he'd kept hidden from them all these years. Then he'd be truly free.

*

Ian poured the can of Fosters into a pint glass and took it into the living room. 'Where did you pinch this?' he asked his brother.

'I didn't pinch it; you can buy those pint mugs any-where now. Anyway, where's mine?'

The brothers had hardly seen each other since Christmas; when one was at the hospital, the other was always working.

'I'm going to miss you, Alex,' Ian said, looking sadly at his elder brother. 'I hope you don't stay away too long.'

'I'll miss you too, and Dad, and Gran. But I have to get away. I think seeing Mum like that has made me re-assess my life, and Christmas Day was the final straw. You just don't know what the future has in store for you; you've got to make the most of each day, before it's too late.'

'I know. You're right, but it seems a bit extreme giv-ing up your job like that.'

'Well I've had quite a bit of time off since Mum had her accident and it's given me time to think. Actually they've been very good about it; Reg said that I could have my old job back any time I wanted it.'

'I doubt if you will. Go back that is. Life's not like that; people don't usually go back, they move on. They change.'

'Maybe.' He looked at Ian and smiled. 'I'm going to miss the Beemer though.'

'Oh yeah, that's the problem with a company car: they can ask for it back.' Ian laughed. 'At least the old VW Golf is mine, even if it has seen better days. Look, Alex, make sure you keep in touch. You've got my email address haven't you?'

'Yes, ianonthetrail@gmail.com; how could I forget?'

'Are you going to the hospital today?'

'Yes, I'm calling in on my way to the airport. Maybe Mum will look at me today.'

'What about Dad?'

'I saw Dad last night. He's fine about it. He says I'm doing the right thing. He says we all have to move on with our lives.'

'Well it's easy to say that, but we can't all give up on Mum.' There was the slightest edge of bitterness to his voice.

'I'm not giving up on her, Ian; she's given up on us. She refuses to communicate with any of us. What more can we do?'

'I know Mum is paralysed, but I think she just needs time to come to terms with her condition,' Ian replied. 'There has to be a way to get through to her.'

'Look Ian, have you never thought that maybe this is what she wants? Maybe she wants us to abandon her and get on with our own lives.' He drank down the last of his beer. 'Maybe she's sacrificing herself for us.'

Ian frowned. 'I don't see it, Alex. Mum knows we love her. Surely she understands how much it hurts us to see her like this.'

'That's just it, maybe she thinks that going to the hospital each day is only making it worse for us. Perhaps she thinks we'd be happier if we stayed away.'

'You're reading too much into it, Alex. It's been six months now. The doctor says unless she makes an effort soon there's unlikely to be any improvement. We have to help her understand that it's important that she tries to get well.'

'Well, I'm sorry Ian. I love Mum, I really do, but I have to get away for a bit. I've got into a rut. I want some excitement in my life. It's time I did some of the things I really want to do.'

'And going half-way round the world is what you want?'

'Yes, I think it is.'

'Okay Alex. I understand. Just don't stay away too long.'

*

Alex could make his way blindfolded to her bedside; nothing ever changed. His mother lay propped up on her pillows, her eyes shut. She'd been dressed in a loose fitting tracksuit, and her feet covered with thick white socks; the bed clothes had been pulled back and folded neatly at the end of the bed. She had all the semblance of being up and ready for the day, but he knew that the day held little for her.

'Hi Mum, it's me, Alex.' He leaned across her, so that if she opened her eyes she would see him. 'I've got some things to tell you.'

He waited but his mother didn't respond. 'Mum, if you can hear me, I know you'll understand. I'm making lots of changes in my life: I've given up my job at Bettericks and I'm going abroad. I know what you're thinking: I've been with them since I left school, my first and only job. I know I earn a lot of money—especially with the year-end bonuses—and I have a company car, but cars and money aren't everything.' He picked up her hand and held it in his own. 'Since your accident I've been looking at things differently; there's so much suffering in the world and here am I spending my days selling sports cars and driving around in a BMW.'

There was still no sign that she could hear him.

'Anyway, I've decided to take some time out and work with VSO. I went up to London last month and had an interview for a job as a small business consultant; apparently my qualifications and experience were just what they wanted. I've had to do a few courses, basic first aid and things like that. And of course I've had dozens of jabs: tetanus, cholera, typhoid. You name it, they've stuck it in my arm; I feel like a pin cushion. But then I don't need to tell you about injections, do I?' He paused again, hoping she would at least look at him. 'They're sending me to Namibia to help set up a number of enterprises in rural communities. I'll get a chance to use my German at last because even though nowadays the main language is English, lots of people still speak German. You know it used to be the official language, that and Afrikaans, until independence in 1990.' He stopped. He couldn't even tell if she could hear him, never mind if she was interested. He felt a well of disappointment opening up inside him. He loved her dearly and yet she couldn't bear to look at him. 'That's about all I know about Namibia, but I'll soon learn,' he added, looking carefully at his mother for just the slightest response. He raised her hand to his face and pressing it against his cheek, continued with his monologue.

'I've put my flat in the hands of a letting agency; that should provide me with some money, though it won't be that much once they've taken their commission. Do you remember my flat, Mum? You helped me buy it. I still have those green curtains you made, and the paisley bedspread.'

He stroked her hand and said, 'I've something else to tell you Mum. I don't know how you're going to take this but it's something I've kept hidden since I was sixteen and I just couldn't leave without telling you.' He paused and putting his mouth close to her ear, whispered, 'I'm gay, Mum. I'm sorry if it disappoints you, but there's nothing I can do about it. At first I tried to fight it but it's not possible. It's how I am and I don't want to keep it hidden from you any longer. I was going to tell you and Dad before I went off to university, but then Peter died and my problems seemed so insignificant. Afterwards there was never the right moment; you had begun to shut us all out and I didn't dare mention it to you. But now I have to say something. I want to live an open life, Mum. I don't want to pretend to be someone I'm not and if that means I have to move away to be who I really am, then I will. I don't know what Dad will say when he knows, or Ian, but I'll worry about that when the time comes.'

He kissed her hand gently and laid it back on the bedcover.

'I have to do this Mum. I know Gran is upset, but I have to go. I'll keep in touch with everyone and they'll tell me how you are. I love you Mum; I wish you would get well.'

At last Teresa opened her eyes and looked straight at him. She blinked her eyelids repeatedly.

'What is it Mum? What do you want?' He picked up the alphabet board that always lay unused by her bed. 'Blink once if you want to use this,' he told her.

Teresa blinked once.

Carefully and laboriously he went through the letters with her until they had compiled her message. It said: 'I LOVE YOU ALEX. IT DOESN'T MATTER TO ME IF

YOU'RE GAY. I LOVE YOU AND I ALWAYS WILL. YOU'RE MY SON.'

'I love you too Mum,' he whispered as he bent to kiss her goodbye, the tears streaming down his face and onto her pillow. 'I have to go now Mum. My flight is at two o'clock. Goodbye and God bless.'

He turned and walked away. He didn't dare look back in case he weakened. It hurt him to leave her but he knew he couldn't stay. He couldn't watch her lying there day after day with no hope of recovery. There was nothing he could do for her. Now he had to build his own life, a new life, free of lies and secrets.

*

If Teresa could have run after him, she would have; he was her first born and although she had fought against it, he'd always been her favourite. The news of his sexuality hadn't surprised her. She'd always thought there was a possibility that he was gay; the signs had been there from when he was a young child, but she'd never said anything. He was right; she'd not been there for him when he needed her and now he, in turn, was abandoning her to her fate. She didn't want him to go. First Peter, then Mark and Michelle, now Alex; her life was unravelling and she could do nothing about it.

What was the point in continuing? Why carry on? She felt angry with the people caring for her. What right did they have to keep her alive like this? She had heard the doctor tell Mark that the tests showed she wasn't in a vegetative state, as though that was something to celebrate. Better to be a bloody vegetable and not know what was happening to you than this, this living hell. She would be better off dead; they all would be better off if she were dead. Alex could leave with a clear conscience, Mark and Michelle could console each other and Ian could get on with his life. Even her mother would be better off, not having to traipse up to the hospital every day and spend hours praying hopelessly to a God who was never going to answer her.

She tried to recall all that she had read about euthanasia, but it wasn't much. It was a subject that appeared in the newspapers on a periodic basis, a polemic that had never been of much interest to her. After all her family were young and all in good health, even her mother— being a devote Catholic—would never contemplate taking her own life, no matter how ill she was. So although she knew that there were people who desperately wanted to end their own lives, legally and painlessly, she had never read any of the details. She would ask the doctor. The next time that silly young woman with her painted smile came with her Ouija Board, she would spell it out to her. She would have to wait until tomorrow now; the woman always came early, just as the nurses were finishing her morning ablutions. Oh well, what did it matter? She wasn't going anywhere anyway. A tear slipped down her cheek and she felt such a wave of self pity that she thought it would drown her.

*

The next morning she could hardly contain her impatience as she waited for the speech therapist to arrive.

'Well you're looking lively today, Teresa,' one of the nurses said to her, gently towelling dry her legs as she spoke. 'It's not often we get a glimpse of those sparkling Irish eyes in the morning.'

Her mother had told them she was Irish. She'd told them all about her, her childhood, her schooldays, even how she'd met Mark. If she'd been able, she would have smiled; there were no secrets when her mother was about. Well apart from that big one: Jimmy's whereabouts. She'd always believed her parents knew where he was. They just wouldn't tell her.

The nurses hauled her up the bed and adjusted the backrest. 'There that's you done. Comfortable?' the younger one asked, putting an extra pillow behind her head.

Teresa blinked once. It was not a very nice job they had to do every day; washing and clearing up after an incontinent, smelling woman in her fifties, who couldn't even acknowledge what they did for her.

'My, you are communicative today,' the other one said, gathering up the soiled bedding in her arms and disappearing from view. 'And here's Miss Jones for your speech therapy. Right on time.'

The round face of the speech therapist came into view; she was still wearing that awful pink lipstick. Why didn't somebody tell her that baby pink lipstick went out in the 70s?

'Good morning Teresa. How are you today? Eyes wide open, I see. Good.'

She didn't expect any answer and seated herself at the end of the bed and set up her board. Usually she had a hard job getting Teresa to cooperate, but today before she even had time to ask her patient any questions, Teresa was blinking her eyes.

'Hang on a minute. You're impatient to get started today. That's good. Okay. Let's start again.'

Slowly, laboriously Teresa blinked out her message to her. She was careful to be precise. She didn't want any misunderstanding. She could see the therapist writing each letter down carefully, but each time she looked up at her, her face was expressionless. If she guessed what Teresa was trying to say, she gave nothing away. At last it was finished. Teresa closed her eyes; she was exhausted.

'Quite a long message today, Teresa. Let me read it back to you and you can tell me if it's correct or not.'

She looked at her piece of paper and read slowly: 'TELL DR STEVENS THAT I WANT TO DIE. TELL HIM I WANT TO KNOW MORE ABOUT EUTHANASIA. IT IS MY RIGHT TO END MY LIFE IF I WANT TO AND I WANT TO. PLEASE TELL HIM.'

She'd added the please because she wasn't sure if Anne Jones would pass her message on to the doctor; she needed her on her side.

'Do you want me to give this message to Dr Stevens?'

Teresa blinked once.

'Okay, I'll do that for you.'

The woman's face was creased with concern. 'You know Teresa, it's early days yet. You mustn't give up hope. I've seen lots of people who feel like you do at first, but then they learn to live with their disability. You have your family to think of, remember.'

Stupid bitch. She *was* thinking of her family. Couldn't people understand? What life was there for her or her family while she was like this?

'Is there anything else you'd like to say to me?'

Teresa closed her eyes. It was too hard.

CHAPTER 13

Mark went to the hospital every evening, straight after work; he would arrive at about six-thirty, sit by his wife's bedside, talking to her about his day until seven-thirty, then get up and leave. That evening Dr Stevens was waiting for him.

'Good evening Mark,' the doctor greeted him at the entrance to the ward.

'Hello doctor. You're working late.'

'I thought I'd stay on so that I could have a word with you. I haven't seen you in some time. Everything alright?'

'No, well I have to work, you know. Life has to go on. I'm here most days at this time, though,' he added. He felt that the doctor was accusing him of something.

'Yes, the nurse told me. Can we go along to my office for a minute or two?'

Mark looked across at Teresa; she lay motionless, eyes closed. 'Yes, of course.'

He followed the doctor along the corridor. What had happened? He couldn't tell from the man's face whether it was good news or bad.

'So what did you want me for?' he asked as soon as the doctor had shut the door behind them.

'Look Mark, we're worried about your wife's mental state. She appears to be cutting herself off from us, and that makes it very difficult to help her.'

'I know. I haven't seen her with her eyes open in a long time. I don't know what else we can do. We take it in turns to visit her; her mother comes every afternoon and one of our sons comes at weekends, but she doesn't know we're here.'

'That's just it; we think she does know you're there, but she's ignoring you, and not just you, the doctors as well.'

'Well can you blame her? She probably can't face this life.'

'To be honest, the only time she wants to talk to us is when she sends messages through her speech therapist to say that she wants to be allowed to die; she's talking of euthanasia. The rest of the time she ignores us. If only we could get her co-operation, we could at least open up some communication links for her. I know the odds are rather long, but in time people do recover some of their faculties. It's ironic you know, doctors used to write off people with Locked In Syndrome; they completely mis-judged the progress that could be made if the patient's will was strong enough. And now here's Teresa, writing *us* off.'

'But you told us that there was no cure.'

'There is no cure, but some improvements are possible. Even if Teresa's body never really works again, the person inside is still the same Teresa; we just need to be able to make contact with her.'

'But maybe the accident has changed that person,' Mark suggested.

'Maybe. I have to admit that your wife's behaviour is not congruent with the majority response of patients with this condition. The usual instinct is to fight to get something of their old lives back, no matter how little. They desperately want the doctors to help them rebuild their links with the world, using whatever technology there is to hand. Most people want to live in the world again, albeit with a severe disability.'

'I see what you're saying doctor: my wife has lost the will to live.'

'Well, I don't think it's quite that. This is what surprises me. She says she wants to die but her brain appears to be reacting to stimuli almost as though she were living a normal life, and not as someone with a death wish. We have done a number of scans now, and there's a lot of activity going on in her brain. The parts of the brain that process data, deal with creativity, make plans and decisions, and those that handle memories and dreams, all these parts are working just as they would in someone leading a normal active life. And, what's more, the amygdala, the part responsible for emotions, is working overtime. It's puzzling.'

*

These interruptions were irritating, but Teresa treated them in the same way she used to treat the television advertising that, with regular monotony, interrupted whatever programme she was watching: she ignored them. She couldn't now remember the precise moment when she decided she would find her own escape from the hell within which she was imprisoned, but that moment had come to her, as clear as a voice in her ear.

Her options were very limited. It was not even possible to commit suicide: she didn't have the mobility to slash her wrists: she couldn't starve herself to death, nor could she whisper in her mother's ear to beg her to help.

She longed for real death, not this death within a life that she had to endure. Seeing her family each day brought her no solace; on the contrary it made her angry and frustrated to be excluded from their world. At first she'd hoped that this anger would subside, that God in his mercy would give her patience and tolerance and make her life easier to bear. But God had abandoned her a long time ago, and every morning when she awoke and found that nothing had changed she became angrier and more frustrated. She found those feelings of frustration harder to bear than anything else. She had to escape from the cruel reality of her life, so she created a parallel world.

*

She has been dreaming about a white house, with a thatched roof and wild fuchsia growing against the walls. She knows it has been a dream, but she continues thinking about it. She walks up to the front door and opens it; inside is a long room with a low ceiling. A peat fire is burning in the fireplace. Teresa walks over to it and sits down thankfully. She realises she is cold and wet, from the rain that has been falling all morning. As she sits there, dozing in the heat from the fire and listening to the sound of the gulls calling outside, a door opens. A boy with brown curly hair comes into the sitting room; he is about six-years-old.

'Mummy. I thought it was you. Can you come and help me with my homework? It's Maths. You know I hate Maths.' The boy twists his face into a scowl as he says it.

Teresa laughs. 'Of course I'll help you Petie, but I'm not doing it for you. You'll never learn if I keep doing it for you.'

The little boy laughs and runs to his mother and puts his arms around her. 'If I get a gold star I'll give it to you,' he says.

Teresa stands up and lets the child take her hand and lead her through the door. They enter a child's bedroom: a single bed is at one end, barely visible under an extravagant array of toys. On the table by the window she notices a box of colouring pencils and some books.

'I thought you said Maths?' Teresa asks. 'It looks as though you've been colouring.' Petie has a lot of holiday homework to do this summer.

'Well, I had to do that too, Mummy. Look I have to learn all my tables before I go back to school. The teacher said so.' He pushes the colouring books to one side and shows Teresa where he's been writing down the tables. 'Can you test me?'

'Alright. Let's see what you've learned.'

'I have to say them first, then you test me,' the boy explains. He sits down by the table and Teresa sits opposite him. The little boy closes his eyes and begins to recite his tables.

Some things never change Teresa thinks as she listens to the sing-song voice of her son repeating the litany.

CHAPTER 14

Ian had meant it when he told his brother he would miss him. They'd always been good friends, mates even, and despite the fact that they lived at opposite ends of the country they always kept in regular contact. Without any discussion, they made a point of being home for family birthdays and Christmas and, since they were teenagers, they'd kept up a tradition of going to the British Grand Prix together, putting the date in their diaries from one year to the next. He hoped Alex would be back from Namibia by next July; Silverstone wouldn't be the same without him.

Their mother's accident had brought them even closer together than ever, and now there was barely a day went by that they didn't speak on the telephone. That was likely to stop now, unless they could communicate by email—he hoped there would be a reasonable internet connection with Namibia. Alex said that he'd be working in Windhoek, the capital, so the communication network should be fine, but you could never tell. He'd have to wait and see.

In the meantime he had a lot of work to catch up on. The regular trips to visit his mother had both affected his work and eaten into his social life. He switched off Radio 3 and sat down at his desk; he had the report to write up from his last field trip.

Ian lived in a rented flat just off Princes Street. When he'd first moved in his mother had come up to stay with him for a week.

'It's very nice Ian,' she said, looking out of the window at the busy street below. 'But it's a lot of money to pay in rent. Why don't you look for something to buy, then you'd have some capital behind you?'

'Maybe,' he replied. But he'd never done anything about it. The creation of the Scottish Parliament had affected the market dramatically; house prices had rocketed and soon even the most modest of apartments was out of his league.

'Why don't you buy something on the outskirts,' she asked. 'What about out by Musselburgh?'

'No, I like it in the centre. This is really very convenient, you know.'

'But it's so noisy and there's so much traffic,' his mother protested.

'Yes, but I like it.'

His mother left it at that.

When he looked back at that week, he realised how much he'd enjoyed showing his mother the city. They'd trudged up the cobbled streets that led to the castle, that dark and sombre birthplace of King James, and bastion of Scottish royalty until the Act of Union in 1707 changed everything. They mingled with chattering groups of tourists from Japan, and tall Canadians, Americans seeking their ancestors, and they stood, shoulder to shoulder with them on the ramparts of this granite outcrop. The sky was filled with dark storm clouds that scudded by, heading out to sea and parting every so often to let a shaft of sunshine light up the panorama below them. His mother loved the way they could turn a corner and there was the sea at the end of an alleyway, or see a distant green hilltop beyond a busy street, just out of reach. He remembered how he took her to see the new Parliament building, and they'd stood arm-in-arm surveying its glass and steel structure.

'Did you say the architect was Spanish?' she asked with a laugh.

'Yes, Enric Miralles. Why?'

'Well, look at those yellow poles. They're exactly like the scaffolding poles they use to prop up buildings on the Costa del Sol,' she explained.

'Yes, I suppose they do look a bit like that. But he's from Barcelona. He did a lot of designs for the Barcelona Olympics back in 1992. His work is very innovative.' Ian's tone had taken on a defensive note.

'Yes, I'm sure it is.'

'Don't you like it, then?' he asked her. 'It has been a bit controversial, you know.'

'Actually, I do like it. It's just those poles that make me smile. Look, why don't we go shopping? I've seen enough monuments and architectural buildings for one day. And besides, while I'm here I'd love to buy some tartan. I might even be able to find an O'Sullivan tartan.'

So they'd wandered down Princes Street and looked in the shop windows, seeking the particular tartan that she fancied, then he had taken her up the hill towards the castle again, this time to have lunch at The Witchery. It all seemed a long time ago now. It didn't look as though his mother would ever be walking up hills again, nor eating in fancy restaurants.

He sighed and switched on his computer. He mustn't let himself become negative about her condition. Even if the others had given up on her, he wasn't going to.

There was not a lot to write about this last trip; he had gone to look at a painting, allegedly by Sir William George Gillies. It was reputed to be one of his early works, a portrait of a woman that he painted on his trip to Italy in 1924. Gillies was part of that group of twentieth century Scottish artists that called themselves 'The Edinburgh School.' He was an eminent artist and highly respected in Scotland, having had an enormous influence on subsequent Scottish painters, as much through his teaching as his work. But in fact, he was actually more famous for his still-life paintings and those expansive landscapes of the Lothian and Fife regions, so Ian had been surprised to hear about this portrait. He'd taken a number of photographs of it, and he now downloaded these onto his computer. Personally he wasn't convinced that the painting was genuine, but it would have to be investigated further. If it were a genuine William Gillies, such an example of his early work would be well worth acquiring for the national collection.

Having written up his report and copied it onto a flash disk that he then stored carefully in his briefcase, Ian turned his attention to the remainder of the evening. It was only six o'clock, but it had been dark for almost two hours; this was the only thing he disliked about living so far north: the cold he could cope with, but the lack of daylight was depressing. He decided to telephone Jenny.

'Hi, it's Ian.'

'Hi Ian. I thought you'd emigrated.'

'Yeah, well. I'm sorry Jenny. I've been rather busy lately.'

'Yes, I'd heard about your Mum. I am sorry.'

'Yeah. Thanks. Look do you fancy a movie or something? We could eat first if you like, or grab something in the pub, when we come out.'

'Ach well, I'd like to Ian, but I'm going out with the girls tonight; Wednesday's girls' night out,' she said with a giggle. 'Maybe some other time.'

'Okay, fine. No sweat. I'll ring you at the weekend.'

'Yes, do that, then you can tell me what you've been up to.'

Ian replaced the receiver and went into the kitchen. He felt like some company tonight, but he couldn't bear going through his telephone book ringing one after the other until he found someone as sad and lonely as himself. He opened the cupboard; there was not much to eat, an unopened packet of rice, some spaghetti and a few jars of sauce. He looked in the refrigerator: even less. Ian was not a good shopper, always waiting until he ran out of something before he replaced it. He thought back to his mother's well stocked kitchen, where the cupboards had always been full of packets and tins—store-room items she called them—and the refrigerator full to overflowing. Michelle used to joke with her, 'If ever there's a national emergency, I'm coming here to stay. We could live for months on all the food you've got tucked away. I think you must have been a squirrel in a previous life.'

Maybe he would just cook the spaghetti and open a bottle of wine. He could usually guarantee to have some

wine in the house, but this was due more to his member-
ship of The Wine Society than his own forethought. He
subscribed to their Wine Without Fuss scheme and each
month they delivered a case of carefully selected wines
for him. All he had to do was pay the bill and drink the
wine. It couldn't be easier. His brother had been quite
critical when he'd told him about it.

'Half the pleasure in wine drinking is making the
selection. It's so satisfying when you realise that you've
discovered a little known wine with great character, and
paid a good price for it. It all adds to the enjoyment,' he
said.

'Well as far as I'm concerned, wine is just for drinking, and if someone can provide me with a regular sup-
ply of good wine at a reasonable price, I'm happy. Half
the time I'm just confused by the array of wines you
find in the supermarkets nowadays: Chilean, Australian,
Argentine, Peruvian. How do I know what's good value
for money?'

'But that's just what I'm saying, Bro. There's so
much to choose from now. It's much more fun wander-
ing along with your shopping trolley and taking your
pick.'

They'd agreed to differ, but whenever Ian was at
Alex's flat, his brother could never resist producing
some 'interesting little wine, from an island just off the
coast of somewhere or other'. Ian wondered if Alex
would find any interesting little wines in Namibia; from
South Africa, maybe?

He knew this trip was something that Alex had to do
and he didn't blame him really, but running away wasn't
going to help Mum. She'd still be there when he came

back —if he came back. He was going to miss his brother.

He took a bottle of French Sauvignon from the wine rack and pulled out the cork. What had happened to his family? He recalled having had a happy and carefree childhood but that seemed a long time ago now. First their little brother had died, now Mum was confined to a hospital bed and Alex had moved thousands of miles away. Dad seemed totally out of it. It was all down to him now; he would have to pull the family back together again.

Ian poured himself a glass of the wine and switched on the television. He felt sure there was a football match that evening. He scrolled down the list of programmes: Celtic was playing Motherwell. He sighed. Well that would have to do. Christ, he was turning into a sad prick: drinking alone in front of the TV.

CHAPTER 15

They had finished washing and dressing Teresa and left her propped up on her cushions to wait for the doctor's visit. They no longer bothered to turn on the television, nor prop books with large print on the lectern by her bed; the nurses had become used to her indifference. But one of them still took the time to look through the selection of music that Ian regularly augmented and, selecting one by Aaron Copeland, fitted the headphones into Teresa's ears and switched it on.

'I don't know why that son of hers bothers,' said her companion, who was attending to the patient in the next bed. 'Hardly worth it, if she isn't listening to any of it.'

'Yes, but he says it's good for her. Therapy,' she explained. 'It's supposed to stimulate her brain.'

The nurse was a keen music fan, and although she wasn't supposed to, she always carried her iPhone in her uniform pocket for that odd moment when she could listen to it.

'Here's Dr Stevens. He's early.'

'Good job we finished in time. It always seems to take longer to sort Teresa out than anyone else,' her companion commented.

'Good morning, Teresa,' the doctor said, approaching the bed.

He looked at the nurse. 'So, Julie, how is she today?'

'Just the same as usual, Doctor. She hasn't opened her eyes yet.'

'Well, make sure you keep them sponged; don't let them get sticky.' He looked at her chart. 'Blood pressure normal, good. What about those bed sores?'

'They're clearing up alright. We've been treating them twice a day and moving her every four hours; it seems to be working.'

'Good.'

He sat down on the edge of the bed and took Teresa's hand. 'Teresa, it's Dr Stevens. I'd like you to open your eyes please. Teresa. Can you hear me?' He removed the headphones from her ears and repeated his question.

Teresa gave no response, so the doctor replaced the headphones and stood up. He wrote something on Teresa's chart.

'I think we had better get the psychiatrist to have another look at her,' he said to the nurse.

He sighed and moved on to the next bed.

*

She is walking along the beach; there is a fishing boat off shore. It is a traditional curragh and there are two men in it. Her husband is there helping the fisherman put down the lobster pots. She knows he's not keen on the sea, but he wants to make himself useful, while they are here. It's summer and this year they have come back to their roots. It's so the children can see where their parents spent their childhood holidays. Tommy and Jack weren't very excited about coming here. Tommy wanted to go on a scouts trip and Jack had his heart set on somewhere warm and sunny. But here they all are and so far they are enjoying themselves. Tommy can't believe how big the beaches are and every day, rain or shine, the boys go surfing in the spectacular Atlantic waves. As for Jack, as soon as he saw the local girls, hanging about in Dingle, he never mentioned Spain again.

She waves to the two men in the curragh. Her husband sees her and waves back. She feels the usual flush of heat as she watches him. He is her love. The one who makes life worth living. She has known him forever; he has always been part of her life. They both knew from the start that they would marry one day and now they have three wonderful boys, all youthful versions of her husband.

There is a dog running ahead of her; he is panting with the heat, his pink tongue hanging out of his mouth and his back feet kicking out sideways. He is a small, reddish brown dog, a mongrel that had found his way to their house the week before. They made some enquiries but no-one has admitted to being his owner. So Petie has named him Foxy.

'He's just like Foxy the fox, in my book at school,' he explains.

Teresa stops, she has reached a sheltered part of the cove. She stops, letting her heavy load drop to the floor. She loves this view; each day it is slightly different. One day, in a certain light she sees the smooth, slopes of blue limestone, another day grey and purple shadows soften the mountains and reveal hidden valleys and mountain passes. She can hear the plaintive sound of sheep's bells and if she screws up her eyes she can just make out their slow moving shapes on the lower slopes. There are times when it is possible to see, in the rounded peaks, a recumbent man's head: a sleeping giant among the rocks.

The locals tell of a time long ago, in the time of Finn McCool, when two sweethearts threw themselves from these rocks in a lovers' suicide pact: Ireland's own Romeo and Juliet. And sometimes —more often than not —when heavy rain clouds fill the sky, it is as though there are no mountains at all; they melt into the misty air.

Today she gives them nothing more than a cursory glance. Today she is going to paint the sea. She sets up her easel. She puts her box of paints and brushes on the ground and tapes a sheet of white paper to the easel. It is good quality paper, Bockingford 300g, hand-made from one hundred percent cotton. She brought it with her. Cheaper paper, that she can buy locally, needs immersing in cold water first to prevent cockling; then it has to be blotted between two towels, and smoothed before being left to dry for at least several hours. She finds this a laborious process that detracts from the pleasure of the painting, so she prefers to buy the more expensive paper in the art shop in Maidenhead. She opens her box and selects the paints she intends to use: French Ultramarine and Light Red. She chooses the brushes: numbers 6 and 14 Round, and a number 1 Rigger.

She looks at the view objectively, seeing it now through the eyes of an artist and adjusts the position of her easel a little to the right; this gives her a clear view across the bay to the Blasket Islands in the distance. They'll provide a good background to the seascape.

She opens one of her water containers; they used to contain orange juice, but she keeps them because they have wide necks and good watertight seals. She mixes up a watery wash of the French Ultramarine on one side of her palette, and a slightly thicker mix of the Light Red and the Ultramarine on the other. She is careful not to over-mix; she wants to be able to see both colours in the wash. This is the part she likes most about painting: mixing the colours. It fascinates her how many shades and hues she can produce from so few primary colours. It is why she prefers to paint in water colour; the transparency of the medium produces such subtle effects. Using the number 14 Round, she paints wide, horizontal strokes of Ultramarine across the paper; in some spots the paint breaks, leaving streaks of white paper visible. She likes the effect and dips her brush into the second mix; she wants this blue-grey colour for the islands.

A series of sharp barks from Foxy distracts her for a moment; he is in the dunes and has tracked a rabbit to its burrow and is frantically digging. A shower of sand sprays out behind him, but he makes little impression on the burrow entrance.

'Foxy. Leave,' she shouts at him. 'Stupid dog, you'll never catch it. It's probably half way across the dunes by now; I bet there's a labyrinth of underground passages and tunnels down there.'

At the sound of her voice the dog abandons his digging and comes and sits by her side, his tail wagging excitedly. She bends down and strokes his head.

'Yes, you're a lovely boy. Now go and lie down and be quiet; I'm trying to concentrate. The boys will be back from the village soon and then I won't have a minute to myself.'

*

Bridget looked at the bedside clock. It was already nine o'clock, but she didn't feel like getting up; her back ached and she was still tired, despite going to bed early the night before. She could hear the cat scratching at her bedroom door; it wanted to be let out. She knew she'd have to get up to see to it. It was Teresa's cat; Mark had asked her to look after it.

'Look Mum, it's not fair leaving the animal on its own all day while I'm at work,' he said.

He always called her 'Mum' when he wanted something. She'd noticed that the first time he came to the house to collect Teresa, and they weren't even related then.

Mark continued, 'Teresa would have wanted you to have it; you know how much she doted on that cat. Besides which, the animal has become used to having someone around all day.'

Bridget had protested but in the end she had no option but to agree. Smokey Joe was a nice cat: very clean and very affectionate, but Bridget didn't want him in her home. She already had her own cat: an ancient moggy that was deaf and almost blind. Princess, as the moth-eaten feline was inaptly called, was, as Bridget had feared, most unhappy at having her home invaded by Smokey Joe. She took to living in the garden shed, and no amount of coaxing from Bridget would entice her into the same house as that Burmese intruder.

'The top o' the morning to you, Smokey Joe,' she said opening the back door and letting the cat out into the garden. 'Now, no chasing the birds, today, if you don't mind.'

That was another grumble she had: Smokey Joe was a great hunter. Only the day before he'd placed a dead robin on her doormat; a small titbit for her breakfast, no doubt. The poor Princess's hunting days were long over and Bridget had got into the habit of crumbling stale bread onto the bird table, and putting out wild bird seed and the bacon rind left over from her Sunday morning fry-up. She enjoyed sitting in the kitchen and watching the birds through the net curtains, but now she wasn't the only one clandestinely spying on the birds from the shadows. Since Smokey Joe's arrival the bird table was hardly visited, except by the bravest magpies and crows.

She filled the kettle with water and flicked the switch. She always needed a cup of tea before she could start the day, but she had barely sat down when there was a gentle knock on the back door.

'Come in Mary,' she called without getting up. 'The kettle's just boiled.'

The scrawny figure of an old woman appeared in the doorway. She held onto the door with one hand and supported herself on an ebony stick, with the other.

'Here sit down. I'll get you a cup.'

Bridget took the woman's arm to help her manoeuvre herself into a chair. She noticed how thin it was and how the skin was bunched into papery folds, the veins standing up like twisted cords on the back of her hand.

'You haven't anything stronger?' the visitor asked, in a wavering voice.

'At this hour? No I haven't. Whatever next, Mary Smith?'

Although Bridget's neighbour looked much older than her, she was actually only in her sixties, but a series of abusive husbands, too many cigarettes and too much cheap whisky had aged her prematurely. The woman sighed and gratefully accepted the proffered tea.

'So how is your Teresa, then?' she asked.

'Much the same,' Bridget replied. She gave this same answer half-a-dozen times a day to concerned neighbours and friends. What else could she say?

'You off to see her today, then?'

'Yes, I usually go after lunch and sit with her for the afternoon.'

'And she doesn't say nowt?'

'No, nothing.'

'What, she just lies there, like in a coma then?'

'Yes, sort of.'

'So what do you do?'

'What do I do? I talk to her; I tell her about my life.'

Nowadays her life rotated around the hospital visits; she knew that Teresa was not going to get better, but nevertheless she felt it her duty to visit her daughter every day. She thought back to the previous day.

*

Bridget had started to tell Teresa about when she'd got married, when she thought she saw her eyelids flickering. She stopped and waited for a moment, but there was no further movement, so she continued, 'As I said, I was barely twenty when I married your father. He was the handsomest man in the village, tall and strong and with the deepest blue eyes you could imagine. His father was a fisherman, like my father and the two of them used to go out in the curraghs together, setting the lobster pots. Do you know, now that I look back, I realise that I must have known your father all my life.'

Bridget paused for a moment to let the nurse check Teresa's blood pressure and make a note on her chart.

Once the nurse had moved on to the next bed, she resumed her soliloquy, 'I never expected Patrick to fall in love with me; I thought he would get tied up with one of those Cork girls, but he didn't. In the summer when I was sixteen he came home for the holidays and asked me to walk out with him. I thought it was just a laugh at first and I didn't really take it seriously, after all he was my brother, Mikey's friend, not mine. We used to walk along the cliffs and he'd tell me about his friends in Cork, and I would read him Mikey's letters. We'd talk about how he was getting on and if the seminary was the right place for him. Well bit by bit it became more serious, and before we knew it we were a courting couple. I never thought it would last, but your father wrote to me every week while he was away, and he came home whenever he could, which wasn't often.'

She stroked her daughter's hand but still she didn't open her eyes.

'That's how we continued for four years,' she said. 'Then one day I realised I was pregnant, so I wrote to Patrick to tell him. He caught the very first train home and that was when we decided to get married. We wanted to do it right away, before the tongues started wagging. I think my Mum and Dad were a bit surprised, but if they suspected anything, they never said. Patrick and I moved to Cork, so he could finish up there and then we moved to London. That's how you came to be born in England, Teresa.

'Your grandmother never really forgave me for moving to London, you know, but there was no work for Patrick in Cork, never mind Dingle. All the young people were the same; they all had to move away to find work. Some went to Dublin, but most went to England. It wasn't much easier in London, though: it was only just after the war and there were still food shortages and it was so difficult to find anywhere to live.'

Bridget stopped and took a drink of water. She knew Teresa wasn't listening. She took out a tissue and wiped her eyes. She tried to remain positive about her daughter's condition but it was hard. Poor Teresa, what a lot of tragedy there'd been in her life. First Jimmy, then poor little Peter and now this horrendous accident. God had given her more than her share of suffering. She took out her rosary and began to pray quietly to the Virgin Mary; she would understand. She would help her get through this.

CHAPTER 16

She has washed the lettuce and arranged it in the salad bowl, now she sprinkles it with a mixture of chopped rocket and basil; she grates some local cheese and tosses it on top, then arranges the tomatoes carefully around the edge of the bowl. She places the salad bowl in the refrigerator to keep cool and measures out oil and vinegar for the dressing. He doesn't like too much oil so she only uses half the recommended quantity, whisking it briskly into a yellow cream with the mustard, sugar and salt. She dips her finger into the mixture and tastes it; it has just the sharp tang that he likes. The steaks are already marinating in the refrigerator and she'll bring them out when he arrives home.

The boys are in bed; but not yet asleep according to the smothered giggles coming from their room. It's hard for them to sleep; the temperature is almost thirty degrees tonight—unusually high for the west coast of Ireland. The locals say it's down to global warming, but they don't complain. She has opened all the windows, but it's still hot in there.

Teresa hears a car pulling up on the gravel driveway. The engine stops and she hears the car door slam. The gravel crunches under her husband's feet. She waits, a nervous flutter in her stomach, anxious to see him.

'Tess? Tess? I'm home.' He comes into the kitchen and sees her standing there. 'There you are.'

She puts down the jug that she's still holding and goes towards him. He puts his arms round her and as she kisses him she can smell the distinctive scent of his body, a strong musky smell that his after-shave cannot hide. Her stomach lurches and she feels the heat from his body inflame her own.

'How are the kids? Did you have a good day?'

'They're in bed, but not asleep. I'm surprised they haven't come out to see you; they must have heard your car arrive.'

'I'll just pop in and see them. How about opening some wine. I could do with a glass; it was a horrendous journey from the airport.' While she and the children were here for the entire six weeks of the school holidays, he could only take three weeks leave. So now, they only saw him at the weekends. It had seemed reasonable enough when they first talked about it but she hadn't realised then just how much she was going to miss him.

After she's opened the wine, Teresa gets out the cast iron skillet and puts it on the heat; she carefully coats it with olive oil and while it's heating she removes the steaks from the refrigerator. They give off a satisfying sizzling sound as she throws them onto the hot skillet.

'My, they smell good. I'm starving. Haven't had any-thing except a few crisps since breakfast,' her husband says as he returns to the kitchen and picks up his glass of wine. 'This is nice. Just what I needed. Now, tell me what you've been up to while I've been away,' he says, giving her his most dazzling smile.

She lays a piece of steak on each plate, before reply-ing. 'Not a lot really. I've almost finished a painting of *the fishing boats; Tommy and Jack have been surfing every single day, and Petie has made a new friend.'*

'Yes, he told me. A boy from the village called Gabriel, I believe.'

'Yes, that's him. A nice kid and his mother is very friendly. I thought of inviting him and his parents over for lunch on Sunday. What do you think? There's another child as well, a girl called Oona; she's about Tommy's age.'

'Sounds a great idea. What's she like, this Oona? Is she pretty?'

'I don't know. I asked Petie but he just pulled a face and said why did we have to invite a girl?' she replied.

'Well Jack will be pleased to have some female company, you can be sure of that.'

This year, their eldest son has woken up to the fact that girls are actually worth talking to. Tommy told her that Jack has a girlfriend at school—that was one of the reasons he didn't want to come to Ireland with them— and he has spent the first few days of the holiday mooning about and sending her long text messages. Thankfully that has stopped now and he seems to be enjoying himself.

She removes the salad from the refrigerator, adding, 'I thought we'd eat outside tonight, as it's so hot. Okay?'

'Perfect. I'll take the salad for you. Any dressing?'

'Yes, in the jug.'

She has covered the old wooden table with a checked tablecloth she'd found in the kitchen. She loves eating al fresco and there are so few occasions that you can do so in Ireland. Tonight is a perfect night. The garden faces south-west and a slight breeze is blowing up from the sea. Any minute now and the sun will sink slowly behind the Blasket Islands; already the sky is taking on a red glow that will soon fade into night.

'The midges are out in force, this evening,' he says. 'Better put that shawl around your shoulders or you'll get bitten.' Carefully he arranges the green shawl so that it covers her bare back and bends down and kisses her neck.

*

'Come on Teresa. Wakey wakey. Time for your exercises.'

Teresa was annoyed at the interruption. Her husband had only just come home and now these stupid nurses were pulling her around in such a way that she was prevented from being with him. Why couldn't they just leave her alone.

'Try to push against my hand. Push. Push.' The nurse tried to encourage her recalcitrant patient to participate in the therapy. She held Teresa's left leg and lifted it off the bed, bending the leg gently at the knee and ankle, trying to encourage some movement. She repeated the process a number of times, then replaced the leg on the bed and started on the right leg.

'Good morning nurse. How is Mrs Rushton today?' It was Dr Stevens, doing his morning rounds.

'Just the same Doctor. Not co-operating at all.'

'What about the bed sores?'

'We're still treating them. They seem to healing, but slowly.' Teresa felt the nurse lift the sheet so that the doctor could look at her back and buttocks.

'Oh, dear. Well, let's try this instead,' he said. There was a pause. 'Here, start with this cream tomorrow.'

She felt him move closer and lean over her. 'Good morning, Teresa. It's Dr Stevens. How are you today?' She could smell his minty breath. What was the point of replying? He knew exactly how she was. The same as every other bloody day.

'Well, I have to admit I'm perplexed. I don't know what else we can do. Even the reports from the physiotherapy unit are discouraging. We have a duty to look after you, Teresa, but without your co-operation, progress is impossible.' He turned to the nurses and asked, 'When does she go down to physiotherapy next?'

'We're just about to take her along now.'

'Good. We need to keep her moving as much as we can,' he said. 'You can see to those bedsores when she returns.'

The nurses waited until he'd completed Teresa's notes and moved on to the next bed, before turning back to Teresa. 'Right, good girl. Here we go.'

The nurses slipped a plastic mat under Teresa's body and deftly swung her off the bed and onto the stretcher trolley. She could have been a sack of potatoes.

That was what upset her more than anything. The impotence, the complete helplessness. She'd always believed she was in control of her life—until Peter's death, that was. Nothing had prepared her for that. Teresa had always looked out for her children, anticipating any dangers, protecting them, keeping them safe—she would never have allowed Peter to go to the river on his own. And he wasn't on his own; he was with his father and he was supposed to be safe. But he wasn't. And there was nothing she could do about it. He was dead and a great hole had opened up in her life. She was powerless to change a thing. Now this. The accident was her fault, she knew. She'd driven like a mad woman, not caring if she lived or died. Her anger had fuelled her and she'd given no thought to the consequences. So now she wasn't in charge of her own life anymore, either. She'd given up control of her body to the caring and kindly nurses. She was indeed like a vegetable: cleaned, prepared and ultimately consumed by her own condition.

The nurses carefully secured the straps so that she wouldn't slip and set off for the gym, chattering cheerfully all the time.

'We've got a surprise for you today, Teresa. There's a new physio, and he's drop-dead gorgeous. Only here as a locum until the end of the month, so we have to make the most of him.' She giggled and continued, 'He's from Dundee and he's got a lovely voice, a bit like David Tennant. Gives me goosebumps, it does. You won't be able to resist opening your eyes today, Teresa. He's well worth a look, I can tell you.'

That was Julie. She was always talking about the men in the hospital. The other nurse was called Nancy— rather old-fashioned name, in Teresa's opinion.

'David Tennant's from West Lothian,' Nancy said.

'Whatever, Dundee isn't far from West Lothian; it's still in Scotland. And he's single,' added Julie.

'How do you know that?'

'Ah ha. I have my sources,' she replied with another giggle. That probably meant that she'd asked him outright; Julie was a very direct young woman.

They arrived at the physiotherapy treatment room, generally known as the gym.

'Hello there. Who's this then?' a man's voice asked, picking up Teresa's notes from the end of her trolley. 'Ah, Mrs Rushton.' He rolled his 'r's softly as he pronounced her name.

'Yes, she has to have physio every morning,' Nancy said. Teresa could imagine her beaming at the young man. 'She's a bit of a difficult one,' she added in a whisper. 'Won't co-operate.'

So that was how they saw her. Difficult indeed. She'd like to see how they'd be in her situation. People just didn't understand how awful it was to be trapped inside your own body and unable to speak to anyone.

'Yes, so it says in her notes. Well, let's see. We'll put her on the tilt table first. Okay, ladies, thank you very much, I'll see to her from here on. You can collect her in an hour.'

When they'd gone he bent over Teresa and said, 'I'm sure you've been on this before, but it's a very good way to stretch those lower leg muscles, so we'll start with that.'

His voice was gentle, so despite her irritation she found herself listening to him. He pushed the trolley alongside the table.

'Hey, Bill, can you give me a hand to move Mrs Rushton across.'

She knew the procedure. They slid a padded plastic sheet under her body and adjusted the height of the trolley until it was the same as the table, then, grabbing the sheet in both hands, they pulled her inanimate body onto the tilt table, strapped it into position with three wide straps and slid a wedge under her feet. When all was secure, he wound a handle until the table tilted into an almost vertical position .

'There we go. I'll let you have ten minutes upright, then we'll do something else. Don't worry. I'll keep an eye on you, but if you have any problem, just let me know.'

She heard him walk away. What a stupid man, even if he did have a sexy voice. How did he think she was going to let him know if she had a problem? She'd been on this rack before and didn't like it. She felt that everything was falling down to her feet and she could do nothing about it. She decided to open her eyes and see where he was. She could hear his Scottish voice talking softly to someone on her left, but her peripheral vision didn't extend far enough to see who it was.

'Ah, Mrs Rushton. Everything alright?' She felt as if she'd been caught in the act of something illegal and shut her eyes immediately, but before they closed she saw his face; the nurses had been right. He was very handsome: blond hair and brown eyes were not a usual combination, but were a very striking one. She wondered if he had a girlfriend.

'I see that you don't want to talk to me then. Well that's okay. I'm used to patients who resent being pushed and pulled about. But the treatment is for your own good, you know. If we don't exercise your muscles, they'll just waste away and you'll never get better.'

She felt his hand push her hair away from her face and tuck it behind her ears. Then he stroked her face gently.

'It would be so much easier if you'd try to help yourself. I know your prognosis is not good; I've read your records. But you know, I've seen people in a similar condition to you make incredible progress. I'm not saying it's easy, nor quick, but some improvements can be made if the will is there.'

He seemed a nice enough man, but she'd heard it all before. He didn't understand how she felt: she didn't want a life as a quadriplegic; what she really wanted was to die. She heard him move away to attend to another patient and gave an inward sigh of relief. Now she would try to return to her dream world, the world where she was whole again, but the tilt table made her so uncomfortable that she couldn't shut it out. Try as she might, she couldn't conjure her new family out of the ether.

Just as he promised, ten minutes later he came back and returned her to a horizontal position. What a relief to spread the weight across her whole body; her back and legs were aching by now.

'I'm going to move you to a treatment table Mrs Rushton; we're going to apply some heat to loosen up those muscles first, then we'll continue working on the legs for a bit. Okay? Just moving you now.'

It was kind the way he explained everything he was doing; she felt less like a useless object and more like a person. The usual physiotherapist was pleasant enough, but she had long ago given up talking to Teresa; she just moved her from one exercise to the next. She heard him wheel a trolley across to her and manoeuvre the heat source so that it lay across her legs, close but not touching. He adjusted the dials until she could feel the heat from the machine.

'How's that? Can you feel any heat yet?' She didn't reply, so he continued, 'Yes, I think that's about right, now. Okay. Ten minutes cooking time. I'll be back when you're done.'

What did he think she was, a piece of sirloin? But she had to admit that the heat was nice; it flowed down her legs and made her feel relaxed and sleepy. She was drifting away to her own world of wide beaches and wild seas, when the machine made a high pitched beeping sound, waking her and alerting the physiotherapist.

'Okay Mrs Rushton, now we'll have a go at those hamstrings,' he said.

Teresa decided to open her eyes for a moment to take another look at him. She was stretched out on a table and could just make out the shape of a large wheel at her side; the man was adjusting some weights and affixing her left leg to the apparatus. He moved the counter weights and her leg lifted into the air.

'We'll do five minutes on that leg, then change over. Okay?' he told her. He continued to ask her opinion, although he must have realised by now that she wasn't likely to give it. He seemed a really nice man, the sort you could laugh and joke with without him taking it the wrong way. In her previous life, she'd have tried to flirt with him, but that was out of the question now. After all, what was she to him? Kind as he was, he probably only saw her as another patient with sores on her bum. How sexy was that? No, no man was ever going to find her sexy again. Her sons loved her; her mother loved her and even Mark professed to love her but no-one would ever be attracted to her again as a woman, not in the way they had before. She'd never been a flirt, not really, but she did like to be the recipient of male attention. It made her feel good. And when she was younger, she'd had quite a number of admirers but she never took up any of their offers; she'd always remained a loyal wife. Her marriage vows were sacred to her and she'd thought Mark felt the same. How wrong she'd been.

'Bill, can you keep an eye on Mrs Rushton, while I look at Sally Reid's arm? I won't be long.'

She couldn't see, but she knew he was gone now. She felt a tinge of disappointment. She could hear him talking to his next patient.

'Good morning, Sally. You're looking ravishing today. Keeping that husband of yours on his toes, I bet. Here, let me have a look at that arm. Let's see how far it will bend back today. Good. Good. You're making great progress. Maybe you should try a quieter horse next time,' he said to his patient.

Teresa couldn't even move to see what she was like but she heard Sally laugh and say something in return.

Bill was now leaning over her. Teresa recognised him; he was a regular nurse in the rehab centre, and although competent, she considered him a bit rough in the way he handled her. He definitely didn't consider her worth chatting to, in fact he never spoke to her at all.

When the leg exercises were over, the Scottish physiotherapist returned. 'Okay, Mrs Rushton, we'll just do half-an-hour of some arm and shoulder exercises now, to loosen those internal rotators in your shoulders, and then you can go back to the ward,' he informed her.

She could hear him instructing Bill in what he wanted him to do. The arm exercises were easier; she was moved to another treatment table and a cushion was placed under her head. She felt him lift her arms and place her hands behind her head.

He left her in that position for about ten minutes, then she heard Bill return and felt him place some weights on her elbows. It was so strange to feel your muscles aching and not be able to move them. Anyway what did it matter if her muscles were wasting if they weren't going to work any more?

She had reached the point where she thought her arms would break off, when the Scottish physiotherapist returned. He removed the weights and replaced her arms by her side, then sat behind her head. She felt him slip his hands under her shoulders and gently start to massage them. Every so often he stopped and held her neck in his hands, supporting the weight of her head and letting the warmth from his hands transfer itself to her muscles. Next he began to apply the slightest pressure, very slowly, pulling the muscles gently, first one way and then the other. It was the most sensuous thing she had felt in a long time.

'How's that Mrs Rushton? Feeling better I hope. You just lie there for a few minutes now and relax. Then we'll lift you back on to your trolley, ready for the nurses.'

It was over.

She was drifting halfway between sleep and wakefulness when the nurses came to collect her. For once she was not in a hurry to get back to her own bed.

'Hi there, Teresa. All loosened up now are we?' Nancy asked. 'Bye Bill, see you tomorrow. Bye Andy.'

Andy. He must be the new physiotherapist. She opened her eyes, but there was no sign of him—all she could see was the ceiling of the corridor flashing past her, as Nancy hurried to get her patient back to her bed. She felt a mixture of anger and sadness as she realised that, as far as Andy was concerned, she was invisible. Her mother had told her once, with great sadness in her voice, that the worst thing about getting old was that you became invisible. Well, she wasn't old yet, but as far as handsome young men like Andy were concerned, she did not exist. If he saw her at all, it was as the sad case of someone with Locked-In Syndrome. The fact that there was a woman trapped inside that wasted body was not obvious to him. That's how it was going to be from now on. All she could expect from people was pity.

CHAPTER 17

For the first time in ages Ian had a date; true it was with Jenny, who was more of a friend to him these days than a lover, but nevertheless he was looking forward to it. He desperately needed a break from work and from his own company. It had all been arranged at the last minute, but he'd managed to get some decent seats for the Il Divo concert at Edinburgh Castle, and was meeting her in the Cock and Bull pub for a drink first. He looked at his watch; it was already seven-thirty and the concert started at eight. He was just about to order another pint of Belhaven Best when a rather flustered Jenny arrived.

'Ach, Ian. I'm soo sorry. I thought I'd get the bus tonight, instead of bringing the car into the city and I just missed it; it was disappearing around the corner when I came out of my flat. I've been standing there for twenty minutes, and I was on the point of going back for the car keys, when the next one turned up. I hope you haven't been waiting long,' she added looking at his empty pint glass.

'Only long enough to sink a pint,' he said and kissed her on the cheek.

'No time at all, then,' she laughed. 'I'll have a glass of wine, please. Red.' She directed this last remark to the bartender.

They took their glasses and sat at table in the corner. The pub was rather crowded now and it was difficult to talk with so much noise.

'So, you're not away south this weekend?' she asked, sipping her wine and wrinkling her nose unconsciously at its bitter taste.

'No. I decided to have a weekend off,' Ian replied. 'I'm going down to stay with my Gran next weekend and we'll probably go to the hospital together.'

'How is your Mum?'

'Well that's just it; she's no better. I don't know whether she's aware of my visits or is just ignoring me, but sometimes I feel that it's a waste of time sitting there for hours on end.'

'If she's not aware that you're there, what's the point of going? After all it's four hundred miles each way.'

'More like four hundred and fifty. But that's beside the point; I can't just give up on her.'

'What about your Dad?'

'Well that's a bit strange. He's never at home when I telephone; I always have to contact him on the mobile. And he's given the cat to my Gran to look after: Smokey Joe, my Mum's favourite.'

'Maybe he's working late, or at the hospital,' she suggested.

'No. I've tried telephoning his office; according to his secretary he leaves at five o'clock sharp every day. I don't think he even goes to see Mum much now.'

'Well, I wouldn't worry, Ian; I expect he's just trying to get on with his life.'

'I think he's resumed his affair with Michelle. It would be just like him; he has to have someone to look after him.'

'Who's Michelle?' Jenny asked.

'She's, or I should say, was, my Mum's best friend. I think they were at school together. Anyway I can't remember a time when Michelle wasn't around. Aunty Michelle, we used to call her when we were small.'

'Why don't you ask him? He might want to talk about it to someone.'

'Maybe. But I'm not sure I'm the right person.'

'Look, Ian, he's a grown man after all; it's his business if he has an affair with an old friend, not yours.'

'I know, Jenny, but how can he screw her while Mum is still lying there in hospital?'

'Yes, I know it seems hard, but you said yourself that it doesn't look as though your Mum will ever recover. You don't want both your parents' lives to be ruined, do you?'

Jenny's own parents had been divorced since she was twelve and she had become very pragmatic about life.

'You're right, I know, but I don't feel comfortable about it.'

'That's probably why he's keeping it from you. Why don't you bring it out in the open next time you see him. If this Michelle was such a good family friend there is no reason why she shouldn't continue to be so. It won't be the same as it was before, but at least you'd all be a lot happier than you are now.'

'Oh, I don't know.'

'Hey, look at the time; it's almost eight. We'd better hurry.'

They swallowed down the last of their drinks and headed up the hill to the castle.

*

Ian's office was located in an elegant Georgian house in Charlotte Square, one of the two broad squares, designed by Robert Adam, that closed off the grid of streets known as Edinburgh New Town. These streets contained some of the grandest houses in Edinburgh but by the twenty-first century few of these elegant buildings were private homes, most had been converted into apartments or offices.

Ian was rarely in his office because the nature of his job meant that he was on the road most of the time, but whenever he returned to file his reports and pick up new assignments, it was with a sensation of pleasure that he entered this building, with its air of elegant simplicity.

He was standing by the window, admiring the Greek Ionic columns of St George's Church at the far end of the square, when his telephone rang.

'Hi, Ian. It's Jenny.'

'Jenny, hi. How are you?'

'Ach I'm fine. Look Ian, I've found the address of that fantastic healer I told you about.'

'Great. Whereabouts is he?'

'She. It's a woman. She lives in Windsor. That's not too far from your Mum, is it?'

'No, not at all. About twenty miles, I suppose. That's fantastic. So what's the address?'

'Right, got a pen?'

'Yes, fire away.'

'Her name is Rachel Hammond, and she lives at Flat 6b, 53 St. Leonard's Road, Windsor.'

'I know where that is: it's near the college.'

'Is it? Well, her telephone number is 01753 888666.'

'So how did you find out about her, Jen?'

'My room mate's from Windsor and she went to med school with her. Small world isn't it.'

'Med school? Is this Rachel Hammond a doctor then?'

'Well, no, not exactly. She trained as a doctor, but never completed the two-year foundation programme. I think she had a bit of a breakdown or something.'

Ian was pleased that Jenny couldn't see the expression on his face. 'Presumably she's okay now?'

'Ach, yes. It was probably just the pressure of her studies. She's been working as a healer for quite a few years now, according to Beth.'

'Beth?'

'My room-mate. Look maybe there's nothing she can do, but it doesn't hurt to ask, does it?'

'That's true. And anyway, if she's been trained as a doctor she'll be able to understand Mum's situation better. I'll give her a ring this evening and see what she says.'

'Good. Let me know how you get on, will you?'

'Yes, of course. Look Jen, are you doing anything this week? Fancy a curry or something?'

'Sounds good. How about tomorrow at seven?'

'Fine. I'll meet you in the Cock and Bull again.'

'Okay, see you tomorrow then.'

'Yes, and don't be late this time.'

She laughed at this last comment and the sound reminded him how her eyes crinkled when she laughed, almost closing, and how her teeth shone, white and strong as the laughter escaped from her slender throat. He felt the warmth of anticipation at the thought of their meeting. It was strange, this cosy friendship that they had. He couldn't quite remember how or why they'd ceased to be lovers and become good friends instead. There'd been no quarrel; they'd just drifted apart, like a couple that had been married too long. His frequent trips to England hadn't helped matters, of course; it was difficult to keep a relationship going when you hardly ever saw each other. Maybe now was the time to rectify the situation.

*

He dialled the number Jenny had given him and put the telephone onto speaker mode while he looked in the refrigerator for a beer. He could hear it ringing and ringing, and was about to hang up, when a soft, English voice said, 'Treble eight, treble six.'

'Oh, good evening. Is that Rachel Hammond?'

'Yes. Can I help you?'

'Well, I hope so. I was given your number by a friend. She told me you were a…' Ian hesitated for a moment. 'She said you were a healer.'

'Yes, that's right. Do you need my help?'

'Well, actually, it's not for me. It's for my mother,' Ian replied and went on to explain about Teresa's accident and her unwillingness to live with it.

'Well, I can understand that. It sounds as though your mother is quite severely depressed about her condition.'

'Does that mean you can't help her?'

'No, not necessarily. Look it's best if you come and see me. We can talk about your mother and then perhaps I can arrange to visit her.'

'That would be great. Oh, you probably haven't realised, I'm calling you from Scotland.'

'Scotland? Where's your mother then?'

'Well that's just it, she's not far from you. St James' Hospital.'

'Yes, I know St James. I've visited a few people there, especially long term patients. So how do we play this then?'

'I'm going down to my grandmother's house on Friday night. Perhaps I could see you on Saturday, if you're free?'

There was a pause while she turned the pages of her appointment book. 'I've got a cancellation at eleven-thirty. Would that do?'

'That would be perfect.'

'Fine. Give me your name and a contact number.'

Ian gave her his name and mobile number, thanked her profusely and hung up. He hadn't felt so positive in weeks.

CHAPTER 18

Mark sat by the river, watching the scullers racing by; the boat nearest to him was pulling steadily ahead, the pink slashes on the blades flashing each time they sliced through the muddy water. A vociferous group of supporters on the opposite bank, cheered the sculler on, one of them waving a flag with a big pink hippopotamus on it. Mark's eyes took in the whole scene, but nothing registered; his thoughts were elsewhere.

He was thinking about his family and there was an empty, sick feeling in his stomach. How had this happened? How had he become caught in a mire of deception and evasion. He was tired of the secrets and the lies; he was tired of making excuses to Ian about why he was never at home when he telephoned him; he was tired of inventing lame refusals to Bridget's offers to cook for him. Even his abandoned house seemed to accuse him: the bed, scarcely slept in, the pillows smooth and clean, the eiderdown immaculate, the refrigerator bare of all but essentials—a few eggs and some UHT milk—and that uniform film of dust a testament to the fact that no-one lived there anymore.

Then there was Teresa. What could he say to his wife, when he was sleeping once more with her friend? He couldn't talk about his day at work; he couldn't tell her about his plans for the evening. He hated to talk about the past, and what was the point in talking about the future? In actual fact there was no conversation when he visited Teresa. She knew he was there but she ignored him. He sat and read his evening paper until a respectable time had passed, then he kissed her on the cheek and left.

He couldn't stand the duplicity, but what was he to do? When he vowed to love her in sickness and health, he'd never envisaged this endless torment; the doctors had said she could continue like this for years. For a moment he wished that his elder son was with him; somehow he felt that he could confess to Alex and Alex would understand. He knew he couldn't tell Ian; he would see it as a betrayal. Ian believed his mother would get well; he couldn't accept the gravity of her condition. All that nonsense about getting a healer to see her. The boy was desperate.

He wondered what his sons thought he did each night on his own; they must know he'd never been one for his own company. Did they guess that he was spending his nights with someone else?

He lit a cigarette and inhaled deeply, feeling the slightly acrid smoke slip down into his lungs. The nicotine rush was instantaneous and he felt himself relax a little. He exhaled and watched the blue smoke curl away across the water.

And what of Michelle? he asked himself. She refused to grasp the fact that he couldn't give up his sons for her. He was genuinely fond of Michelle, and she was wonderful in bed. Given time, he told her, his sons would understand; they just had to be patient. It was not as if he were an old man, after all; he was only fifty and still pretty virile. What else was he supposed to do? Even if

Teresa recovered, it would take years for her to regain her mobility; she would be in her sixties at least. With a slight shiver, he realised that he had begun to think of Teresa in terms of the past and it was then that he knew that their life together was really over.

An old man sat down on the bench next to him. By way of introduction he told Mark that he was tired; he'd just pushed his grandson all the way along the tow path from Belcher's Bend.

'Belcher's Bend? That's up past the lock isn't it?' Mark asked politely.

He was pleased to have a distraction; his own train of thought was leading him nowhere and only making him depressed.

'Yes, that's right. Must be 'bout a mile, I'd say.'

'No wonder you're tired.'

The small boy regarded Mark with interest and smiled at him.

'Hello, and what's your name, then?' he asked the boy. The child gurgled something unintelligible.

'That's Davy, my grandson. His mother works on Mondays and Wednesdays; just a little part-time job to bring in a few bob. So I gets to look after him. My wife used to have him, until she got ill. But I don't mind; he's a good little chap. We have a nice time together, don't we Davy?'

The child chuckled excitedly and started waving his chubby fists at some ducks that were waddling up onto the path in anticipation.

'Oh, here're the ducks, Davy. Shall we give them some bread?' the old man asked, pulling a plastic carrier bag out of his pocket and extracting a piece of stale bread, which he gave to the boy.

'No, don't eat it Davy. It's for the ducks. Look throw it like this.'

His grandfather tossed another piece of bread to the steadily advancing ducks and the boy clapped his hands in glee as one of them caught the bread deftly in its mouth and greedily gulped it down. Davy now seemed in danger of capsizing his push-chair in his excitement; he lifted his arm as high as he could and threw his own soggy morsel of bread in the general direction of the river.

'Has your wife been ill for very long?' Mark asked, trying to estimate the old man's age. He guessed he was probably about seventy-five.

'About a year now. She had a stroke. I kept her at home as long as I could, but about three months ago I had a bit of a turn myself, so the social worker suggested we put Ruby into a home.' Tears filled the old man's rheumy eyes, so Mark said nothing, just continued to watch the ducks pecking in the grass along the bank for any missed crumbs.

After a moment the old man continued, 'I hated doing it, putting my poor Ruby into a home, but there was no other solution. It's a nice place,' he added. 'She has her own room; well there are only two others in there with her, so it's almost like her own room. And the nurses are very kind. They have to do everything for her, you see. She's completely paralysed down her left side, but she can talk a bit, which is nice. I go to see her every day, and tell her what Davy and I have been doing. I'll tell her about meeting you today.'

'Not a lot to tell there,' Mark said with a laugh. He stood up. 'Well, I must be going. Nice meeting you. Bye Davy.'

The child waved his hand at Mark, then returned his attention to the ducks.

For moment Mark was reminded of Peter. He'd loved the river. That was the problem. He always wanted to go fishing with him. Teresa said he was too young, he'd get bored, but Mark had convinced her he'd be alright. And he had been, until that evening. He rubbed at his eyes, instinctively trying to erase the sight of his beautiful son when they pulled him out of the weir.

*

She was, as usual, lying silently in her bed, eyes closed, the television on the wall opposite unheeded. She appeared so peaceful, sleeping contentedly. But he knew she was awake.

'Hi Teresa, it's me, Mark.'

He leaned across her so that if she did open her eyes she would see him, smiling down at her. Usually it was a meaningless gesture as she normally gave no sign of recognition at his presence. Today, however, her eyes opened and looked straight at him. There was no warmth in them. She knew. She could see through him, see him for the fraud he was. He stepped back, startled at their brightness, at the intensity of those green irises.

'Teresa, you're awake. How are you my love?' A pointless question, he knew, but old habits were hard to break.

She blinked at him rapidly, urgently. What was it? Did she want her board? He picked up the board of letters from the end of the bed and held it before her. She blinked again; that must mean that she wanted to tell him something. He picked up the pointer and proceeded to move along the line of letters until she blinked, then he wrote down the corresponding letter. This was deadly slow. No wonder she hardly ever bothered to communicate with them; it was so tedious. He smiled at her encouragingly and copied down her message. So intent was he on watching for her eye movements that he had no idea what she was saying to him until the final full stop. He looked down at the message and his heart stopped.

'MARK, I WANT YOU TO HELP ME DIE. I CANT LIVE LIKE THIS. YOU OWE IT TO ME TO HELP ME. PLEASE HELP ME DIE. I HAVE SPOKEN TO THE DOCTOR AND HE WONT HELP. THERE IS ONLY YOU.'

He put down the board and leaned towards her, whispering in her ear, in case anyone should overhear him.

'Teresa, my love, I can't. I can't do that to you. I know this is all my fault but don't ask me to do this. I can't; I just can't.'

She began blinking again, rapidly. Once again they went through the laborious process of writing down her message.

'I UNDERSTAND HOW YOU FEEL BUT IT WILL BE SO EASY. I HAVE THOUGHT ABOUT NOTHING ELSE FOR DAYS. ALL YOU NEED TO DO IS GET HOLD OF SOME MORPHINE AND SLIP IT INTO MY FEEDING TUBE. NOBODY WOULD KNOW IT WAS YOU. THEY GIVE ME MORPHINE WHEN THE PAIN IS BAD. THEY WOULD THINK

IT WAS AN ACCIDENTAL OVERDOSE. PLEASE
MARK. YOU OWE ME THIS. THEN WE WOULD
ALL BE FREE.

'I'm sorry but I can't.' He bent down and kissed her
forehead. Her face was so drawn and pale, the hollows
in her gaunt cheeks more pronounced than ever. She
stared at him for a moment then squeezed her eyes shut.
All communication was over. He sighed. Was that all
she had to say to him? He would do anything to help
her, but not that. The boys would never forgive him.

*

Mark knocked on the front door and waited for a moment before opening it with the key she'd given him.
Michelle put her head around the kitchen door to see
who it was.

'Darling, why do you always do that? There's no
need to be so formal; this is your home too,' she said,
coming over and giving him a kiss. 'Here let me take
your coat. So, how was Teresa today?'

'No different. The doctor's talking about getting the
psychiatrist to look at her again.' He couldn't bring himself to tell her what Teresa had asked him to do.

'Well, I can't see what good that will do if she isn't
communicating with anyone.'

'I suppose they just want to try something else.'

'Come and sit down. I'm just making us a chicken
curry.'

'Yes, I could smell it as soon as I got out of the car,'
he said, laughing. He caught her around the waist and
hugged her, kissing the back of her neck, affectionately.
'Shall I open some wine?' he asked.

'Please. But Mark, do stop asking for permission to do things; you're not a guest. Just do what you want.'

'Okay, sweetheart, but I still don't feel comfortable poking around in your house.'

'Would you sooner I came to live with you?' She looked at him, but he avoided her gaze. 'No, you wouldn't, because then Ian might find out about us. And that would be awful, wouldn't it?'

'Now, don't start on that, Michelle. You know I love you, but it's too soon for us to tell the boys. They're both very fond of you, but that could change if they thought you were taking advantage of their mother being in hospital.'

'Is that what you think, Mark? That I'm taking advantage of Teresa's illness to seduce you?'

She went to the cupboard and took out a packet of rice.

'Of course not. I'm just saying what it might look like.'

She didn't reply; instead she carefully measured out the rice and poured it into a saucepan of boiling water. Only then did she turn to look at him.

'Mark, please remember, it was *you* who telephoned *me*. You made the first move. I had resigned myself to the fact that our love affair was over. I wasn't happy about it, but I'd accepted it.'

'I know Darling, but I was so lonely.'

'Lonely? Lots of people are lonely. You don't jeopardise your marriage and your family because you feel lonely. I love you Mark. I thought you loved me.'

'I do love you. I wouldn't be here now if I didn't love you,' he replied. He stifled a sigh. They'd been down this road before. Why did it have to be love? Why couldn't she just settle for sex?

'Look Mark, I want us to live together as a couple. I'm tired of lying to our friends; I haven't even told my mother about us.' She was on the point of tears.

'We are living together,' he protested.

'No, we're not. You may be sleeping here, but your official home is still in Gatsby Terrace. You arrive here each Sunday evening with your suitcase of clothes for the week and you leave on Saturday morning with the same suitcase. You won't even allow me to do your washing. That's not living together.'

'I thought you didn't like doing things like washing and ironing,' he said, realising at once how lame it sounded.

'Look, Mark, don't let's argue over this. Just bear in mind that one day you'll have to decide what you're going to do with the rest of your life. Try not to leave it too late.'

The rattle of the saucepan lid reminded them of the rice. Michelle adjusted the flame and left it to simmer while she set the table.

'How about this bottle of Australian Chardonnay? We don't want anything too delicate with curry, do we?' Mark suggested.

'Sounds fine. Pour me a glass now, would you. A big one.'

CHAPTER 19

The next morning, after Mark had left for work Michelle remained sitting at the breakfast table. She'd had a terrible night; after the usual lovemaking, which had seemed more perfunctory than usual, she'd lain awake for a long time thinking about her life. She remembered checking the clock at two o'clock and again at three; finally, when the pale light of dawn was starting to creep through the curtains, she had fallen into a dreamless sleep.

Michelle was an only child; her mother had given birth very late in life, after having already resigned herself to a childless marriage. Then to both parents' delight Michelle had been born, not only sound and healthy, but also very beautiful. She had blonde curly hair and big blue eyes, and would sit in her pram, which her mother always parked just outside the door of their small terraced cottage, smiling and gurgling at all the passersby. They were enchanted with her. She grew up in a home with little money, but an over abundance of love.

When she was fifteen her father died. He was already seventy and years of hard work and heavy smoking had taken their toll on his not very robust body. A long, painful period of emphysema followed by pneumonia had delivered the coup-de-grace. Michelle was heartbroken. It was her best friend, Teresa, who helped her through that painful time.

She and Teresa had been inseparable until Teresa had met Mark when, inevitably, they had at first drifted apart. But the ties of their friendship proved too strong and when Teresa and Mark married, she had begun to see more of her again.

Michelle had been just twenty-one when she began having trouble with her periods. At first it was irregularities: lateness, heavy bleeding that lasted two weeks and soaked her clothes, debilitating pain that caused her to cancel engagements, then nothing at all for a couple of months. The doctors suggested she change her contraceptive pill, but her condition didn't improve. They suggested the coil—a fairly new device then—they even advised no contraceptives at all, but her suffering continued. In the end, worn down by the machinations of her own body, she agreed to a D and C. They cut out the tumour they discovered, snuggled deep inside her womb and the D and C became a hysterectomy. It was not until many months later that the full significance of their action hit her: she would never be able to have children now.

Once again Teresa had been a caring friend. She refused to leave Michelle at home to mope and so began a pattern that would last many years. Michelle was included in almost everything that the Rushtons did. The children came to regard her as part of their family and called her Aunty Michelle; they became the children she couldn't have. The Rushton family filled her life.

Inevitably she had boy friends; she had been a beautiful child and had grown into a particularly attractive young woman, or so she was told by the numerous young men who courted her. But none of her liaisons turned into marriage; no-one was quite her Mr Right, and besides, she was replete with the family she had. She regarded Teresa as her sister and Mark as her brother.

Michelle struggled to remember the exact moment when she knew that she was in love with Mark. If the truth be told, she'd always loved him a little, since they had first met. She remembered with surprising clarity the evening when she had first seen him: he was playing badminton at the leisure centre. As she watched him moving agilely around the court, never taking his eyes off the shuttlecock as he moved back in anticipation of an overhead lob, or leaned in towards the net to smash it at his opponent's feet, she felt an instant physical attraction to him. There was something very masterly about this man. Who was he? He was tall and tanned and lean; the muscles in his arms and legs were firm and well defined, and he had a smile that lit up his face each time he scored a point. A grubby sweatband kept his long, black hair from falling into his eyes and his socks were odd: one white and one blue.

She was standing there watching him, when Teresa came up to her. She had just won her singles match, and her face and arms were gleaming with sweat.

'Hi, Michelle. I see you've discovered my secret.'

'Your secret?' Michelle was perplexed.

'Yes, my new boyfriend.'

'What, the one with the odd socks?'

'Yes. Gorgeous isn't he?' She remembered feeling a surge of disappointment when Teresa told her that.

Michelle drank the remains of her cold coffee. She didn't feel like going to work today; she'd telephone and say she was sick, then she'd go and visit Teresa. She had stayed away too long.

*

Teresa was propped up on her pillows, when Michelle arrived. Her eyes were closed and she seemed to be oblivious of the young nurse who sat by her bed, holding her hand and gently moving it back and forth.

'Hello,' Michelle said softly. For some reason she felt the need to whisper so as not to disturb anyone. 'I've come to visit Teresa. Is it convenient?'

'Oh, yes. No problem at all.' The nurse abandoned Teresa's hand and got up. 'Come and sit here. You can exercise her wrists if you want. It'll give you something to do as I don't expect you'll get much response from her.'

Michelle sat down and took Teresa's hand. It was cool and damp; the skin was soft through lack of use. She looked enquiringly at the nurse.

'It's easy. Just move the hand back and forth slowly a few times, then try rotating it a little, first one way then the other. Then you can try opening and shutting the fingers. Don't force it, just move it gently. It's important to try to keep her joints supple, but as she has no voluntary movement it's down to us,' she explained. 'If you need anything just ring the bell.' She indicated the bell-pull at the head of the bed.

Michelle began to move the hand very gently. The nurse was right, it was easier to have something to do while she spoke to Teresa.

'Hello Teresa. It's me, Michelle.' She waited, but there was no response from her friend.

'I'm sorry I haven't been to visit you very often. I didn't know if you'd want to see me or not.'

She stopped, unsure of what to say next, but she continued working the wrist in a slow rhythmic motion. After a few minutes she placed the hand back on the bed and picked up Teresa's other hand.

'Look Teresa, I'm so sorry. I really am. The last thing I ever wanted to do was hurt you. Really. You're my best friend. I've always loved you Teresa, but I love Mark too. I can't help it. I've loved him for years and never told anyone.' She paused, then continued, 'You can't imagine what it's like to love someone so desperately and know you can never have him. I used to watch you and him together and feel so envious. Then when you had the boys, I could hardly bear it. At first I didn't want to see you. I tried to find a boyfriend, someone of my own, but it didn't work; I couldn't stop thinking of Mark. I even considered marrying Bob, just to get away from you all. Do you remember Bob? He was a nice guy; he went to Australia to work as an engineer. But in the end I couldn't go with him. So I decided to be content with my role as Aunty Michelle.' She tried to keep the bitterness from her voice. 'And in a way I was content. I saw Mark; you and I remained friends and I began to love your sons as though they were my own. Sometimes I would fantasise that they were mine, mine and Mark's. But believe me, in all that time I never said anything to Mark. I promise you. It was my secret.'

She replaced Teresa's hand on the bed and stroked it gently. The knuckles protruded from the skin, which hung so loosely from the bone that she could pinch it between her finger and thumb. Someone had removed

Teresa's wedding ring, but the indentation of the years lingered on. She ran her finger along it.

'I would never have told him how I felt, but then one day we were alone together and everything changed. You were staying with your mother. He didn't know when you were coming back or even if you'd be back. I still don't really understand how it happened. We were just swept away with passion. Of course we knew it was wrong, but it didn't feel wrong; it felt wonderful. It wasn't just that it was exciting; the secrecy, the stolen moments, the cryptic messages, sure they kept it alive, but I felt there was something more, something deeper. I was so happy that I couldn't even feel any guilt. I couldn't think of anything except when I would see him again.

Well that was until we got caught—Ian and Alex saw us— and then I came to my senses. I realised that too many people ran the risk of getting hurt, people I loved. You especially. So we both agreed to end it. I was even thinking of moving to London to make a fresh start; I'd started looking at flats in Wimbledon. But then you had your accident.'

She sighed and took up Teresa's other hand. 'Now I don't know what to do. He needs me Teresa. I don't think he loves me, certainly not as much as I love him, but he needs me. He can't cope on his own. I know he still loves you, but he can't bear to see you like this. It's destroying him.' She waited, unsure what to say next. 'Teresa, please forgive me. Truly, I never meant to hurt you.'

She wished Teresa would give her some sign, but her friend lay motionless, caught in her own nightmare.

*

Once Michelle had left, Teresa opened her eyes. Someone had cleaned away the cobweb around the light and with it the dead fly. At last. How was it, with so much to bear, that a little thing like a dead fly could irritate her so much? How strange was the human mind. She went over all that Michelle had said and tried to examine her own feelings. When Mark had told her about his affair with Michelle she had felt betrayed, not just by him, but Michelle too. Her best friend. You didn't do things like that to your best friend. She tried to harden her heart and find it in herself to hate her but it was impossible. Disappointment, betrayal, pain, yes all of those were there but not hate. She knew Michelle had not acted from malice; however misguided her actions, they were not intended to hurt her. Somehow she had convinced herself that it was alright, that if nobody found out about them then nobody would get hurt. And nobody would have got hurt if Mark hadn't had an attack of conscience and wanted to confess all. How stupid he could be at times. Was his conscience clear now? She doubted it very much.

She wondered if he'd told Michelle about her message to him. Probably not. Michelle had been full of talk about how they were going to help her get better, make her life worth living again. Very noble but why didn't they just leave her alone? Why didn't they all just leave her alone?

CHAPTER 20

Bridget was delighted when Ian telephoned to ask if he could stay. He'd told her that he would arrive on Friday night, quite late, so not to prepare anything for him, but she'd wanted to do something, anyway. When he was younger, Mark and Teresa would bring the boys round to stay with her every Saturday evening while they went out, and she always cooked them their favourite dinner, shepherds' pie. She'd now made one for Ian just in case he was hungry; she'd prepared it that morning and popped it in the oven as soon as he arrived.

She looked across at her grandson; his red hair was longer than usual, making him look younger. He reminded her of her father—in the days before his head was as bald and shiny as a billiard ball and all that remained of his red hair were his thick, rufous eyebrows.

'So what do you talk about Gran, when you go to see Mum?'

'Well, I usually tell her about my childhood in Kerry, about her grandfather and her grandmother, and generally what it was like to be alive in those days. Things were very different then. It was another world,' she said with a slight sigh. 'Then sometimes I talk about when she and Jimmy were small and the tricks they used to get up to. Every summer I used to take them to stay with their grandmother in Kerry, you know. They loved it there.'

'Jimmy, who's Jimmy?' Ian interrupted. He put down his knife and fork and looked at his grandmother quizzically.

Bridget looked away and hesitated before answering, 'Oh well, I suppose it doesn't matter much now. Jimmy is your uncle.'

'My uncle? I didn't know I had an uncle. What do you mean Gran, a real uncle or just someone we called uncle?'

'Well, not a real uncle; a sort of second cousin. He was my sister Dorrie's son, but he lived with us from when he was about four-years-old, so we thought of him as our son. He always called us Mam and Dad.'

'But he was really your nephew?'

'Yes, I suppose so, although I never thought of him like that.'

'What happened to his real parents?'

At this a pained look crossed his grandmother's face. 'We were his real parents,' she said. 'The only parents that cared for him.'

'So, what happened to your sister? Dorrie?'

'Oh Dorrie was a bit of a rebel, and a terrible one for the boys. We all knew she'd end up in the family way; it was inevitable the way she carried on. My poor mother could do nothing with her. Anyway one day, when she was just turned sixteen she ran off with this lad from Derry. They went to England to look for work. Then the next thing we knew she wrote to my mother to tell her she was expecting Jimmy. My mother wrote and wrote, but we heard nothing until the baby was born. I must say I was surprised. I quite expected Dorrie to have an abortion as she was in England and it was so easy to do there. Then we had another letter to say that the father had left her. He'd gone off with some English woman. So my mother persuaded her to come home and bring little Jimmy with her.'

'So how did he end up living with you and Grand-dad?'

'Well Dorrie wasn't really cut out for motherhood; she did the best she could, but she was hopeless with him. She soon returned to her old ways: out every night and drinking more and more.' Bridget paused, then added, sadly, 'I think she was a very unhappy woman, you know.'

'So what happened?'

'Well in the end, she said she couldn't carry on like that; she was dying from boredom. She wanted to go back to London. My mother didn't want her to take Jimmy with her—I remember Dorrie being very re-lieved at that—so we said Jimmy could come and live with us here in Maidenhead, just for a bit you know, until she got herself straight. He'd just had his fourth birthday and he was such a lovely wee boy. He had the same curly red hair as my father.'

'So what about my Mum? Had she been born by then?'

'Oh yes, your Mum was about two-years-old. She loved it when Jimmy came to live with us; he became her big brother. You see,' Bridget explained, 'when Tere-sa was born I'd had lots of problems; I was in labour for thirty-six hours and they had to do a forceps delivery to save the baby. I lost so much blood that the doctors ad-vised us not to have any more children; they said I might not survive next time. You know it was a lot riskier in those days if there were any complications. So, despite the fact that we'd set our hearts on having a son, Patrick wouldn't hear of us having any more.'

'So that's why you took in Jimmy?' He made it sound a bit selfish of them, but Bridget made no comment.

'Have you finished?' she asked, indicating his plate with the remains of the shepherds' pie.

'Yes, thanks. It was lovely Gran, but I'm not really hungry tonight. Sorry.' He followed her into the kitchen. 'So this Jimmy was Mum's cousin then? If he was like a brother to her, why haven't we ever met him, or even heard of him before?' Ian seemed to be having difficulty taking it all in. 'Are you sure your memory's not playing tricks with you, Gran. You're not confusing him with one of your own cousins, are you?'

Bridget gave a little toss of her head at this remark. Just because she was old, why did they assume there was something wrong with her memory? Her memory was as good as anyone's.

'Jimmy was what you might call the black sheep of the family; I suppose he took after his mother in that respect. We haven't heard from him in a long time.'

She wiped her eyes with the edge of her handkerchief. It made her sad to think of Jimmy. Now it seemed she was going to lose two children. 'Look, why don't I make you another cup of tea?' she asked.

Ian perched himself on the pine table by the window and watched as she bustled around the kitchen. Bridget tried to focus on the task in hand but she couldn't get Jimmy out of her mind. It had broken her heart when they'd had to leave him.

'That Smokey Joe is a nuisance, you know. He won't leave my bird table alone.' She indicated with a wave of the tea cloth, the place under a lavender bush, where the cat was crouched motionless, eyes fixed intently on a sparrow that had just alighted on the bird table.

'That's what cats do, Gran. Anyway, tell me some more about Uncle Jimmy. Why didn't Mum mention him to us? Didn't she like him?' he asked.

She looked at her grandson. What had she done? She should never have mentioned Jimmy. Ian would be like a dog with a bone now until he got to the bottom of it. That was Ian. He'd always been like that, even as a lad; he had to know the ins and outs of everything. 'Oh, your Mum loved him. That was half the problem.'

She refilled his teacup and took out a clean one for herself, then sat down on a wooden chair, next to him. 'They were inseparable when they were young, your Mum and Jimmy. She loved having a big brother, and Jimmy was such a soft one, he didn't mind her trailing around behind him everywhere. He took her to the park when he went to play football with his friends, and she would sit behind the goal cheering him on. Your Mum was always a bit of a tom-boy; she could climb trees and ride a bike—all the things the lads could do—and your Granddad taught her how to fish. I often thought she preferred Jimmy's company to that of her girlfriends.' She took a sip of her tea then continued, 'Of course it was different when they were at school; he had his friends and she had hers. In fact when Jimmy took the eleven-plus, he went off to The Sacred Heart Boys School, so they didn't see a lot of each other during term time. But they still had the holidays.'

'So where is he now?' Ian asked, insistently.

'We don't know. That's the truth. As I said, nobody's heard from him in years.'

'But what about when Granddad died, didn't he get in touch then? Didn't he come to the funeral?'

'No. Well we had no way of letting him know.' Bridget couldn't speak for a few minutes; she was thinking of the fact that Jimmy was not only unaware that his grandparents were dead, that Patrick—the only father he'd ever known—had died, that his real mother had died of liver failure when she was only forty and now, that Teresa was seriously ill. If anything happened to Bridget, who was there left to tell him?

'What about your sister, Dorrie? Didn't she know where he was?'

'Dorrie? No. By then she was an alcoholic and spent most of her time shut away in a clinic run by the nuns, trying to dry out.'

She thought back to the last time she had seen her sister: the rebellious beauty gone forever and in its place a wasted body and hollow eyes. She lay in a hospital bed, her stomach swollen and her skin yellow and she hadn't recognised Bridget.

'Maybe it's time we tried to get in touch with Jimmy,' Ian said at last, interrupting her reverie.

'I told you, we don't know where he is. He's probably gone abroad,' she snapped. 'Anyway, what good would it do? Your mother won't forgive him anyway.' It was impossible to hold back the tears now. 'I don't want to talk about it anymore, Ian.'

'Sorry. I didn't mean to upset you, Gran. Why don't I tell you who I'm going to visit tomorrow, morning?'

CHAPTER 21

The next morning Ian parked near Windsor Castle and walked along Peascod Street, until that ancient road turned into St Leonards Road. He had no trouble finding Rachel Hammond's house; it was exactly where he'd thought it would be: at the end of a row of red brick Edwardian houses right at the point where the two roads merged. He arrived punctually at eleven o'clock, and as he mounted the stone steps that led to a carved wooden door inset with frosted glass, it opened and a man in a raincoat and a flat cap came out. He nodded at Ian, and set off down the road. Ian wondered if he were a patient; if so, he looked particularly sprightly. The man had left the door open, so Ian knocked lightly and went in. The long narrow hallway was made to seem even longer and narrower by a row of chairs that were arranged along one wall; there was a stairway of dark, carved oak at one end, with a stair runner so bare in patches that the wood showed through. Worn by the tread of people seeking a miracle, desperate for a second chance? As he was surveying the scene, a woman's voice called down to him.

'Is that you, Ian? Come on up.' A smiling face looked down at him.

'Rachel?'

'Yes, come up, do.' Her voice was even more melodious than on the telephone. He climbed the stairs towards the sound. A doorway stood open on the landing allowing a shaft of sunlight to lighten the gloom. He went in.

Rachel Hammond was standing by the window, the light creating a halo around her. At first he found it difficult to focus on her, but when she moved closer, her hand outstretched in greeting, he could see her quite clearly. She was a woman in her early thirties, tall and slim, with black hair that already had some grey showing in it and dark brown eyes. Her nose was small and straight and her face was almost the shape of a perfect heart. She was not at all what he'd imagined—although if anyone had questioned him on what exactly he'd imagined a faith healer to look like, he would have been hard pressed to answer.

'How nice to meet you Ian. Please come in and sit down.' She gestured towards an armchair opposite her.

He watched her, slightly fascinated; she seemed to glide rather than walk and there was a serenity in her smile that he'd only ever seen once before, on the face of an elderly nun in a convent outside Stirling, when he'd gone to look at a chalice that was of special interest to his department.

'Thanks,' he said, sitting down with his back to the window.

Her consulting room was light and airy; it had been painted in a restful shade of blue and there was a rug of the same tone covering the parquet floor. A variety of pictures decorated the walls: a large photograph of an Indian guru dominated the wall in front of her desk and there were various seascapes and paintings of clouds and woodlands. All very restful. The windows were tall, imitations of Queen Anne sash windows, painted white, and with fine Venetian blinds which she now pulled down, cutting off the view of the houses opposite. 'A little more private,' she said, by way of explanation, as she sat down.

At first she didn't speak, just sat regarding him curiously, the gentle smile still on her lips. Normally this situation would make Ian feel uncomfortable and he would instantly fill the silence with whatever came into his head. Instead he sat waiting, aware of a stillness in the room. He could hear his own breathing and was aware of the weight of his body pressing down on the chair.

'Well, Ian,' she said at last. 'How did you come to know about me?'

Ian explained of his connection with Jenny, and her help in contacting Rachel.

'Ah, yes. I remember Beth; a lovely girl. So she's a doctor in Edinburgh now?'

'Yes, at the Royal Infirmary, I think.'

Rachel didn't speak for a moment then said, 'Tell me about your mother.'

He repeated what he'd told her on the telephone.

'What else can you tell me about her? What sort of life did she lead before the accident?'

'A pretty ordinary sort of life, really,' he answered, going on to explain Teresa's life as he saw it: that of a devoted wife and mother. He wondered if he should mention his suspicions about Michelle and his father, then decided against it. As far as he knew his mother was unaware of their affair.

'So, she was perfectly happy?'

'To be honest, I don't think so. My little brother died five years ago. She took it very badly at the time and hasn't really been the same since. Of course I've been living away from home most of the time, in fact ever since I went off to university at eighteen,' he added. 'So I don't really know if she'd been happy or not.'

'So, you would only see what she wanted you to see?'

'Well, yes, but everything seemed normal to me. Yes, she was sad about Peter, but apart from that she never talked to us about him, or about anything very much, if it comes to that. She was wrapped up in her own life.'

'Forgive me for saying this, but young men are not the most observant when it comes to their parents' relationships. They usually have too much else on their minds.' She laughed softly.

'I can't argue with that.'

He realised that she was right; he knew nothing about what his parents went through after Peter died because he was always out with his friends. Even before he went to university he was never at home, except to sleep—and not even then at the weekends. He'd left it to Alex to deal with his parents while he went blissfully on with his own life. He knew it had been his way of coming to terms with Peter's death, but now, with hindsight, it seemed selfish.

'What about her relationship with your father? She's still married I take it?'

'Yes my parents are still married. Well that's difficult to answer. She blames him, you see, for Peter's death. He'd taken him fishing.'

'Peter is the brother who died?'

'Yes. He drowned.'

'That's very sad. Is there anything else that has happened in her life that could be affecting her?'

Apart from the fact she's completely paralysed? Ian thought bitterly.

'Well, I've just learnt from my grandmother that my mother had a cousin, who disappeared when she was young. I believe she was very fond of him; according to my grandmother he was like a brother to her, yet she's never mentioned him to any of us.'

'That's interesting,' she said, 'I wonder why not?' She sat quietly, her hands resting in her lap, palms upwards, her back straight and both her feet firmly placed on the ground. She closed her eyes. Was she thinking, or meditating? He waited. After a few moments she spoke again. 'Well, Ian your mother has experienced a lot of sorrow in her life and maybe it is despair that is taking away her will to live. I think I should visit her. I won't be able to help her physically, you realise that, but I hope I can do something to help her emotionally and spiritually.'

Ian felt a surge of disappointment at this. He realised then how desperate he'd become; he'd been hoping for the promise of a miracle.

As if she had read his thoughts, she said, 'I'm sorry Ian; I'm not in the miracle business. I may be able to help your mother, but so much will depend on whether she wants to get well. We all have this enormous power within us, and we can choose to use it positively or negatively.'

'Yes, I understand,' he said. 'So when would you be able to visit her?'

'Tomorrow?'

'That'd be great. The hospital is quite quiet in the afternoons; there're no doctors' rounds and the nurses usually leave the patients to their own devices.'

'Fine. I'll meet you at the main entrance at three o'clock.'

'Good. I'll be there.'

Once again he noticed how the light created the semblance of a halo around her head.

*

Ian heard from Alex each month when he sent an email account of his activities, and he would always make a point of reading it to his mother.

'There's a newsletter from Alex, Mum. Shall I read it to you?' He didn't wait for a reply. They had all become used to her silence by now.

'Hi Guys,' he began. *'Well it's been three months now, a quarter of the way into my contract, and we're just starting the dry, winter season. It's the nicest time of the year—so they tell me—and it certainly is more pleasant than when I arrived. The days are warm and sunny, but at night it gets very cold; the temperature is often below zero. I seriously wondered if I'd be able to stay the course when I first got here. The temperatures were in the mid-thirties and the humidity was over sixty percent. A bit of a shock coming here straight from an English winter. But they did say it was hotter than usual this year. I have to admit I miss the English countryside. I expect your cherry tree is in blossom right now, Gran, and the wisteria will be coming into flower, Dad. There's not a lot of rain in Namibia, much of the land is desert or scrub, so there're no lush woodlands, like at home.*

They've planted trees and flowers here in the capital, which is almost European in style with its clean wide streets and pavement cafes, but even here they don't like to waste the water. Still it's a very beautiful country for all that. Lots of tourists come here just to see the scenery and the wild life conservation parks. Might be worth a visit some time Ian, what do you think?'

Ian paused for a moment and cleared his throat. Was Alex suggesting he go out to visit him? It sounded like a nice idea; he'd have to think about it. He continued reading: *'I spend much of my free time at the coast. It's not so sunny there; they get a lot of fog and cloud because of the cold currents that come up from the South Atlantic, but there's hardly any rain and the entire coast-line is desert and quite spectacular. The beaches are a bit like the ones we used to go to in Cornwall when we were kids, only much, much bigger and the sea can be quite treacherous. It's not for nothing they call this stretch The Skeleton Coast. And they're quite deserted. I've bought myself a surf board, just a cheap one, not one of those flashy things that the kids all use at home. Sometimes I go down to Swakopmund with a couple of friends for a bit of surfing: a South African lad called Samuel and a girl from Australia. We also do a bit of snorkelling together. Some of the reefs are wonderful; the water is so clear and the fish are incredible, like nothing I've ever seen before. Josie, the girl from Australia, says it's nowhere near as good as the Barrier Reef, but then the Aussies are a bit like the Americans with their "bigger and better" attitude, so I don't take too much notice of her.*

How are you all keeping? I hope your physio' is going well Mum. I want to see some progress by the time I get back; so you'd better get to work on it.

My German is improving. I was amazed how much I actually remembered; it just all started coming back to me as soon as I arrived. And it's been really useful, especially when people want to discuss something behind my back. They get quite a shock when they realise the Englishman can understand them. Some speak Afrikaans and there are a number of indigenous languages as well, but English is the official means of communication. That's what I speak at work.

They've given me an old breakdown truck to get around. It's a far cry from the Beemer, but it suits these roads. My job is pretty interesting: I spend part of the week in Windhoek, giving seminars and running workshops on such exciting things as writing business plans or setting out a marketing strategy. The rest of the time I go out visiting small companies on a sort of free consultancy basis. I either go to Walvis Bay, where the fishing industry is located, or I visit the outlying farms. There's a big drive to encourage ostrich breeding at the moment. Have you ever tried ostrich steak Ian? You'd like it; it's just like beef steak, only healthier—less cholesterol.'

Ian stopped reading for a moment. 'Well that's amazing. I never thought Alex would eat ostrich. Actually Mum, I've had ostrich steak. Don't you remember I had it that time when you and I ate at The Witchery, when you came to Edinburgh to check up on me. It was a bit tough, if I remember rightly. Sorry, Alex, give me Aberdeen Angus any day.'

He picked up his iPad again. 'R:ght, where was I? *That usually means I have to drive for hours through the bush. It's very interesting, but hot and dusty. It would be a lot better if the damned air conditioning in the truck worked properly.*

You wouldn't recognise me Mum: I've lost at least a stone in weight, and I've never been so brown. I think it's the effect of the wind as much as the sun. They'll be taking me for a native soon.

Oh, in answer to your question Ian, I drink South African wine, when I can afford it. They do grow grapes here, quite a big export item actually, but no wine worth the name.

Well, not much more news. Drop me a line when you can, Ian and let me know how everyone is. I miss you all. Take good care of Mum,

Alex.'

Ian closed his iPad and said, 'Sounds as though he's having a good time, Mum. No need to worry about him, anyway. I'm glad to hear he's lost some weight; I thought he was starting to develop a bit of a paunch, before he left. All those business lunches.'

Ian chattered on to his unheeding mother, until the false cheerfulness of his monologue grated even on his ears.

'Oh, by the way, Gran dropped a b:t of a bombshell last night: she started to tell me about when you were a girl and about your cousin, Jimmy.' He stopped in surprise; his mother was regarding him solemnly with her big eyes. It was so long since he had seen them open that all he could think of was the intensity of their colour; twin pools of liquid green. He bent close to her and whispered, 'Don't worry Mum, I know how much you loved him. I'll find him for you.'

*

After Ian had gone, Teresa lay for a long time thinking about what he'd said. It was so long since anyone had mentioned Jimmy that she almost felt that he'd never existed, that he was a figment of her imagination. Yet all this time her mother must have known how she felt about him. Why hadn't she spoken to her about it? All those years and she had never even said his name, until now. She hadn't told her anything about him, so why had she told Teresa's son?

CHAPTER 22

After leaving the hospital, Ian decided to drive past his Dad's house to see if he was home. As he turned the corner into Gatsby Terrace, he saw his father's Volvo parked outside their house. He drew up behind it, and was just about to get out, when the front door opened and Michelle came out; she looked upset. He pulled the car door shut and waited until she went past, her high heels clicking on the pavement, unaware that he was sitting there watching her. Once she'd turned the corner and was out of sight, he got out of the car and went up to the front door and knocked. It opened instantly.

'Oh. Ian. It's you,' his father said, obviously disappointed at the sight of his son.

'Yes, who did you think it was? Michelle?'

When his father didn't reply, Ian walked past him into the hallway.

'It's nice to see you Ian. Bit of a surprise though; I wasn't expecting you this weekend. You should ring first you know. You were lucky to catch me in.' His father continued talking, as he led the way into the kitchen. 'Cup of tea? Coffee? Beer, maybe?' He avoided looking at him, concentrating instead on taking two mugs out of the dishwasher.

'Just coffee. I'm driving.'

'So, been to see your Mum, have you?'

'Yes, I have actually,' he replied, deciding not to mention his visit to the healer.

Ian struggled to control his feelings: a mixture of anger, disappointment that his father was so weak, satisfaction at being right in his assumptions and pity for his mother. He remembered his conversation with Jenny and decided to take her advice.

'Dad, wasn't that Michelle I just saw leaving?'

His father continued to prepare the coffee. His back was towards Ian, so Ian couldn't see his face. 'Could have been. She's just left. She'd called in to ask after your Mum.'

'She didn't look very happy. In fact, I'd say she'd been crying.'

'Well, you remember Michelle, she gets very emotional. She was, sorry, is a good friend of your Mum.'

Ian sat down at the kitchen table. 'Look Dad, you can tell me. Are you and Michelle still having an affair?'

There, it was out. The question that had been plaguing him for weeks had been asked. However he still didn't feel comfortable questioning his own father in this way. It seemed like role reversal; it used to be his father who asked him the awkward questions.

His father turned to face him, but at first he didn't answer. He placed the coffee pot on the table and sat down opposite his son, then he said, 'Well, I suppose you were bound to find out sometime. I just didn't want to tell you until we had some better news about your mother.' Then he went on the explain that it was on that fateful night when he'd confessed to Teresa about their affair that she'd run out of the house, and set the whole train of events in motion.

'But you said you'd broken it off?'

'Yes. I had.'

'So why did you tell Mum? What was the point of upsetting her?'

'I was so ashamed of what I'd done, I suppose.'

'Really? If that was the case, why did it start up again?' Ian couldn't keep the sarcasm from his voice.

Ian listened to his father's story of loneliness and frustration, of his fear of a future on his own, and his dread of having to look after a severely disabled wife. It was strange that he never once spoke of being in love with Michelle. It was all about him.

'So, why was Michelle upset just now?'

'She wants me to tell you and Alex about us. She wants it all out in the open.'

'And what about you Dad? What do you want?'

'Oh, Ian. I don't know. I don't want to lose her, but I can't face telling everyone yet.'

'What you mean Dad, is that you can't face everyone thinking you're a selfish, callous sod.' Ian gulped down some of the scalding coffee. 'I can't believe it. You've given up on Mum. It's not as though she's dead, for God's sake. And even if she had died in the crash, it would still be too soon to be setting up home with someone else. But she's not dead and she's going to get better. And how on earth are we going to encourage her to get better if she finds out that you and Michelle are living together?'

Ian knew he shouldn't be saying these things, but he felt so angry with his father that he couldn't stop himself. He was shouting now and he'd stood up in his rage, knocking the table and spilling his coffee. His father remained seated, his head bowed, meekly accepting his son's criticism.

'How could you Dad? Don't you love Mum? Did you ever love her? Wasn't she a good wife to you?'

'Look Ian, It's hard to explain. I'm just the sort of man who needs to have a woman in his life,' he began.

But Ian wasn't listening. 'I don't think you even love Michelle. I think the only person you love is yourself.'

'Your Mum's very unhappy,' his father began. 'She wants...'

'Of course she's unhappy. Not only is she a bloody quadriplegic, she can't even communicate with her family. Wouldn't you be unhappy if you were in her situation?'

Whatever his father had been going to say, he never finished it and asked instead, 'So, what are you going to do Ian?'

'What am I going to do? Well I'm not going to tell Mum, for sure, nor Gran, and what's the point of worrying Alex, when he's half-way round the world. No, Dad, I'm going to do nothing. You should be asking yourself that question, not me.'

'I ask myself that question every day, son.'

His father looked so sad and lonely, that Ian felt his anger abate. He had a quick temper like his mother, but also like her, it soon subsided. What had Jenny said? It was not really his business. Who was he to say what his father should or shouldn't do. He sat down again at the table, and mopped at the spilt coffee with a serviette. They sat in silence for a while, then he said, 'Did you get an email from Alex?'

'I don't think so. I'll check later.'

'Well, if not, you can read mine. I'll forward it to you.'

'Thanks.'

'I'd better get off now. I'm staying at Gran's for a couple of nights.'

He'd planned asking his Dad to go out for a meal that evening, but now it hardly seemed appropriate.

'That's nice for her. She'll enjoy the company.'

Once again Ian was struck by the man's loneliness. After all his parents had been married for over twenty-five years and, for most of that time, had seemed very happy. His father had never had to come home to an empty house before, nor had to wonder what to prepare for his meals; everything had been taken care of by his wife: the bills, the laundry, the shopping, the garden, his sons' schooling. No wonder he missed her. She'd been the driving force in their family. The engine at the heart of their lives.

'By the way, Dad, did you know that Mum had a brother?'

'A brother? No, I'm sure she didn't. I've never heard anyone speak of a brother. Why do you ask that?'

'Gran was telling me about Mum's childhood, and she said she had a brother. Well he was actually her cousin, but he grew up with them and she thought of him as a brother.'

'Died did he?'

'No, just disappeared.'

'I think your Gran is confused. I'm sure your Mum would have mentioned him at some point over the years, even if he was dead. Your Gran had a lot of brothers and cousins herself, maybe she's confusing him with one of them,' he suggested.

'Maybe. Just thought I'd ask.'

*

She leans on the gate and watches Tommy sauntering up the lane. She can hear him calling Foxy, who has made a detour into the hedgerows looking for rabbits. He's a tall boy for his age, and the summer sun has turned his creamy skin a light shade of coffee.

'Mum. Can we go to the fair?' he calls even before he reaches her.

'What fair's that?' she asks. She's not a great fan of fairgrounds but the kids love them.

'It's the Kerry County Fair. Haven't you seen the posters about it? Everyone's going. There's a bouncy castle, and donkey carts, and a dog show—we could take Foxy—and a pet farm. It's the big event of the year. We have to go. You could take your paintings. People take all sorts of things. Or you could enter the baking competition. Oona's mum is going in for that.'

She laughs. 'Do you really think they give a prize for burnt fairy cakes?'

It's a family joke that Teresa's baking isn't very successful. In the early days she'd tried to bake sponges and cakes but they never turned out as well as her mother's. Then one day Jack had returned from school with a bag of cakes that he'd bought at the school bazaar.

'I thought you'd like these Mum. You know, we could buy cakes and then you wouldn't have to worry about burning them any more.' It was very sweet of him, but

she got the message and has never attempted cake making again.

'Okay, slow down. When is it exactly?' she asks her excited son.

'Next Sunday. Do say we can go. Dad'll be here; he can come with us,' the boy continues.

'It sounds a nice idea, Tommy. I'll talk to Oona's mum and find out more about it.'

'Great. What's to eat?'

She smiles. Tommy's thoughts rarely stray far from his next meal.

CHAPTER 23

After Ian left, Mark went into the lounge and poured himself a large whisky. He sat by the French windows that opened out onto the garden. It had been a cloudy day, one of those grey, nondescript days of which there seemed to be so many, and although it was still only early evening, the sky was darkening. He decided against sitting outside.

What bad luck that Ian had arrived just as Michelle was leaving. He'd asked her not to visit him at home, for precisely that reason. He drank some more of the whisky. Maybe it was for the best: at least it was out in the open now. This was what he needed to make him face up to his responsibilities; he would talk to Bridget and he would email Alex. Reminded of his eldest son, he opened his laptop. Maybe he should write to him straight away before his courage failed him. He began:

My dear Alex,

I enjoyed reading the email you sent to Ian. You seem to have settled in well. The job sounds interesting; pity it's not making you any money. I know; that's not the point of voluntary service. Well at least it's only for a year and then you can get back on the career path again.

Your Mum is just the same. The doctors say she isn't making any progress at all. I can't understand her; she's being completely non-co-operative. I go to see her each day and your Gran and Ian visit as well, but it's all a waste of time. She doesn't want to see any of us.

Mark stopped typing. He couldn't tell Alex about Michelle yet. He needed to speak to her first. She'd said it was all over between them, that she didn't want to see him again. He felt sure she didn't really mean it, but there was no point in upsetting everyone for nothing if she was serious about severing their relationship.

He thought back to her visit. This time she'd been annoyed because he refused to go away with her for a few days break. She'd showed him the details of a small hotel in Cornwall. He had to admit that it looked very tempting, but he didn't want to complicate his life further, he told her.

Michelle worked in a large travel agency in London; it was part of a national group. Most of her work was organising business travel: flights, conferences, trade fairs, limousines, theatre tickets, anything the business-man needed for his trip, but every so often she came across one of those special deals that were on offer to agency employees. The previous month she had tried, unsuccessfully, to get him to go to Venice with her. It was an excellent offer, she told him: three nights in a four-star hotel in the centre of the city for only three hundred pounds each, including flights. She'd been so annoyed that he wouldn't accompany her, she invited a friend from work to go with her instead. Mark had lied and said it was because of pressure of work, but he knew she hadn't believed him.

He finished the last drop of the whisky and refilled the glass. He calculated that he had at least four weeks holiday due to him; when he returned to work on Monday he would arrange to take a week off and suggest that they go away somewhere. He would try to make it up to her.

Mark was woken from his reverie by the telephone ringing. He put down his empty glass and went across to answer it.

'Mark? It's Michelle.'

'Hello Michelle. I was going to telephone you; we need to talk.'

'Oh. Okay Mark. Why don't you come over and I'll cook us some supper?'

'Can you come over here? I've had a couple of whiskies and don't fancy driving.'

'Yes, alright. If you're sure?'

'Yes, I'd like you to come, Michelle.'

'Okay, see you in about half-an-hour.'

Mark replaced the receiver and poured himself another whisky. I'd better make that the last, he thought.

No matter how he tried to shut it out of his mind, his wife's desperate plea kept coming back to him. She didn't want to live; that was obvious. She had shut herself off from the world since the accident happened. The only thing it seemed that she really wanted, was to die, to escape from the tomb in which she found herself trapped. Could he really deny her that? But how could he do it? Euthanasia was a crime in Britain. He would go to prison if he were caught. He tried to remember what he'd read in the papers about a woman who helped her paraplegic son to die. It had gone to court and been headline news for a few days. But what had happened to her in the end?

If he went ahead with it, how would he get the morphine? He was pretty sure you couldn't just buy it over the counter. And which doctor could he find who would give him a prescription? No he'd have to think of another way. He needed something foolproof. Something completely undetectable. The doctors would have to think it was natural causes, her heart giving out or something like that. The next time he was with Teresa he would talk to her about it. If she was adamant that was what she wanted, then he would do it for her.

*

It took Michelle less than half-an-hour to drive the short distance to Gatsby Terrace. She'd been sitting by the telephone all evening, wondering whether to ring Mark and apologise, and when she at last summoned the courage to do so, he'd not given her the opportunity to speak. So she freshened her make-up, grabbed her coat and keys, and left.

However when she arrived at his house, she didn't immediately go to the door, but remained sitting in her car with the engine running quietly, trying to calm her racing heart. It was important that she didn't become too emotional, she told herself; she needed to talk to Mark calmly and rationally. After a while she felt calmer and ready to face him, so she switched off the engine and made her way up the drive to his front door. She hesitated a moment more before ringing the bell, but then, when she saw his shadow through the glass, her heart began to beat wildly again.

'Hi Michelle,' Mark said, kissing her cheek and taking her coat from her.

He smelled of whisky. She hoped he hadn't had too many; it would make talking to him so much more difficult.

'Come into the kitchen and I'll pour you a drink,' he said, leading the way.

That afternoon was the first time Michelle had been in his house in a long time, and here she was again, twice in one day. She thought back to the previous occasion she'd visited Gatsby Terrace, just before Teresa's accident: they'd been shopping together in Oxford and had come back laden with packages and flopped down in the lounge, moaning about their aching feet and the crowded shops. Mark had brought them both a large gin and tonic and watched as they opened their purchases, giggling like a couple of schoolgirls on Christmas morning. What a long time ago it seemed now; so much had changed since then.

'Chardonnay alright?' he asked.

'Yes, that's fine. Thanks.' She sat down at the kitchen table and sipped her drink. 'Mark, I...' she began, keeping her eyes firmly fixed on the surface of the table.

'No, don't say anything yet. I want to talk to you first.' He sat down opposite her and took her hand in his own. 'Ian came to see me this afternoon, just after you left. He saw you leaving.'

'Oh, God. What did he say?'

'Well, in typical Ian fashion he came right out and asked if we were having an affair.'

'What did you tell him?'

'What could I tell him? I told him the truth.'

'Oh, Mark.' Michelle didn't know whether to feel pleased or upset. This was what she'd wanted, to have everything out in the open, but she'd wanted Mark to make the first move not wait until they were found out. She looked at Mark, hoping for some clue to his feelings on this. 'How did he react?'

'Angrily. What did you expect? His mother's in hospital and his father is fucking her best friend. That's how he sees it.' Mark stood up and started to pace about the kitchen.

Michelle began to cry softly. She was very fond of Ian, even more so than Alex. She knew that for all his brash candour he had a very kind heart, and she hated the thought that he would turn against her.

She wiped her eyes and asked, 'Is he going to tell Alex?'

'He says not. But it doesn't matter one way or the other. I'm going to tell him myself and then I'm going to tell Bridget. I can't keep living like this; I want to get my life back. They will all come to terms with it eventually.'

'But what are you going to say? Exactly?' Michelle was beginning to feel nervous. She was unsure of where Mark was going with this; was he going to tell them that their relationship was a thing of the past or the future?

'Well, that rather depends on you,' he said, sitting down again and looking directly at her. His voice had softened and there was almost a look of pleading in his eyes. He stretched across and took her hand again.

'What do you mean?'

'Well, I know I've not been very fair to you. I've been too concerned with what people would say, instead of thinking of your happiness. You don't deserve to have to skulk around in this hole-in-the-corner manner.'

Michelle refrained from commenting; she hadn't seen it as skulking. That made her feel cheap.

'It's time we started behaving like any other couple. After all it's not as though Teresa is going to get better. The doctors all agree that there's no cure for her condition. She could even die. And anyway, I doubt she even really knows what's going on.'

'She is conscious. Of course she knows what's going on.' Michelle thought of her friend lying there in her hospital bed, unaware that they were discussing her like this. Life was so cruel. 'So what do you propose?'

'Good word that.' He laughed as he said it, and the warmth of his sudden smile caused her stomach to lurch in a familiar way.

'That isn't what I meant. I mean what are we going to do?'

'Well I think I will put this house on the market and move in with you. It's far too big for just two of us here, and anyway it has too many memories. I want us to make a fresh start.'

'But you can't sell Teresa's home. The boys won't agree to it.'

'It's got nothing to do with the boys. It's my house. I'll do what I want with it.' Mark looked angry now.

Michelle realised that he was frightened. He had no idea how to cope with Teresa's situation. Everyone was looking to him for support and advice and he couldn't give it. He was like a child who just wanted it all to be over with. Sell the house. Move on with their lives. But it couldn't be like that.

'I know, but it was their home,' she said gently. 'Even if they have no legal right to the house, they're going to feel some strong emotional attachment to it. You'd be removing yet another part of their childhood.'

'So what do you suggest? The only alternative is for you to move in here. Do you think they would like that any better?'

'No, I suppose not. But please, Mark, before you do anything, talk to them. Let's take it step by step.'

'Alright, but I thought you wanted things to change. That's what you've been telling me, over and over again.'

'I do, but let's not rush in and upset everyone needlessly. I would hope we could stay friends with Ian and Alex. I don't want to become their enemy and you don't want to lose your sons.'

'Yes, you're right. What about if I move my stuff to your place first?'

'Yes, that's fine. Then you can just lock up this house for a while. After all you don't know if you might need to sell it in the future to pay for Teresa's care. It might be best to wait a bit to see what will happen.'

'I know. There are so many things to consider. I just don't know where to start.'

'No-one knows what the future has in store, Mark,' she replied, thinking of her friend.

'Well I know one thing: I'm going to spend my future with you.'

Michelle smiled at him. This was the nearest he had ever got to being romantic.

'Anyway, what did you want to talk to me about?' he asked, remembering their earlier conversation.

Michelle sipped some more of her wine before replying, 'I went to see Teresa. I told her about us and I asked her to forgive me.'

'Did you get any reaction?'

'No, but I'm sure she could hear me.'

'The doctors say she can hear alright, but it's whether she bothers to listen.'

'I stayed for a while, just sitting there, massaging her hands, and I thought: This is my best friend and here she is all alone, trapped in her lifeless body; she can't speak to me, she can't accuse me of betraying her, she can't tell me she forgives me. And I realised then that you and I are the ones who have to help her. We caused this awful thing to happen, so we have to help put it right.'

'It's no good Michelle. She doesn't want help, not from us, not from the doctors, not from anyone. She wants to die.'

'That doesn't matter. She needs help; the nurses and doctors can't do it all. And maybe, if we're lucky, with time she will start to respond. I know, if the roles were reversed, she would do it for me.'

'Maybe. I don't know. What sort of help are you talking about anyway?'

'Care, love, attention, all that sort of thing. I was talking to one of her nurses and she told me that she needs much more physiotherapy than they can possibly do in the rehab unit. We could sit with her and exercise her feet and hands. They will tell us what to do, so we do it properly. We could wash her hair and do her nails.'

'Oh yes, Teresa was always very proud of her nails,' Mark said more to himself than to her.

'We could read to her. I'm sure there's lots that we could do to make her life more comfortable,' she continued. 'We could even try taking her out. And we would feel better about ourselves.'

'Well, it sounds fine, Michelle, but I think you're being very optimistic, and anyway how do we fit it all in? We both work and you commute every day and don't get home until late—and that's when the trains are on time. We're not bloody saints, you know. Nor miracle workers.'

She looked at him; he was still very negative. Perhaps it was the whisky talking. 'We can work on that. I may even ask for a transfer to Wycombe, and then I'd be right on the doorstep. The important thing is that there's someone to look after her. We can't expect Ian or Bridget to take it on.'

'Ian's too far away.'

'And he's too young. He needs to live his own life without the constant worry of his mother. And Bridget is getting on now.'

'Yes, she's aged a lot this last year' He seemed to be agreeing with her, at last. 'Okay, sweetheart, we'll give it a try. But don't expect too much. I don't think people with her condition have a great life expectancy.'

'I don't expect anything. As I said, whether she wants our help or not, she certainly needs it.'

*

Later that night, after Michelle had left, Mark returned to his email to Alex. He was glad she'd come round; he now had a much clearer idea of where they were going. It was not going to be easy and he didn't expect his sons to applaud his actions, but he felt more confident now that—in time—they would forgive him for his infidelity. What they surely wouldn't forgive was what he was going to do next.

CHAPTER 24

Ian couldn't forget the way his mother had looked at
him when he mentioned her brother—or cousin, whatever he was; he'd obviously been very important to her.
And if that was the case then finding him might be the
key to unlocking his mother's cage of indifference. He
needed to find out more about this man and the only
people he could ask were Bridget and his mother. It was
unlikely his mother would tell him anything so, much as
it pained him to do so, he was going to have to pressure
his grandmother into telling him everything. He needed
to know more if he was going to help his mother regain
her will to live.

*

Bridget was sitting in the kitchen when he arrived, with
Smokey Joe purring away, on her lap.

'Ian. You're early. I thought you were going to spend
some time with your Dad?'

'I did call round, but he was about to go out, so I
popped in to see Mum and then I thought I'd come back
here.'

'Well, it's lovely to see you. To be honest, I'd be glad
of some company tonight. Talking about the past has
made me feel quite down.' He saw that she'd been crying.

'Sometimes it helps to share things with other people,' he began, wondering how he would tackle the subject of Jimmy. But before he could begin, his grand-

mother looked straight at him and said, 'You're right. There have been too many secrets in our family. We've always been great ones for keeping things to ourselves. I think it's time I explained some things to you.'

Ian poured himself some tea and waited for his grandmother to continue. She stared down at the table for a moment with a look of indescribable sadness on her face. At last she looked up and, with a sigh that carried the regrets of a lifetime, said, 'It was our fault. We should have realised they were too close. But you don't always see what's right under your nose, do you?' Ian didn't reply, so she carried on, 'It was when we were all staying at my mother's, during the summer holidays. It was 1980; Jimmy had just had his fifteenth birthday. My, but he was a grand boy, full of life, and so handsome. Well, he and Teresa were down in Finlay's cove, where they always went—it was called that because many years before a fisherman called Terence Finlay was drowned out at sea and his body was washed up in that cove, just two miles from his own cottage. Can you believe that? Well, anyway, they went down to the cove as usual to swim and look for crabs, and generally play about, just like they'd done for years. It was one of those pretty little coves that you can find all along the west coast, with a bank of jagged rocks stretching out into the sea—that's where they'd find the crabs, in those rocks. Well, the cliffs at this point were not too high and it was easy enough to scamper down the bank. Even I could do it in those days.' She smiled at Ian, her blue eyes twinkling at the memory of her youth. 'And there was a cave, just above the high water mark—a smugglers' cave, Jimmy liked to call it, and it probably was, once upon a time—which was always their favourite place to play, and I suppose we just didn't realise how quickly they were both growing up.' She paused. Ian wasn't sure where this was leading, but he was starting to feel uncomfortable. 'So that particular day—it was a Friday—they were in the cove as usual, when the two Brady sisters saw them. I don't know what my two were doing, but according to Siobhan Brady they were both naked. I expect they'd been swimming and taken off their bathing suits and laid them on the rocks to dry. We'd never made a big thing about nakedness in our family,' she added. 'But then, Siobhan, the evil-tongued creature, said she saw them kissing. May God forgive her.'

'So that's why Jimmy went away?' Ian interrupted.

'Well, it wasn't only that. We never got the whole story, you know, just what the Brady girl had to say. Teresa was too upset to speak and Jimmy just clammed up tight.'

'So what happened?'

'Well, they say that Maisie, the older one and an even nastier piece of work than her sister—God rest her soul—climbed down the bank and sneaked up on them. When they saw her, she ran off, screaming that she was going to tell Father O'Connor what they were doing. She started running towards the cliff, but Jimmy, who was a very fast runner, set off after her and cut off her escape, so she headed off along the rocks, hoping to clamber up the cliff at the far end of the cove, where the bank had collapsed. And that's when it happened.' Bridget stopped and wiped her eyes. Reliving the events of that day was upsetting her badly.

'When what happened, Gran?'

'This freak wave, it came from nowhere and swept across the rocks, lifting Maisie up and pulling her out into the sea.'

'My God. What did they do?'

'There was nothing they could do. They were all too shocked. Even that Siobhan was silenced for a while. Jimmy ran to Mrs Doody's shop and she rang the coast-guards, but there was no sign of Maisie anywhere. That part of the coast has some awful vicious undercurrents; she must have been towed straight out to sea.'

'So, did they ever discover her body?'

'Oh, yes. It washed up the next week at Ventry. Oh it was a terrible thing, so it was.'

Ian reached across and patted his grandmother on the shoulder. 'Was there a police enquiry?' he asked.

'Not really. The Garda were informed, but everyone agreed it was just a terrible accident.'

'And Jimmy?'

'Well, of course, Siobhan told her version of events and soon all the tongues in the village were wagging. Then Father O'Connor came to see us. It was awful.' She sighed. 'In the end we decided it would be best if Jimmy stayed in Ireland with his grandmother for a bit and Teresa went back to England with us.'

'But how could you and Granddad just leave him behind?'

At this accusation, Bridget couldn't hold back the tears that had been gathering and let them flow freely down her careworn cheeks.

'Oh, Gran, I'm sorry. I didn't mean it to sound like that. I'm just a bit shocked by all this.' Ian went over to his grandmother and hugged her to his chest. 'Look it's a long time ago, Gran. I'm sure you did what you thought was best, at the time.'

Bridget pulled herself away from her grandson's embrace. 'I didn't want to leave him, but your grandfather said we had no option. He said it was the only way to stop it before it went too far. They were in love, you see. We didn't know what else to do. Father O'Connor was breathing down our necks; he threatened to tell Father Riley, our priest in Maidenhead, if we didn't do something to keep Jimmy and Teresa apart. We just didn't know what to do for the best; we couldn't leave Teresa, so we had to leave Jimmy.'

'But what about Mum, what did she say?'

'Oh, Teresa was distraught. She cried and screamed. We had to lock her in her bedroom to stop her running away, and then when we got home to England she refused to speak to us for months. She wrote to Jimmy every day, but he never got her letters; my mother intercepted them all.' She took a deep breath before continuing, 'Then eventually she came to terms with it, but she never mentioned Jimmy's name again. I think she felt he'd abandoned her.'

'And Jimmy?'

'Well I thought it would be just for a few years. You know, until they'd passed through the adolescence stage. I thought he'd find a girlfriend and then things would be alright. But they weren't. It was awful for him there. Everyone blamed him: they said it was his fault that Maisie had died. They tormented him about Teresa, and even when my mother sent him to school in Cork, the accusations followed him.'

'Poor guy. He must have had a hell of a time.'

Bridget didn't reply to this comment, instead she continued with her tale, 'Then one day, when he was seventeen, he just upped and left. He told no-one where he was going and he's not been in touch with anyone since.'

'Just disappeared?'

She nodded.

'What's that, thirty-five years ago? He could be anywhere by now.'

'Yes. I don't even know if he's still alive.'

'Well, I suppose that explains why Mum has never mentioned him. I wonder if she ever thinks of him?'

'I doubt it. As I said, she has never even spoken his name in all these years. And I've never dared speak to her about him, in case I upset her. I'd lost one child; I didn't want to lose another.'

'Do you have any photos of him?'

'There might be a couple in the album, but we didn't have a camera in those days, so I doubt if there are many. There should be one of him as a baby, some-where.'

Bridget blew her nose and wiped the remaining tears from her eyes. She looked calmer now, as if telling the story to Ian had released something inside her.

'Well, Gran, let's see if we can track him down. I think we'd all like to know where he is.'

'It's all very well for you to say that Ian, but how do we find him? Your Granddad and I, we made lots of en-quiries, but nobody had heard of him.'

'Yes, but nowadays it's a lot easier to find people. There's so much data collected on everyone these days.

Anyway, I've got some friends in the police force, maybe they can help. I'll start making some enquiries next week, when I'm back in Edinburgh.'

CHAPTER 25

The next morning Mark set off for the local library. He still hadn't come to terms with what Teresa wanted from him but he couldn't get her angry eyes out of his head. She was suffering, of that there was no doubt, but he couldn't see how he could be the one to help her. He was sure it was illegal, a criminal offence. For a moment the thought went through his mind that maybe this was her way of punishing him. She would be released from her torment and he'd go to prison and spend the rest of his life regretting his actions—all of them.

'Can I help you?' a young librarian asked him.

'Yes, I'm writing an article on euthanasia and I wanted to look up some details on the current legal situation here in the UK,' he replied.

'Well if you like to use the computer I'm sure you'll find a number of references to euthanasia and in the meantime I'll see what journals we have with relevant articles.'

He directed him to a bank of computers and gave him an access card. It was still early; the library had only just opened and the usual crowd of students that dominated the computers was absent. He could have used his laptop at home but he didn't want to risk the boys, or Michelle, seeing what he'd been doing—he knew none of them would approve of his actions.

Almost immediately he found an article on a man with Locked-In Syndrome who was fighting for the right to die. He was only slightly older than Teresa and his situation was very similar: he couldn't speak and, like her, he communicated by blinking his eyes. Nothing else worked. But he wasn't terminally ill; that was the problem. As Mark read on, article after article, some pro-euthanasia, others virulently against it, he realised what an ethical dilemma it was. If Teresa had been linked up to a ventilator or some apparatus that was keeping her alive, it would have been possible to turn off the life support machine and allow her to die. But she wasn't. She was breathing unaided, her heart and internal organs were functioning and her brain was alert. To end her life would need a lethal injection and this would be viewed as murder. One was considered passive euthanasia and was not a crime, the other was active euthanasia and against the law. But morally what was the difference? Surely if you switched off the breathing machine and the patient died, no matter how ill he was, the cause of his death was someone switching off the machine?

He thought back to his own father's death. Mark and Teresa had been away on holiday, walking in the Lake District when they received a call from his mother. His father had collapsed and was in hospital. By the time Mark arrived his father was in ICU, connected to a life support machine and unconscious. He stayed like that for a week, with Mark and his mother by the bedside, day and night, but he seemed unaware of their presence. Then one night the doctor stopped to talk to them.

'It's no good,' he said. 'We can't take him off the ventilator. We've tried and each time his heart is put under too much strain. I'm sorry to have to tell you this but he is not going to recover.'

They'd looked at him, not really comprehending. 'It's best if we switch off the machine,' he continued.

Mark's mother understood then. 'But he'll die if you do that,' she said.

The doctor had nodded gravely. 'He won't suffer,' he said.

'But...'

'It's for the best. His only prognosis is to remain permanently connected to the ventilator; it's only that that's keeping him alive.'

Mark remembered putting his arm around his mother and repeating, 'It's for the best, Mum.' The best for whom?

They stayed with him until the end. It hadn't been quick. His old man's heart hadn't wanted to give up without a fight and beat strongly for a while until, at last, it petered out and stopped. He was dead. Was that murder? They had never even considered the question at the time. He was Mark's father and his life was over. What else could they have done for him?

Once they'd had a dog, a big, hairy cross between an Alsatian and a Schnauzer, that used to follow Mark everywhere when he was a boy. A car accident left the dog unable to walk, so they'd had him put down. Mark had cried buckets at the time but he knew that his friend was suffering and even as a child, he understood it was for the best. If it was permitted to put a family pet out of its misery then why not a human being?

He scrolled to the next page. What about other countries? Maybe she could go to another country to die. He vaguely remembered seeing a few minutes of a TV documentary on assisted suicide some years ago. Teresa had turned it off; she never liked any of those programmes about ill-health and death. Where was it? Switzerland? He typed in a few key words and waited while Google gave him yet another list of options. Eventually he found what he wanted. Yes, he could take her to Switzerland. There was even an organisation to help him: Dignitas. Or Holland. It was legal in Holland. That was another option. As he read on he realised it was still not that simple; he would still be breaking UK law. It was illegal for someone to help a person commit suicide. He found a recently published report by a group called Dignity in Dying, which pointed out that assisted dying was beyond the reach of the average person. The fees were around £10,000—a lot of money but something he could manage—and then there was the cost of getting a seriously incapacitated woman such as Teresa to Holland, or Switzerland. What was even more difficult was getting the co-operation of the doctor to give you the patient's medical records. It was an administrative minefield. The enormity of the task suddenly hit him. How could he take her out of the country without the rest of the family finding out what he was doing? She couldn't travel alone. And from his talks with Dr Stevens he couldn't see him being very helpful. Without his assistance, it was impossible.

'I've found you a few journals that might help,' the librarian said, putting a pile of magazines on the table next to him. 'There're also a couple of books you might like to look at; they're reference only, I'm afraid.'

'Thanks.'

He continued scrolling through the plethora of articles offered up by Google until one caught his eye. It was about a study undertaken in 2011 by a Belgian doctor and according to the heading, not all patients with Locked-In Syndrome wanted to die. It seemed that some were resigned to their limited life state. He frowned, thinking of Teresa's angry eyes. That seemed difficult to believe. As he read he realised the sample taken by the researchers was fairly small, with less than seventy worthwhile results and these included, naturally enough, only those who could communicate in some way. Nevertheless the results were interesting because the suggestion was that, as time went on, people adjusted and learned to adapt to their condition. Some of those who responded indicated that they felt almost as well as they did before they became locked-in. Were the authors of the article saying that assisted suicide shouldn't be offered to them on this basis? He read on. No, it seemed to be about a question of time; the suggestion was that the patient needed time to adapt to his new state and then, if he still wanted to die, he should be allowed to.

Time. Teresa had been in a locked-in state for over a year now. How much time did they mean? Since her accident time had dragged for him—every day a torture. What on earth must it have been like for Teresa? Would she really learn to adapt with time?

He shut down the computer, picked up the books and journals and moved to a quieter part of the library. His head was spinning; he felt more confused than ever.

Maybe Michelle was right, maybe they should concentrate on keeping Teresa comfortable and wait to see what happened.

*

Teresa has decided to take Foxy for a walk. She has planned to start a new painting today of some ruined cottages she has discovered. They've obviously not been lived in for years; the roofs have collapsed and the wooden doors and windows disappeared long ago in a forgotten fire, only the stone walls remain, their white paint still blackened from the fire. A scarlet fuchsia grows through the gaping windows and winds its way along the wall; pink and blue hydrangeas dominate the gardens and a solitary dog rose grows by the gate. It will make a lovely composition and if she starts it today, it could be ready for the County Fair. She wasn't going to enter anything—she hasn't done very much painting since she's been here; just a couple of watercolours— but the boys have insisted. As Jack put it, she might be a crappy baker but she is a wonderful painter. He'd even collected an entry form for her, so now she has no choice. A solitary sheep has climbed onto a wall and is busily grazing on the plants that have rooted there. She thinks the sheep would make a nice touch to her painting, so decides to take a few photographs of it. Although she prefers to paint "live", as she calls it, because then she can appreciate the changing tones of light, it is always useful to have the odd photograph of the scene, so that she can make some adjustments at home. And anyway that sheep isn't going to wait around all day for her to paint it.

But she doesn't feel very creative today; she's bored: the children have gone to play with some friends in the village and it is only Tuesday; her husband won't be back until Friday; it seems an age to wait.

She looks again at the empty windows of the cottage and a feeling of melancholy comes over her. No-one has lived here for years. The place is deserted; she is all alone. She photographs the scene from a number of angles and heads for home.

CHAPTER 26

Healing Hands? Where had she heard that expression before? She couldn't remember. Anyway what on earth did Ian think he was doing now? Was this woman supposed to be the new Jesus, about to tell her to pick up her bed and walk.

Teresa felt the woman's hands on her head, the warmth slipping across her forehead and down her neck, like summer sunshine. Gradually her irritation ebbed away and her whole being seemed to be concentrated on the source of the heat. How long the woman stayed like that she didn't know, but after a while she became aware that she'd changed her position and was now standing by her side. Although she didn't touch her, Teresa knew she was passing her hands across her body, casting out whatever demons she thought were inhabiting her. It was all very peaceful, but useless.

Still she had to hand it to Ian; he was determined. Despite her irritation, she felt pleased that Ian was fighting so hard for her. She'd felt like laughing when he'd brought the crystals and placed them around her bed, explaining what each was supposed to do; well she certainly needed some positive energy. The music therapy was actually very soothing; she loved music anyway and if he thought it was helping her, so much the better. And she liked the poetry. She wasn't sure it was doing her much good but the fact was that so many of the poems seemed to speak to her directly. Did Ian realise that or was it just by chance he chose those poems?

As she thought about her second son, she realised that the straws he was clutching at were as much for his own benefit as hers. Ian was not ready to let her go. It made her sad to think of his suffering but it was nothing compared to hers. And now he was going to look for Jimmy. How on earth did he find out about him? Her mother, of course. But what exactly had she said to him? Teresa felt a tingle of excitement; maybe she should make a point of listening to her mother's ramblings the next time she visited her, just in case there was an explanation.

She became aware of the woman speaking. She had a soft, musical voice. 'I think that's enough for today. I'll see you next week.'

Teresa felt the woman's hand on her forehead again. It rested there for a moment then was gone. She had to admit that she felt different. She went over in her mind what had happened while the healer was there. Not a lot; she hadn't spoken to her and she hadn't tried to massage her unresponsive limbs. She hadn't done very much at all and yet Teresa felt more at peace; it was if the woman had released some knot of tension inside her. Perhaps Ian wasn't so daft after all; perhaps these alternative treatments were helping her to feel more relaxed. But what they weren't doing was making her whole again. No-one could do that. The doctor had admitted as much.

*

Ian walked with Rachel to her car. The woman had said very little to him since she'd arrived, her attention had been focused wholly on his mother.

'So, what do you think?' he asked.

'About what?'

'My mother. What do you think her chances are?'

'Ian, I've told you; I can't do miracles. Your mother's condition is serious. I read the doctors' notes and their prognosis is not good. This condition is not really reversible, but I have known people make incredible progress.'

'And in my mother's case?'

'Your mother needs a reason to live. I told you that from the start. If the will to live isn't there, she will die. Maybe in a few months. Maybe in a few years. It's important that you find something that will give her hope. At the moment she is resigned to her fate. She sees no possibility of a different future and she doesn't like what that future holds.'

'She wants to die,' he interrupted. 'The nurse told me; she's asked the doctor to help her.'

Rachel looked serious. 'All I can say is that if we can help her recover her will to live, then she may make some progress. I will do what I can.'

'Will you come to see her again?'

'Yes, of course. Next Sunday if you like. I can come every week. But I can also be doing a lot from home.'

'From home? What do you mean, like distance healing?'

'Something like that.' She smiled at him kindly. 'Don't worry Ian, you're doing all that you can to help your mother,' she said. 'Look, I must go now. I'll see you next Sunday at the same time.'

'Okay. And thanks, Rachel.' He watched her drive her blue Corsa to the end of the parking lot and turn right, before he got into his own car. He was extremely tired, as if he'd been doing some vigorous exercises, and he had an overwhelming urge to sleep.

*

As he crawled through the traffic on the M1 he thought back over the weekend: first, the revelations of his grandmother and then his father. It all left him feeling disorientated: too many secrets. Ian was a straightforward young man, not given to subterfuge; it made him uncomfortable.

He switched on the car radio and skimmed the channels until he found something soothing: "Songs of the Auvergne". He recognised the voice of Victoria de los Angeles, one of his mother's favourites. He would try to download it for her before he saw her next. As soon as he thought it, a doubt crept into his mind: was the music therapy actually working? He wasn't sure. Nothing seemed to be working. Maybe he was wrong. Maybe she would never get better. Was it possible he was just being stubborn, refusing to face what everyone else seemed to have accepted? Maybe it would be kinder if they let her die. Would he want to live like that? He knew the answer. Instantly he was angry at his own weakness. No, he wasn't going to let that happen. What was it Rachel said? It was important for his mother to have hope. Hope. He was going to give her that hope. He was going to give her the will to live; he was going to find her brother for her. He was no longer looking for a miracle. Rachel had convinced him that what was required was something more within his grasp. Finding Jimmy was going to be the key to her recovery; he was sure of that.

A lorry overtook him, the driver honking his horn, impatiently. Ian pushed all further thoughts of his mother to the back of his mind and turned his attention to the traffic. He ought to have left earlier; Sunday evening was the worst possible time to be driving home. The road works were causing an enormous tailback that wound its way northwards like an articulated worm, never reaching twenty miles an hour.

'God, I'll never be in Edinburgh before midnight at this rate,' he said aloud, regretting his decision to save money by driving down in his own car.

*

The next day Ian rose early, despite his late night. He was due to drive up to Aberdeen to attend a furniture auction; they'd received a tip that one of the local lairds was selling off some of his possessions. Ian's job was to check that nothing of national importance was on offer. It would take him about an hour and a half to get there, and he had some personal things to attend to first.

When he'd told his grandmother he had contacts in the police force, he was actually thinking of one particular contact: Andrea, an ex-girlfriend who, in the end, had preferred her job to him. They had been dating for almost a year when she'd received the opportunity to move to Aberdeen with a promotion to sergeant. She'd promised to keep in touch and he'd said he would visit her often, but neither had happened. Nevertheless he was excited at the prospect of seeing her again.

He dialled the central police station in Aberdeen and asked for her by name.

'Yes, Sergeant Forbes speaking.'

'Hello, Sergeant Forbes, this is a voice from your past.'

'Ian, how lovely to hear from you.'

'You recognised my voice.'

'Well, I'm not a sergeant for nothing you know.' She laughed.

'How are things? You sound happy.'

'Great. They couldn't be better. I love it here,' she replied.

'You don't miss Edinburgh then, or your old friends?'

'Well I suppose I don't really. I'm too busy to keep up with my new friends, never mind worrying about old ones. Anyway why the call? I'm sure you haven't rung just to see if I'm missing you.'

'Well, I did hope you might have missed me a little bit, but no, you're right, I've rung for a favour.'

'You know me, hen; if I can help, I will. What is it?'

'I need to trace a missing person,' he began and then explained about Jimmy.

'Right. It's a bit of a long shot, you know. How many years is it? Thirty-five?'

'Yes, I think so. He disappeared in 1982.'

'Okay. Let's see what we can do. Did anyone report him missing at the time?'

'No, I don't think so. He was living with his grandmother in Ireland then. I think he was pretty unhappy, so nobody was really surprised that he left.' Ian told her about the events that had led up to Jimmy's exile.

'Yeah, sounds pretty miserable, poor kid.'

'I think his parents made a few enquiries, but nothing official.'

'Okay. What's his full name?'

Anticipating these questions, Ian had gathered as much evidence from Bridget as he could. He pulled out his uncle's birth certificate.

'James Patrick O'Sullivan.'

'Pretty common name, unfortunately. Date of birth?'

'The third of July 1965.'

'Where was he born?'

'Burnham, Slough.'

'I thought you said he was Irish?'

'His parents were Irish and he lived in Ireland a lot of his life.'

'Father's name?'

'Not known.'

'Mother's name then?'

'Dorothy Margaret Sullivan.'

'Not much to go on, but it will have to do for now. I'll see what we can come up with. Have you any reason to think he may have had trouble with the law?' she asked.

'Not really. But as he was only seventeen when he disappeared, it is possible.'

'What do you want me to do if I come up with any-thing?'

'Well, I've got to come up to Aberdeen today, to go to an auction. Any chance we could meet for lunch?'

'As things are at the moment, yes. But I can never tell what might come up. Let's say two o'clock at Frasers. It's only ten minutes away from the station.'

'Police station?'

'Aye, of course.'

'Okay, two o'clock it is.'

'Got to go. Bye hen.'

Ian smiled to himself as he replaced the receiver; she always called him hen. Andrea was from the Borders and her accent was softer than the Edinburgh accent. He tried to picture her at her desk in her blue uniform; she'd been a pretty girl, with short, black hair and brown eyes that sparkled with interest at everyone and everything. Her face was wide, with a strong jaw that spoke of determination and her pale skin had the lightest dusting of freckles. Yes, she was a pretty girl.

*

Andrea was sitting at a table by the window when Ian arrived, slightly out of breath from running from the carpark.

'Hi. Andrea. You look great. You haven't changed a bit,' he said when he saw her.

It was true; she was as lovely as ever, despite the tiny lines that had appeared around her eyes. She flushed with pleasure at the complement.

'Neither have you, still a lot of blather, I see.'

'Where's the uniform then? I expected the full regalia.'

'I'm actually off duty now. You didn't expect me to slip out of work to see you, did you? Anyway, I would frighten away all the customers.'

'I suppose I didn't really think about it,' he admitted. 'Well, did you find anything?'

'Yes, surprisingly, but let's order first, then I'll take you through it.'

Ian was too elated at the prospect of locating his uncle to concentrate on the menu. He ordered a salad and a seafood platter. He fancied some wine, but decided against it; Andrea knew he had to drive back to Edinburgh and she wouldn't approve. The preliminaries over, he returned to the question of his uncle: 'So, don't keep me in suspense any longer. What have you found?'

'Like I said, it was surprisingly easy. He was in the police files for stealing a car when he was seventeen. It was in Liverpool and it must have been just after he ran away.'

'So what happened to him?'

'Well, he served a six-month sentence in a Borstal correction centre, then nothing more was heard of him. He certainly didn't get in any more trouble with the police.'

'So that's it then?'

'Well, not quite. I thought his name sounded familiar, and now I know why.'

'Why?' Ian could feel his impatience rising.

'James O'Sullivan. He's the golf pro' at Elshie.'

'Elshie?'

'Elshie Golf Club. It's on the Fife coast. He's been there for ten years. He had a bit of success in the PGA tour when he was younger, but never got into the big money, so became a club pro' instead.'

'How do you know it's him? Like you said, James O'Sullivan is a very common name.'

'I got this off his web page.' She handed Ian a printed sheet. 'It may not be him, but it's worth speaking to him just in case.'

Ian read the sheet aloud, 'Born in 1952, English of Irish parents. Took up golf when he was twenty, after spending a couple of years at sea on a cruise ship. Unmarried. Been at Elshie since 1996. You're right; it could be him. But what made you think of him in the first place?'

'My Dad's a member at Elshie. I've played there lots of times with him. Jimmy's a really nice guy; he's very popular with the members.'

'I'd forgotten that you played golf. So you're still knocking it about?'

'Not really. I just don't get much time with the job, you know. And I'm working to get a transfer to become a Detective Sergeant, so that takes up a lot of time too.'

'Andrea, this is fantastic. I don't know how to thank you.'

'Better save your thanks until you see if it's the right James O'Sullivan.'

CHAPTER 27

When Ian arrived home there was an email waiting for him on his computer; he clicked on the flashing icon to see who it was. Alex. There was an attachment with it: a photograph of a young black man, wearing jeans and a tee-shirt. He sat down to read his brother's letter:

'*Dear Mum, Dad, Ian and Gran,*

Hi again. Hope you are all keeping well and Mum is making some improvement.

Everything here is fine. In fact, better than fine: I'm in love. I've met this wonderful South African guy called Baruti. He works in the South African Embassy here in Windoek and we met at a reception for overseas aid workers. I know you're going to find this a bit of a surprise or maybe not. Maybe you realised that I was gay and just didn't want to say anything. But either way, I hope you will be happy for me. I've got some leave coming up in a couple of months so I've persuaded him to come back to England with me, to meet you all. I just know you're going to like him.'

'My God. Maybe we knew? I don't think so, Bro. You kept that a pretty close secret. So big brother is gay. Well I never,' Ian muttered aloud, then resumed reading.

'*I've got a new flat. It's a lot more comfortable than the old one, which was basically just a room that I rented in someone's house. This one has a bedroom, a sitting room, kitchen and bathroom: all mod cons in fact, and best of all, it's own front door. Actually it's quite luxurious by Namibian standards, although you'd be hard pressed to swing a cat around in it.'*

'I wonder if Baruti has moved in with him?' Ian mused.

'I have been travelling around quite a bit. Baruti and I went camping one weekend in the Namib Desert. I don't really have the words to express how magical it was. The desert is red, vast red sand dunes that stretch for miles and miles; and it is totally uninhabited. At night the sky is black; there are no secondary lights from cities or even villages to minimise the blackness. That weekend there was no moon, only the light from the stars. It's hard to describe what it was like to lie there on the sand and look up at an alien sky: no Plough, no Orion's Belt, no Seven Sisters.

All the local aid agencies are getting excited about the proposed visit of Doris Klugg, the German film star. She plans to visit a number of schools and hospitals in the area. I can't say I had ever heard of her before, but she seems to be pretty big in Germany. She's got this charity concert next month in Hamburg to raise money for African children. It's going to be televised internationally, so you might see it. You might even see some footage from our schools, because she's bringing a film crew here with her.'

'I bet she is. Great publicity after all,' Ian muttered. 'Well, we'll have to look out for it. You never know we might get a glimpse of you as well, Bro.'

'The German Embassy are putting on a grand reception for her and Baruti has been invited, so I'll probably be going along as well. Chance for some free bubbly.

Don't have much more news. I'm due to meet Baruti and Sam—he's another aid worker, like me—for a beer in the Bavarian beer garden in the main square at six. Another reminder of the German heritage in this part of the world—but this is one I like.

Love to you all. Sorry to spring my news on you in this way, but I couldn't bring myself to tell anyone other than Mum before I left. You all had enough on your minds without worrying about my sexual proclivities.

Let me know how Mum is getting on, Ian.

See you all soon, I hope, Alex.'

His brother had added a postscript, '*PS: Ian, I was gob-smacked to hear about Mum's cousin. How could she keep it a secret all these years? I hope you can trace him. Maybe he will be just what Mum needs to cheer her up. Sorry I'm not there to help you Bro. Keep me posted, okay? Alex.'*

He was gob-smacked? What else did Alex think they would be when they read his email? And his brother was a fine one to talk about keeping secrets—he'd kept his own well enough. Maybe it was a family trait. Ian had nothing against gays—he certainly wasn't homophobic—but he was angry with his brother for keeping it from him. Didn't he know him at all? Did he really think he wouldn't approve? He slammed the lid of the computer shut and went into the kitchen to pour himself a glass of wine.

His anger gradually abated but now he felt disappointed with his brother. He'd thought they were close, as close as brothers could be, when they lived at opposite ends of the country. He'd been wrong. He sipped the Cabernet Sauvignon and tried to remember the last time he'd spent time alone with his brother. It was probably last Christmas. They'd both been pretty drunk and he thought Alex wanted to tell him something, but instead of listening to him, he'd kept rattling on about how they were all going to have to pull together to get Mum well. That and a lot more drunken rubbish. Well, it sounded as though Alex was happy with his new love. Ian wondered what his plans were. Did he intend to stay in Africa? He was pretty sure his brother had originally said his contract was for a year, and now he was talking about coming home on leave. Ian didn't like the sound of that.

Ian printed a copy of the email and the photograph and put them on the table; so Alex was basically leaving it up to Ian to tell the rest of the family. He'd told Mum, but that wasn't hard; she wasn't going to say much to him with her Ouija board, was she? No, the hard part he'd left for Ian. He started to smile as he remembered that was just the sort of thing he used to do when he was a teenager—he'd get Alex to go in first and make excuses for him. When he pranged Dad's car, he even got Alex to say he was driving it. So now it was his turn to be the mediator.

What was his grandmother going to make of it? She'd be intrigued to hear he was in love, but with a man? He thought of his brother and imagined him chuckling to himself as he typed the email. He'd have known how amazed they'd be to learn about Baruti. It now made sense. Alex hadn't had a girlfriend since he left college; Ian tried to recall her, but all he could remember was that she'd been a quiet girl, with hair the colour of a dormouse and she played the violin. He couldn't remember what reason Alex had given for the break-up, but now it seemed obvious.

*

Ian went into work early the next morning; he wanted to see what was scheduled for him for the rest of the week. Although it was barely eight o'clock, Fiona Scott, his research assistant, was already at her desk.

'Morning Ian. This is early for you. Could ye nay sleep?'

'Hi, Fiona. Yeah, something like that.'

He headed for the coffee machine. 'Want a coffee?' he asked.

'Please. I've been here since seven and I'm parched. Canna face breakfast so early.'

'Breakfast? I thought you survived on a fag and a cup of coffee?'

'Ay that's true, but canna face the coffee too early. Pure nicotine is all I can handle at that hour.'

She abandoned her computer and came over to join him.

'Any idea what Andrew wants me to do this week?' Ian asked. Andrew was their boss. The customary practice was to have a team meeting first thing on a Monday morning to discuss the work for the week. He knew that Andrew wouldn't have been pleased that he'd missed it the day before.

'I made some notes. I'll sort them out for you afterwards.'

She pulled out a pack of cigarettes and a lighter, and arranged herself halfway out the open window. The non-smoking rules were a challenge to Fiona.

'There'll be hell to play if Andrew catches you,' Ian said, handing her the coffee.

'Nay problem. He's never in afore nine,' she said, a smile of satisfaction crossing her face as she inhaled deeply.

'Mind you don't fall,' he said, only half joking. They were on the third floor and it was a sheer drop to the pavement below.

He sat at his own desk and opened up his computer. There were quite a few emails to deal with, including one from Andrew. He read it, *'Ian, Bit disappointed you couldn't arrange your visit for **after** the team meeting. Try not to miss next week's, please. Need you to go to St. Andrews this week to look into something. Fiona's got the details. Andrew'*

'What's this about St. Andrews?' he asked her.

Fiona finished the last of her cigarette and closed the window. She collected a sheaf of papers from her desk and pulled up a chair beside him.

'Och well, I don't think it's anything much, but Andrew seems to think it's worth looking at.' She passed him an old photograph of a grey stone house, with a conical tower covered in ivy.

'What's this?'

'It's Kirkaldy Tower, just outside St. Andrews. The laird is selling it at a public auction next month. Andrew thought we should take a look at it first, to see if it's worth preserving. He reckons too many of these old hooses are being sold to Sassenachs, and the first thing they do with them is rip out all the interiors and modernise them.'

'Well people don't want to live in these draughty old houses with ancient plumbing and woodworm. It's quite understandable.'

'Aye, but he reckons there's something special about this one. Dates back to Jacobean times. He wants me to research its background for you, but in the meantime you're to go up there and take some pics.'

'What, of the house? My job is to look at the furniture.'

'I know, but he thinks there's a very fine hall screen, and he also wants you to photograph the staircase and some of the moulded ceilings and wall panels. He thinks they may be planning to remove them and sell them separately.'

'Fine. Is the address in here?'

'Aye, there it is. The address is St. Andrews, but it's on the road to Cupar. Stick the postcode in your Sat Nav and you'll nay have a problem.' She moved across to her own desk and continued with her work.

Ian opened a map of the east coast of Scotland. Elshie was not very far; it was on the A917, by the coast. It was not on a direct road to St. Andrews, but he calculated that he could afford to make the detour and still be at Kirkaldy Tower by eleven.

'Right. I'm off. Could you ring and let the laird know that I'll be with him by eleven.'

'Any message for Andrew?'

'No, just tell him where I've gone. I'll see you later this afternoon to collect whatever you've found out.'

'Okay. Bye'

*

For once the traffic across the Forth Road Bridge was flowing smoothly, and Ian soon reached the junction for the A92, and before long was driving towards Elshie. The country road twisted and turned, affording glimpses of the slate grey sea at every bend and taking him through small villages with white painted cottages and traffic calming schemes. Before long he was driving through the old fishing village of Elshie. Although he'd never been there before, he recognised it at once: its picturesque harbour wall, the cobbled streets and rows of brightly painted fishing boats appeared in numerous postcards and paintings of the area. Since the emergence of the huge factory ships, much of the local fishing was in decline; sons no longer joined their fathers fishing for haddock and lobsters, they went to Peterhead and joined the fishing fleets. Now many of the fishermen's cottages were owned by painters and potters, weavers and jewellery makers, their front rooms turned into craft shops, their English accents blending with the local brogue.

Elshie Golf Club was at the far end of the village and it was not much after nine o'clock when he parked his car in the visitors' carpark. The clubhouse was a large white building with a gabled roof, covered in grey slates. It seemed curiously out of character with the rest of the village. Checking carefully that he'd parked in an area designated for visitors, he followed the direction indicated to the Pro Shop. As he approached, he felt a nervous tightening in his stomach at the anticipation of finding his uncle.

'Good morning, can I help you?' A young girl with her hair tied back in a ponytail, was sitting behind the counter, filing her nails.

'I'd like to see James O'Sullivan,' he said.

'Jimmy? He's teaching at the moment. Can I help?'

'No, I don't think so. I want to talk to him about some lessons,' he lied, using the first excuse that came into his head.

'Oh, I can help you with that,' she replied, putting her nail file away and pulling out a big appointment book. 'When did you want to see him?'

'No, well actually, I need to speak to him first. I'm not sure if it is lessons I need after all.' He knew he sounded ridiculous, but the girl didn't seem to notice.

'Well, he'll be about twenty minutes,' she said. 'You could have a coffee in the clubhouse and I'll send him over when he gets back. He's got nothing else booked until eleven.'

'Fine, I'll do that.'

As he was leaving the girl suddenly thought of something and called after him, 'You're not a rep, are you? He won't see reps without an appointment.'

'No, I'm not a rep,' he assured her.

The clubhouse was old and smelled of a blend of stale cigarette smoke, furniture polish and beer. It didn't seem to have been painted in a long time, but the old wooden floor gleamed with years of patient polishing. The walls were hung with trophy boards, carrying the names of former champions and the years of their successes—the earliest from the beginning of the twentieth century, making the club over a hundred years old. He was impressed.

He sat down at a table by the window overlooking the eighteenth green. After a few moments a uniformed waiter came over to take his order, and while he waited for him to bring his coffee, he surveyed the room. There were two elderly men sitting in one corner, drinking tea and eating toast, but otherwise the bar was empty. Was this the environment that Jimmy had lived in for ten years? It seemed dull and musty; everything preserved in rules and regulations and furniture polish. There were notices everywhere: No smoking, No walking on the putting green, Gentlemen must wear a jacket in the clubhouse after seven o'clock, Gentlemen only, Ladies are requested to enter by the side door, Members Only, No practising on the first tee... The instructions seemed endless.

'Anything else, sir?' the waiter asked.

'No, thank you. That's fine.'

He turned his attention back to the course. Elshie was a traditional links course and to the untrained eye it was hard to distinguish one hole from the next; all Ian could see was a long expanse of yellowing grass that was presumably the fairway, bordered by sand dunes and wind-blown bushes. There was not a tree to be seen. Two balls landed on the eighteenth green; then a third hit the green and ran on into the bunker. He could see three figures coming down the fairway towards him, their golf bags slung over their shoulders. As he watched them approach, heads down, bent into the wind that was whipping across from the sea, one of them stepped into the bunker and played his shot to the green; the ball rose into the air in a cloud of sand and landed just past the hole, where it spun back, narrowly missing the cup. Ian heard cries of admiration from the other players and the sound of applause: a man wearing a tweed cap had stopped to congratulate the player on his shot.

As he drank his tepid cup of coffee, he considered taking up golf. Maybe a few lessons wouldn't be such a bad idea. It didn't look a very hard game to play, despite what he'd heard, and it seemed a shame to be living in Scotland—the birthplace of golf—and not even try to play the game. Well, if this man was his uncle Jimmy, he'd ask him for some advice.

All of a sudden he was aware of someone standing behind him. 'Good morning. Did you want to see me?'

A tall man, in his mid-fifties was looking at him quizzically. It was the man in the tweed cap.

'Are you James O'Sullivan?' he asked, his mouth suddenly dry.

'That's me. How can I help?'

He had an unusual accent, as though he'd travelled a lot; Ian could hear a Scottish lilt, but there was something else as well. The man removed his cap and sat down next to him. He was going bald, Ian noticed, and what hair he had was cut very short, but it didn't disguise the fact that it was the same rusty red as his own.

'Well I'm not sure that you can help me,' Ian began. He took a deep breath. This wasn't easy. 'You see I'm looking for someone called James O'Sullivan and I thought you might be the man.'

The smile disappeared from the man's face. 'And why might you be looking for a James O'Sullivan?' he asked.

'It's a family matter: his cousin is ill and we want to contact him.'

'Well, I don't have any family, so you've obviously got the wrong man. Sorry.' He started to get up.

'No, please don't go yet. Look my name is Ian Rushton.'

He held out his hand and felt the man's firm grip as they shook hands. There was something in his manner that was too defensive; it gave Ian the impression that he wasn't telling him the truth.

'Let me explain some more,' and Ian started to tell the story of his mother's accident and how she had become locked into her own world.

'So what do you expect this cousin of hers to do?' James O'Sullivan asked.

'I don't know exactly, but we've tried everything. The doctors say that she could make some progress if she wanted to, but she doesn't want to.'

'Maybe she'd sooner be dead,' the man said, then seeing the distress in Ian's eyes at his harsh words, added in a softer tone, 'You know sometimes life is just not worth living. Have you thought of that? Why do you want your mother to go on living when she's obviously so unhappy?'

'I don't know. Everyone else has resigned themselves to the fact that she'll never get better, but I can't accept it. While she's still alive I want to do everything possible to help her.'

'I can see that, but are you sure it's for her sake, or is it for yours?'

Ian didn't reply. That was a question he'd never asked himself and one he knew he couldn't answer.

'Look, Ian, I really am sorry, but I can't see how I can help you. There are lots of James O'Sullivans in the world. It's not an uncommon name, you know. What makes you think he's in Scotland?'

'Well I have to start somewhere, and your background seemed to fit. None of us ever knew about this cousin until my grandmother let it slip last week. It seems to have been a complete family secret; even my father never knew. When my Gran told me the story I just felt I had to do something to find him; not just for my mother's sake, but for his too.'

He told him everything his grandmother had related, including how his mother had written to Jimmy repeatedly until, finally convinced that he had abandoned her, she stopped. He left out the part about them being naked on the beach—after all, it was only hearsay.

'So why did nobody try to find this lad when he ran away?' James O'Sullivan asked, clearing his throat as though he had something caught in it.

'Well my Gran said that they made lots of enquiries, but got nowhere.' Ian was beginning to think that maybe he'd found him. If it wasn't him, why would he be asking so many questions?

'What about the police?'

'They said it was likely that the boy'd just run away and there was nothing that they could do. They said he'd turn up when he was hungry. It doesn't sound as though they took it very seriously.'

'What makes you think your mother would be interested in seeing her cousin after all these years, Ian?'

'I think my mother loved her cousin very much. I've told you how she refuses to respond to any of us when we visit her, well when I told her I knew about Jimmy she opened her eyes and looked straight at me. I knew then I had to do something. It was the first time I had seen her eyes open in months.'

'So what is your mother's name?'

'Teresa.'

'Teresa,' the man repeated softly. 'My sweet Tess.'

Ian felt a surge of adrenalin at the sound of the man repeating her name; he'd been right after all. This was his Uncle Jimmy. 'So she is your cousin?' he asked.

'Yes. But God knows how you found me after all these years.'

'Well thank God I did. Oh this is terrific.' Ian was so elated, he couldn't keep still. He stood up. 'So what shall we do now?'

'Hang on, Ian. Not so hasty. I have a lesson at eleven, and the rest of the day is fully booked. I can't go shooting off anywhere today.'

'No. No, of course not. Look I've got to be in St. Andrews by eleven too. What about if I come back and see you one evening and we can talk? I only live in Edinburgh. It's not far.'

'That's sounds good. How about tomorrow, sometime after six?'

'Fine. I'll come here shall I?'

'No, better to come to my house and we can talk in private. It's not far from here; I'll give you the address.' He pulled out one of his business cards and wrote on the back of it.

'Right then. See you tomorrow.'

'Oh, by the way Ian, how is your grandmother?'

'Gran is fine, but Granddad died a few years ago.'

'Yes, I know.'

Ian didn't ask how he knew; he could ask all the questions he wanted the next time.

CHAPTER 28

Teresa lay awake thinking about her family. Ever since Ian had said he would find Jimmy, she had been unable to stop thinking about him. If anyone could find her brother it would be Ian; he was so determined. But did Jimmy want to be found? Was he even still alive? It had been so long since she'd seen him. They hadn't even had the chance to say goodbye, just torn apart without a word; they might as well have ripped out her heart.

She felt tears fill her eyes, but could do nothing to wipe them away. She wasn't sure she wanted Jimmy to be found. Not now. How would he react to her helplessness? And how would she feel if he re-entered her life? She would have to leave the cosy world of Petie and Tommy and Jack and face the empty void that was reality. She wasn't sure she could do that.

Michelle's visit had disturbed her too. She'd tried to ignore her presence, to cut her out and return to her fantasy life, but her friend's persistence had prevented her. She was angry with her. Why had she come to see her? It was easier to hate her when she stayed away. She recalled Michelle's words. So she loved Mark, did she? Well she could have him. Did she think she was the only one who'd ever been in love? Did she think that love was easy? Painless? Well Teresa could assure her it was not. And why did they want to tell her their problems? Why did they want her absolution? She was in no position to help them; she couldn't even help herself. But try as she might, Teresa couldn't maintain her anger against Michelle. After all, she was only grasping at some small happiness while she could. Lying there in her bed, caught between the nightmare of her present life and the solace of her dreams, she'd had plenty of time for reflection. She knew her husband was not a bad man, only a weak one. And she understood weakness when it came to being in love. Michelle was right: he would never be able to cope on his own; he needed someone to love him and Teresa couldn't do it. She'd tried. My God she'd tried. But when he'd let Peter drown that had been the end for her. She knew she could never love him after that. But hate them? What good did it do to hate them? She felt her heart softening towards her husband and her best friend.

*

She awoke to see Julie, the nurse, standing over her. 'Good morning Teresa. The doctor wants you to have a scan this morning; it's been a while since your last MIR so he wants to see if there is anything going on in that pretty little head of yours. But first of all we'd better get you cleaned up.'

The nurse set to work washing her body and changing the king-size nappy that was her permanent apparel. Instead of dressing her in her usual cotton tracksuit, she covered her body in a blue gauze smock.

'We'll get you dressed later, sweetie,' she told her. She combed her hair and rubbed some sweet smelling cream on her face and hands. 'There that's much better. Right, off we go.'

Calling one of the other nurses to help her, she manoeuvred Teresa onto the trolley and set off for the radiology department.

Nowadays Teresa actually enjoyed her morning bedbath; the nurse was a very pleasant girl and would chatter away all the while about her life outside the hospital. It was so removed from Teresa's own existence that she could listen to her without the usual painful memories getting in the way. What she enjoyed most was the sensation of feeling clean for a short while, without the all pervading smell of her own body fluids. How she would have loved to have been able to soak in a hot bath for an hour or two.

Teresa had had an MRI scan before, but it had been before she regained consciousness, so she was unprepared for what was to happen. As she was pushed into the room she could just make out a large cream cylinder at one end. A woman in a white coat came to meet them and helped the nurse place Teresa's body on a concave surface. They pulled a strap around her and tightened it into place, so she wouldn't fall. Then the woman in the white coat bent over Teresa and fitted a set of ear-defenders to her ears. She smiled at Teresa and patted her face.

Teresa could hear the nurse speaking to the woman but couldn't make out what she was saying. Suddenly she seemed to be alone and moving slowly, inch by inch, into a giant tube. She felt the panic well up within her, an irrational terror at this further incarceration and silently screamed for them to stop. She was inside the machine now, the inner surface of the tube only inches from her face and then the noise started. Despite the ear-defenders the noise was deafening, like a team of pneumatic drills trying to break through her skull. She closed her eyes and wished she could die.

*

The door to her bedroom bursts open and a small figure hurls himself on the bed beside her.

'Mummy, what time is Daddy coming home?' Petie is so excited he begins to bounce up and down on the bed.

'Don't do that Darling, Mummy has a terrible headache.' It's like a hammer inside her head.

'But when Mummy?'

'His flight gets in at six.'

'Can we go to the airport to meet him?'

'Yes, I expect so. It depends how I feel. Now run along and play. I just want to rest a little bit longer.'

Her youngest son snuggles up beside her and kisses her. 'I'll stay here Mummy and look after you. I won't make a sound.' He places his small, warm hand on his mother's forehead and strokes it. Teresa knows Petie will not be able to keep still for long, but lets him lie there beside her anyway. She closes her eyes and tries to sleep.

'Mummy, are you asleep?' Petie whispers after a while.

'No, Petie, I'm not asleep,' Teresa replies patiently. The pounding in her head is unremitting.

'Well Mummy, you know the County Fair is on Sunday.'

'Is it?'

'Yes it is. You know it is. There're going to be fireworks.'

'*So? I suppose that means we'd better keep Foxy in then? He doesn't like fireworks.*'

'*No, I mean, yes, we'd better keep him in, but that isn't what I wanted to say Mummy.*'

Teresa smiles to herself; she enjoys teasing her son.

'*Can we go, Mummy?*'

'*Go? Go where?*'

'*Oh, Mummy.*' *Petie is getting frustrated with his mother now.*

'*Can we go to the County Fair?*' *he asks.*

'*Do you want to go then?*' *Teresa feigns surprise.*

'*Yes, Mummy. And so does Tommy. And Jack. We all do. You know we do.*'

'*Are you sure you want to go? You wouldn't prefer to stay at home with Foxy?*'

'*Nooo.*' *The child is bouncing up and down on the bed again. He has now realised that his mother is joking.*

'*Of course we can, Darling. That's why I've been so busy painting.*'

'*Are you going to win, Mummy?*'

'*Who knows, Petie? Who knows?*' *She closes her eyes again.*

Petie realises that he will get no more from his mother and slides off the bed. 'I'm going out to play,' he says, closing the bedroom door behind him.

Once he has gone, the house seems quiet without him. She opens her eyes and stares at the ceiling. For a moment panic seizes her and she is unable to move. Where is everyone? Why is she alone? Where have they all gone? Where is Petie?

*

The noise had stopped and she could feel someone lifting her back onto her bed. She opened her eyes but saw only the flash of ceiling lights and overhead ducting as she was whisked quickly along the corridor.

'We'll just drop her back and then go for some lunch,' one of them said—a male voice.

She didn't recognise him. Was it someone new or just a technician from the radiography department?

'Okay, but I have to get her settled in first. That'll take a few minutes; she's not easy you know.'

It was Julie. She was a jolly young nurse; Teresa had become very fond of her, in a way. Even though her words were blunt, Teresa knew that she was a very caring young woman, who did her best to make her comfortable. She wondered where they were going to go for lunch. If only she had that choice. Where would she go? To the little Italian place in Bromley Road, where she and Mark went on their first proper date? Or maybe for an Indian meal. The memory of prawn Dansak and Peshwari naan rushed back to her, causing her mouth to salivate; she could feel the saliva run down her chin.

'She's dribbling,' the man said.

'Hang on then.' Julie's face moved into view as she bent over her and wiped the corner of her mouth with a tissue. 'There, that's better. I expect that's us talking about food, isn't it, Teresa?' She smiled at her.

She was a pretty young thing. No wonder the owner of the other voice wanted to have lunch with her. Suddenly Teresa felt very old; no man would be interested in taking her to lunch now.

'They'll be bringing her meal round soon, anyway,' the male voice added.

'Not for Teresa,' Julie told him. 'She still can't swallow. It's all through a tube for her.'

'God, poor sod. What a life.'

She heard Julie hiss at him and whisper: 'She's not deaf you know.'

'Sorry.'

They were back in her room; they pushed her bed into its usual station and Julie wound up the back rest so that Teresa could see. The male voice belonged to a rather pimply, but not unattractive youth wearing the white uniform of the lab technicians.

'Here we are Teresa. I'm off to lunch now; I'll be back in about an hour. Is there anything I can get you before I go?'

Teresa blinked twice, slowly, to tell her 'No.' The nurse put the headphones in Teresa's ears and switched on some music: Bartok. Soothing, piano music, just what she needed after the ordeal in the scanner.

'Dr Stevens will be along later to give you the results. Bye for now.' She smoothed the covers over Teresa's legs and left with the young man.

'Doesn't say much, does she?' he said.

*

Teresa had been dreaming about food when a gentle touch on her arm woke her. She opened her eyes and saw the doctor leaning over her.

'Sorry, did I wake you?'

He sat down on the edge of her bed and pulled out the manilla folder that contained her notes. 'I've got your results here. Not bad, not bad at all.'

So, can I go home now? she wanted to ask.

'There is no deterioration in your condition since the previous scan and in fact, it's possible to see signs of more activity. Which is good.' He flicked through the notes, nodding his approval as he did so. 'Yes, pretty stable.'

What was he talking about? All he was really saying was that things were still the same. So what if they hadn't deteriorated? She wished they had, then she might die and be free of this torment.

'What we need to do now is try to get you more active. I shall speak to your physiotherapist and see if he can increase your sessions with him.' He smiled at her.

What awful teeth he had. With the money that he earned you would have thought he would have had them capped. She was suddenly aware of her own teeth. The nurse cleaned them for her daily but she always had a horrid taste in her mouth. Just one more irritant in her daily life.

She blinked at him rapidly.

'What is it Teresa? Do you want the board? That's good.'

She blinked once. He held it up for her and waited as she spelled out her message.

'EUTHANASIA.'

'Now what do you mean by that? I've already told you that euthanasia is against the law in this country. I won't hear any more of that talk. You mustn't give up Teresa. It's early days yet. We'll continue your treatment and I'm sure you'll soon start to feel more comfortable with your life.'

She wanted to laugh at that—if only she could. Did he really know what he was talking about? How could anyone be comfortable when they were unable to speak, to eat, to drink, to move, to do even the simplest things for themselves? She indicated that she wanted to tell him something.

'WILL I EVER GET BETTER?' she asked.

She felt sorry for him; he looked so sad. It couldn't be easy for him to have patients that he could do nothing to help.

'Teresa, I've tried to explain that we don't really have enough expertise to put you back together as you were before, but that doesn't mean that you have to give up all hope.'

She was angry now. She blinked rapidly at him.

'What is it?'

She spelled out: 'WILL I?'

'The truth is Teresa, I don't know. Most people never recover from your condition. Some die. But there is a lot we don't know about the brain and there is always a possibility that you could be a case in a million and make some improvement. As I started to say, your results are no worse; they may even be a fraction better.'

Teresa stared at him for a moment then closed her eyes. It was pointless. He couldn't help her, not to live nor to die.

CHAPTER 29

Jimmy lived in a quiet street in the centre of Pitten-weem, another of those picturesque fishing villages that like Elshie bordered that translucent northeast coast. Ian parked his car in the carpark by the harbour and climbed the steep cobbled street that led to Jimmy's cottage.

'Good, you found it alright. Come in, do.'

'Thanks.'

Although Ian was not very tall, he still had to bend down in order to enter the cottage.

'Nice place. Looks pretty old,' he said, looking around at the whitewashed stone walls of what seemed to be the only living room. Jimmy was obviously a man of few possessions and simple taste. If he'd been told to move out in a hurry, it wouldn't have taken him long to gather together the few items that Ian could see in the room.

'Yes, it's one of the original old fishermen's cottages. Nothing's been changed, except the plumbing. Look, come and sit down. Can I get you a drink? Tea? Beer?'

'A small beer would be fine.'

Ian sat down on an old leather armchair and looked around him. The only ornaments in the room were a number of framed photographs on the stone mantle-piece above the fireplace. While Jimmy got the beer, Ian got up and picked one of them up. It was of his mother. But not of his mother as a twelve-year old, but when she was about twenty. He picked up another one: it was of his grandmother and his mother, standing together outside a shop he vaguely recognised. His mother was holding the handle of a pram. He looked at another one: this one showed his mother at about forty, with him and Alex. He knew when that one had been taken; they'd been to the circus that afternoon. It had been Alex's birthday. And there was one of his mother and Peter, taken by the river. He put the photographs back and sat down again.

'Here you are.' Jimmy sat down opposite Ian and said, 'So, you're Tess's son, then.'

'Yes.'

'What about the other boy?'

'Alex? He's gone to work with the VSO in Namibia,' Ian replied and went on to explain how Alex had reacted badly to his mother's accident.

'I can understand that,' Jimmy said. 'Sometimes things are so hard to face, all you want to do is get away and try to forget they ever happened.'

'Is that what you did?' Ian asked.

'Yes, I suppose I did. I couldn't bear it any more in Ireland; I had to get away. I stole some money from my grandmother's purse, packed a few clothes and hitched a lift to Dublin on one of the fish lorries. God, did I stink of fish by the time we arrived.' He smiled at the memory and drank some of his beer.

'What did you do then?'

'I bought a ticket to Liverpool.'

'Why Liverpool? Did you have some friends there?'

'No. I knew no-one, but the shortest, and the cheapest, crossing was to Holyhead and from there I hitched another lift to Liverpool. Not on a fish lorry that time.'

'So that's where you got into trouble with the police? Liverpool?' Ian asked.

'How do you know about that?' A frown passed across his uncle's face, like a sudden cloud on a sunny day. 'And come to think of it, how did you manage to find me?'

Ian felt a surge of embarrassment at prying into this man's life, and explained how he'd asked an old friend to help him.

'It's amazing, you can never get away from the past, no matter how much you try,' Jimmy said, a slight touch of bitterness in his voice. 'Anyway, no matter. You're here now.' He paused , staring into space for a minute, then continued, 'Borstal was probably the best thing that could have happened to me at the time. I hated it there. It was worse than the Christian Brothers. Well, almost.' Once again the twinkle had returned to his eyes. 'But it gave me time to think. There was a man there who was determined to help boys get on the right road, so to speak; he would help them find jobs, arrange for them to have somewhere to sleep, even give them clothing or the odd bob or two. I wanted to travel, to find something that would get me away from everything; so when my sentence was up and he told me about this job on a cruise ship, I jumped at it.'

'On a cruise ship?' A good way to disappear.

'Yes, it was perfect. I had my board and lodging free and I was able to save up most of my pay—there wasn't exactly a lot to spend it on, anyway. They worked us pretty hard, the hours were long and we didn't have a lot of free time to go ashore. Then there were the tips. The passengers weren't supposed to tip us directly; the company preferred to add a service charge to their bills and dish it out to us at the end of the voyage, but there was always some old lady who would take a fancy to you and slip you a fiver from time to time.'

'Where did you go?'

'Mostly round the Mediterranean: Venice, Istanbul, the Greek Islands. It was great for a young lad; I loved it. And of course I was used to the sea, because I'd often been out with my grandfather, fishing. I never suffered from sea sickness, not once—if you can survive the sea around the west coast of Ireland you can survive anything.'

'So how long were you on the cruise ships, then?'

'Oh, a couple of years I suppose. Then I decided I wanted a change. I had some money saved, so I went to the south of Spain and bummed around for a bit. That's where I got into golf. I got this job as a caddy at a posh golf club in Marbella. At first I was just a glorified bag carrier, trailing around behind these rich old guys, but then I started to play in my spare time. I soon picked it up; in fact it came quite naturally to me. There was a golf pro there called Fred Styles—you may have heard of him.' He waited for Ian's response.

'No, I don't think so. I don't know much about golf.'

'Well, he was pretty famous in the fifties; won a few majors. Anyway he was the pro there then and he took a shine to me. I think he could see I had the makings of a decent golfer and so he made it his business that I learnt to play the game properly.'

'What happened then?'

'Well, it was his idea, really. He said I should go back to England and try to get my professional's card. So that's what I did. I got a job as the assistant professional at a club in Maidenhead and once my handicap was down to scratch I applied for my player's card and joined the tournament circuit.'

'Maidenhead? That's not far from where we used to live.'

'I know.'

Ian pointed to the photographs. 'You've known where we were all these years, but you never got in touch,' he said, failing to keep the accusation out of his voice.

'There wasn't really much point. I thought your mother didn't want to see me: she'd never written, nor answered my letters. I didn't want to upset things. After all she was a married woman now,' he added.

'But it wasn't her fault,' Ian protested.

'I know that now. But I didn't then. I thought she'd sided against me.'

'And what about Gran? Why didn't you contact Gran?'

Jimmy didn't reply.

'So how did you take those photographs?' Ian asked. He was beginning to think his uncle was a stalker.

'Once I moved to Maidenhead, it wasn't hard to track down Bridget and Patrick. They'd only moved house twice in their lives. I made some enquiries at our old house in Slough and soon had their new address. Then one day I saw Tess there, and I followed her home. Easy really.'

'What a lot of wasted years,' Ian said, suddenly. 'Why didn't you at least speak to her? Why stalk them?'

'I wasn't stalking them; I just wanted to see that they were okay. But you're right; they were wasted years. You have to realise something Ian—although you may not want to hear this. I love your mother, and I've never loved anyone else. But she is my cousin. They were right to keep us apart; there was no future for us. We could never have married or had children like a normal couple. And then you and your brothers would never have been born. Think of that. It was for Tess's sake that I kept away. I didn't want to ruin her life.'

Somehow it didn't seem so shocking to Ian anymore. They'd only been children after all, two cousins locked in a forbidden love. What did it matter now, when his mother lay helpless in her hospital bed?

'Did you never marry?'

'No. I've had a few girlfriends over the years, but nothing serious. Like I said, it's your mother I love. And I always will,' he added.

Ian couldn't help wondering if he would still feel the same when he saw her emaciated body in its invariable blue tracksuit and white socks, propped helplessly on her hospital bed.

'So how did you end up at Elshie?' he asked, eager to move the conversation on.

'Well I was reasonably successful on the tour, but I could never hack it on the last day. Four days straight competition is hard on the nerves; I usually did well the first two days, then the pressure would get to me and I'd start dropping shots; it was the putting mainly. I made some money on the tour, but never won any big trophies, so in the end I decided to give it up and become a teaching pro.'

'But why up here, in Elshie?'

'Well, the old pro retired, that was one reason, and the other...' He paused and drank some more of his beer. 'The other was because I was becoming a bit obsessed with Tess again. You're right; I felt I was turning into a stalker, hanging around her street, hoping to catch a glimpse of her. Especially after your little brother drowned. I felt so sorry for her; it was all I could do to stop myself rushing round there to comfort her. Then I realised it had to stop. I thought if I lived far enough away I would have less opportunities to see her and I might get over my obsession.'

'But would it have mattered, after all those years? As you said, my mother was married by then.'

'Probably not. But there didn't seem much point dragging up the past.'

'So you haven't seen her since you moved up here?'

'No. The last time I saw her she was on her way to her father's funeral.'

'You didn't know about the accident then?'

'Not till you turned up out of the blue. What exactly is her condition now? You keep talking about "Locked-In Syndrome." What is that, some kind of coma?'

'No, she was in a coma for a short time, and then when she woke up we found she was totally paralysed. At first we thought she was brain dead too, but then they came up with this Locked-In Syndrome diagnosis. It's like she's trapped inside her body; she can hear and see, but cannot move anything except her eyes. It's like being in an inner state; her mind and her memory all function perfectly, but she is physically unable to communicate.'

'My God, that must be horrifying for her.' He stood up and walked across to the window. 'My poor, darling Tess,' he murmured. 'I can't believe it. What a dreadful thing to happen to her.'

'We think that's why she's withdrawn from us. She's unable to communicate with us, so she ignores our presence.'

After a few minutes, Jimmy turned to face him. 'Just like me. She's running away from reality, in the only way that she can.'

'Yes, I suppose she is.'

'What do the doctors say? Is there no cure?'

'No, there's no cure, but they have developed some techniques to help people in her condition to communicate.'

'So why aren't you using them?'

'We've tried, but Mum won't co-operate. When she can be persuaded to write anything with her message board, all she says are things like: "Leave me alone" or "I want to die." The doctors are frustrated by her behaviour; they say she could make some progress if she'd only make the effort.'

'So that's why you wanted to find me. You think I might be able to motivate her to get well?'

'I doubt if she will ever get well, but anything would be better than seeing her lying there with her eyes shut the whole time.'

'Well Ian, you might as well know this. I'll do anything for your mother. Just tell me what you want me to do.'

'I want you to come and visit her. I want you to talk to her. Tell her what I've been trying to tell her for months, that we all love her and want her back, no matter how disabled she is.'

'Okay, I'll give it a try. Give me a few days to re-organise my diary, then I'll take some time off and come down to see her. When are you going to visit her next?'

'At the weekend.' Ian suddenly felt embarrassed. 'I've got a healer coming to see her on Sunday afternoon,' he added. He saw Jimmy raise his eyebrows in surprise, but he made no comment.

'Okay, I'll try for Saturday.'

'You could stay with Gran. She's got a couple of spare rooms. I usually stay with her.'

'What about your Dad? Don't you stay there?'

'Actually, it's not very convenient for him at the moment. And anyway Gran likes the company.' He didn't want to be disloyal to his father, so he didn't explain further.

'Alright, I'd like that. You'd better prepare her first. I don't want to give her a heart attack by suddenly appearing unannounced.' Jimmy stood up and stretched. 'How about another beer?'

'Thanks.' Ian felt he needed it; the meeting had been surprisingly emotional for him and his throat felt very dry. It wouldn't have taken much for him to have started crying.

*

As soon as he arrived back at his flat, he telephoned his grandmother. He could tell by the way she answered the telephone that she thought it was bad news.

'Hi, Gran. It's only me, Ian. Don't worry, it's not bad news. I just wanted to speak to you.'

'Ian. It's after ten o'clock.'

'Yes, sorry Gran, I hadn't realised it was so late.' In his excitement to tell her the results of his search he'd forgotten that she went to bed at nine-thirty.

'So what is it that can't wait until the morning?'

'I've found him Gran. I've found Jimmy.'

At first his grandmother said nothing. He could imagine her blue eyes brimming with tears. When she spoke at last, he could hear her struggle to remain calm.

'Where? Where is he?'

'He's working up here in Scotland.'

'Did you speak to him? Are you sure it's Jimmy?'

'Yes I had a long chat to him this evening.'

'But are you sure it's him? You've never met him remember. How would you know if it was him or not?'

'It's him alright, Gran. Don't worry. Anyway you'll see for yourself soon enough; he's coming down to see you on Saturday.' Again there was silence. 'Gran? Can you hear me? Is that alright if he stays on Saturday? I'll be there as well.'

'Do you think that's a good idea, Ian?' His grandmother sounded a bit shaky.

'Are you alright, Gran?'

'Yes, I'm fine. Just a bit surprised. It takes a bit of getting used to, the idea that I might see him again. I've wished for that so often. So many times. You've no idea.'

'I'll be down on Friday evening as usual. Jimmy said he would ring and tell us when he'd arrive.'

'I thought he was dead, you know. But that didn't stop me looking for him all the time. You'd be surprised how many men look like him from behind, how many times I thought I saw a glimpse of him only to be disappointed. I used to try to imagine what he would look like now, whether he had grown more like his grandfather or whether his father's features had taken over.'

'He's gone bald, Gran, but he's still got some red hair.'

'Bald? I never imagined him bald.'

'Look, Gran, don't upset yourself. You'll see him on Saturday and then we can talk,' he reassured her.

'Alright.'

'Goodnight Gran.'

'Ian?'

'Yes?'

'You're a good boy, Ian.'

'Thanks Gran. Goodnight now.'

*

Bridget didn't want to go back to bed; her sleep had been disturbed and now she felt wide awake. When she replaced the receiver she felt faint, as though she needed to sit down. Her hands were trembling. She went into the kitchen and filled the kettle from the kitchen tap. A cup of tea was what she needed to settle her nerves. She sat at the kitchen table waiting for the kettle to boil and replayed Ian's words in her mind: 'I've found him Gran.' He'd found Jimmy. She just couldn't believe it; how could it be true after so many years? She hoped it wasn't a cruel hoax; someone who thought there might be some money in it for them if they pretended to be Jimmy. She had read of those things in the Sunday papers. But then she knew Ian was pretty shrewd; he would have known which questions to ask this man, to make sure it really was Jimmy.

Her stomach was churning with emotion; she didn't know whether to feel elated or sad. He had come back to her many times in her dreams; dreams from which she awoke—her pillow wet with tears—to realise that it was only an illusion and weep some more. So many years had passed. They'd missed so many years of his life: not knowing where he was, if he were alive or dead, grieving but unable to bury their grief, searching every day for some small clue as to his whereabouts, dreading that telephone call that would bring them closure and always, always hoping for a miracle. Now they had the miracle, but it was too late for her Patrick. She remembered how much he'd missed Jimmy, and how he'd blamed himself for not doing more for him. He was a man who never said very much, but she could see the hurt in him, there deep in his eyes, the tiny flickers of pain when anything reminded him of Jimmy.

And Jimmy had done this to them; he'd left without a word. No word in thirty-five years. How could he have let them suffer so? She'd been convinced he was dead; she'd told herself he would never have stayed away so long if he'd been alive. All she'd needed was a postcard from him, a telephone call, something to tell them he wasn't dead. She felt a sudden anger against him for all the suffering his disappearance had caused, and then just as quickly let the rage dissipate. She put her head down onto her arms and cried. The grief that had been building inside during all those long years came spilling out onto her blue and white kitchen tablecloth: tears for her son, once lost and now found, tears for her dead sister and her unhappy life, tears for her husband who had never stopped blaming himself for his son's disappearance, tears for her daughter confined to a hospital bed for the rest of her life and tears for herself, the silent witness to all their pain.

PART 3

CHAPTER 30

Mark couldn't stop thinking about what Teresa had said. She wanted to die and she expected him to help her. As she'd reminded him, it was because of Mark and his infidelity, that she was where she was today. Why did she have to say that? Surely she could see how sorry he was. Hadn't he told her over and over again how he regretted his actions, how he'd do anything to make it right? And this was how she expected him to make it up to her, by murdering her? She'd even worked out how he was to do it. Morphine. Painless enough, but where could he get it? Steal it from the hospital? It wouldn't be that easy. Surely they kept all the drugs under lock and key. What about the internet? They said you could find anything on the internet these days; you just had to know where to look.

It was too late to go to the library, so he pulled out his laptop and opened the browser. When he typed in morphine, dozens of sites came up, telling him of its properties and the dangers of misuse. Nothing about how to get hold of it. Then he typed 'How to buy morphine' and pressed the enter key. To his amazement the computer displayed a list of places where he could buy morphine without a prescription and even pay by credit card. He might have been buying some new shoes; it was so simple. He scrolled through the alternatives until he came to one that looked reputable and, before he knew it, he'd purchased enough morphine to kill a horse, and paid for it. It would take a week to arrive.

Mark deleted the history, closed the computer and sat back. He couldn't stop shaking. What had he done? Did he really mean to murder his wife? No, he mustn't think like that. It wasn't murder. She was ill and she was never going to get better. She wanted this. It was the least he could do for her. He knew she was right; if it hadn't been for him she would never have rushed off into the night and had the accident. He was the only one who could help her. He was the only one to put it right.

'Oh God, what am I going to do?' he groaned and putting his head in his hands, he began to cry.

*

When Ian arrived at the hospital on Friday evening, he was surprised to see Michelle sitting at his mother's bedside; she was holding Teresa's hand and talking to her quietly.

'Hello, Michelle. What are you doing here?' he asked, and bending over his mother kissed her on the cheek. 'Hi, Mum. It's Ian.'

He looked around for a chair and spotted a spare one by the door, which he pulled up next to the bed and sat down opposite Michelle.

'Hello Ian,' Michelle replied. 'I thought I'd call by and give your Mum a bit of massage.'

Ian realised that as she spoke to him she continued to massage his mother's hand and fingers.

'Right.' He felt uncomfortable with her there; he wondered if his father had told her about their conversation. 'So how are you? It's a while since I've seen you,' he said, at last.

'Well everyone's been so busy, haven't they? But I'm okay, thanks.'

They sat in silence for a while, both looking at the inattentive Teresa, while they wondered what to talk about.

At last Michelle spoke, 'I believe you and your Dad had a chat last week.'

'A chat? I was round there, if that's what you mean?'

'He told me that you know about us, him and me.'

Ian looked nervously at his mother. Was she listening to them? You could never tell.

'Don't worry, I've explained it all to your mother. I've told her that I'm in love with Mark and I've asked her to forgive me.'

Ian said nothing.

'Don't look so shocked Ian. These things happen. I never wanted to hurt anyone, believe me.'

'Did you get any response from Mum?' he asked at last.

'No, but I'm sure she heard me. I think she'll forgive me in time.'

Ian didn't know what to say; he felt like a young boy again, tongue-tied. He thought back to the previous evening; he and Jenny had gone to the cinema together. He'd told her that his suspicions about Mark and Michelle had been correct, but she'd just told him to live with it. What had she said exactly? 'It's their life, Ian. There's nothing you can do about it, so just make the best of it. It's not hurting your mother, after all.' But she didn't know that. Maybe his mother was hurting. Maybe

Michelle's confession was the last straw. Still Jenny was right in one respect—it was none of his business.

'So what are you and Dad going to do?' he asked, keeping his voice as neutral as possible. He could have been asking her the time of day.

She looked at him and smiled. She had a lovely smile; it started with her lips and spread slowly across her face, bringing a sparkle to her blue eyes. 'Your Dad is going to move into my house, for the moment.'

'So what will he do with our house? Is he going to sell it?' Ian asked. Surely not. It was too soon to be closing so many doors on their shared past. After all, his mother was ill, not dead.

'No. He's not going to do anything for now. He'll just shut the house up. Maybe in the future he may need to sell it to pay for your Mum's care; we don't know. There's no point in being too hasty.'

The relief he felt when she said that must have shown on his face because Michelle put her hand on his shoulder and said, 'Don't worry, Ian. It's your home too. He won't do anything without discussing it with you and Alex first; I'll make sure of that.'

'I suppose we'll have to think about Mum's future, one day.'

'I know this is hard for you, Ian, but I hope we can remain friends. And please try to forgive your father. Don't hate him. He's not a bad man you know, and he does love you. Don't make him choose between us, please.'

'Michelle, I don't hate Dad or you. It's just hard to take it all on board. My life seems to have disintegrated, broken into hundreds of pieces and I'm unable to bring any of them together again. Just give me time.'

Michelle turned her attention back to Teresa. She grasped the left knee in one hand and with her other took hold of Teresa's ankle. Slowly she worked the lower leg back and forth, exercising the knee joint.

Ian watched her for a moment then asked, 'Michelle, did my Mum ever tell you about her cousin Jimmy?'

'No, I don't think so. I don't remember the name. Why?'

'Well, apparently she had this cousin that she was in love with, but her family kept them apart.'

'Really? No, I never heard anything about that. I'm a bit surprised though, because Teresa and I used to tell each other everything.'

That was a lie. She never told Mum when she was screwing her husband, did she? 'Well, nobody had heard from him in thirty-five years.' Ian paused. Was his mother listening? 'I've met him.' He looked at his mother. Would she open her eyes again? No. She lay there motionless.

'You've met him? How did you meet him?'

'It's a long story. Anyway he's going to come down and see Mum, tomorrow.' Still her eyes remained shut. Ian felt the disappointment bitter in his throat.

'Does he know about her accident?'

'Yes, I've explained it all to him, but he still wants to come.'

'I suppose you're hoping it will make a difference to her.'

'Well it might. It's worth trying anyway. We won't know if we don't try.' He could tell from Michelle's tone that she didn't share his optimism. 'Is Dad coming here tonight?'

'Yes, he said he'd be over about seven. Why don't you come round for some supper? You could tell him all about this Uncle Jimmy.'

'Gran's expecting me. She'll have cooked something, I'm sure, but I'll come round afterwards, if you like.'

'That would be nice. Say about nine? We'll have a drink.'

'Fine. I've got an email from Alex. Dad will like to see it.'

'You remember where I live?'

'Yes. Bretstone Road, isn't it?'

'That's right, number twelve.'

Ian walked around to the other side of the bed and leaning over his mother whispered in her ear, 'I'll see you tomorrow, Mum, and I'm bringing you a surprise.' He stood there, looking at her for a moment, then kissed her gently. He hated leaving her, but he also hated to stay and see her so helpless.

'See you tonight then, Michelle.'

'Okay. Bye Ian.' She continued exercising Teresa's knee.

*

Michelle was just about to leave when Mark arrived.

'How is she?' he asked.

'Not good. She refused to look at me today. I can't understand it. Yesterday she was fine. We watched some telly together and she used her board to tell me what she wanted. It was very encouraging. Today she doesn't want to know.'

'She was having a scan this morning, maybe that's unsettled her,' Mark told her.

'Oh, by the way, Ian called in. He's coming over later for a drink. He says he's got an email from Alex. He'll bring it over.'

'Why doesn't he forward it to me? That's what he usually does with Alex's emails. Never mind, it'll be nice to see him.'

'Look I've got to go; I need to get to the shops before they close,' Michelle said, buttoning up her coat.

'Okay, I'll see you at home.' He was reluctant to give Michelle a kiss, even though Teresa was lying there with her eyes screwed shut. Instead he smiled at her.

He waited, listening to her heels clicking on the hard floor until she'd gone, then picked up Teresa's hand and said, 'Hello Teresa, it's Mark. I've been thinking about what you asked me.'

She opened her eyes and looked at him.

'Believe me, I know how you feel. This is no life for you but I really don't know what I can do to help you.'

Teresa snapped her eyes shut.

'No, listen to me, please. I want to help you, of course I do, but it's not as easy as you might think. It's against the law here in the UK. I'd have to take you somewhere like Holland or Switzerland, where it's legal and I can't see how I could do that without Ian and Alex finding out. And then there's your mother; it would break her heart.'

Again the frantic fluttering of her eyelids. He picked up the board. What a clumsy way of talking to her; it was so slow that she could only communicate with simple words. No nuances of the English language for her. How frustrated she must feel.

'IT IS MY LIFE,' she spelled out to him. 'NOT THEIRS.'

'Yes, my love, I know it's your life but that won't stop the people who love you being very upset. The boys would never forgive me. Their mother would be dead and their father would be the one responsible. How on earth could they cope with that?'

'MARK, PLEASE.'

It had been unbearable watching her suffer before but now it was worse; she truly seemed to believe that he could help her end her pain.

'Ah, Mr Rushton, I'm glad to see you're here. I'd like a quick word, if I may.'

It was Dr Stevens. Mark hurriedly wiped Teresa's slate clean before the doctor could see what they'd been talking about.

'Teresa's not herself today, I'm afraid. She's rather down,' he said.

Mark nodded. 'Yes, I'm aware of that.'

'She had an MRI scan this morning and the results are much as we expected.'

'What does that mean?'

They both looked at Teresa, who was, for once, listening intently.

'There is no sign of deterioration in her condition and there are plenty of indications that parts of her brain are very active.'

'Is that good?'

'Let's say, it's not bad news; it's just probably not the miracle that you'd like to hear about. I've explained it all to Teresa.'

'And what was her reaction?'

'Your wife's very depressed. She doesn't want to continue with her life and to be honest, I can understand why. However, as I've told her, and as you're probably aware yourself, there is nothing we can do about it. It is our job to care for our patients and preserve life; if we cannot cure them then we must make their lives as comfortable as possible.'

'Are you sure there's nothing you can do, doctor?' Mark cannot believe he is asking this. What does he want the man to do, give his wife a lethal injection? Well it would let him off the hook if he did.

'All we can do here is continue caring for her as we have been. What you and her family need to do is give her a reason for living. You wouldn't believe how important that is. I've seen people just fade away and die for no more reason than they didn't want to live. Teresa needs to regain her will to live or she probably will die, anyway.'

'Is that so bad, if that's what she wants?'

'There are many arguments for and against euthanasia and I don't care to enter into one them with you now. The hospital's position is clear; euthanasia is against the law. End of story. My personal opinion doesn't come into it.' The doctor stood up. He looked annoyed.

'Of course Doctor; I understand.'

'As I said, the best help you can give your wife is to encourage her to cooperate with the hospital staff, who are all trying to do their best for her. Talk to her, spend time with her, give her a reason for living.' He shook Mark's hand. 'You know where to find me if you have any other questions.'

'Thank you, Doctor.'

Once the doctor had left, he sat down again next to Teresa. She was staring at him.

'You heard what he said, Darling. There's nothing that he can do.'

A tear rolled down her cheek, and for a moment he was tempted to tell her of his success in getting the morphine. No, if he did that, then he was committing himself to going through with it. It was too soon. Anyway just because he'd bought the damned stuff, didn't mean he had to use it; it wouldn't arrive for a week and she could change her mind before then. No, he'd keep it as a last resort, although how he'd manage to give it to her, was something he still had to work out. He looked at the network of tubes and catheters that were connected to her body. If this was to happen—and he prayed to God it wasn't—he would have to pay closer attention to how the nurses administered Teresa's drugs. Was he really ready for that?

'Oh don't cry, please don't cry. I will help you, Teresa, I promise, but not yet. It's too soon, much too soon. Let's wait a bit and see if things improve. Let's try and do it the hospital's way first. Maybe we could get you to come home. Would you like that?'

His wife shut her eyes. She wasn't going to talk to him again that evening, he knew. If he wasn't going to help her to die then she didn't want anything to do with him.

It had been the same when Peter died. It was as if she was the only one who was heartbroken about his death. She turned inwards and shut everyone else out, him included. She blamed him of course. He blamed himself, although everyone else said it was just a tragic accident. He should never have taken a six-year-old fishing by the weir—he knew that now. But Peter was a sensible boy. He was desperate to fish there and had been nagging him for ages to take him along. Mark had just bought a new licence to fish Hurley Lock—there'd been some salmon spotted there at the time—and it seemed a good idea to take Peter along for the day. Of course Teresa wasn't keen that Peter should go, but no-one could refuse Peter when he'd set his mind on something, not even her. So Teresa had made them some sandwiches and they'd set off for the day.

It had all gone well until he'd been distracted by a call on his mobile. He still was not clear in his own mind what happened next. They were on the riverbank, upstream from the weir. He could remember Peter calling out to him, telling him he'd caught something. But Mark was still arguing with the man from the garage who wanted to overcharge him for some repair work. Peter must have tried to net the fish himself and lost his footing. The next thing Mark realised was that Peter was in the river, being swept downstream towards the weir. He'd jumped in after him but the current was so strong that he was unable to reach him. It all happened so quickly that he had no chance of saving his son.

He looked at his wife. He had been responsible for so much of her suffering. He adjusted the sound on the television for her, straightened her pillows and left. There was nothing more he could do at the moment.

CHAPTER 31

Bridget had never felt so nervous before; she couldn't settle to anything. For the twentieth time she looked at the kitchen clock, then checked it against the clock in the hall; they were identical. Ian had said he would arrive at eight, after he'd visited Teresa. It was still only a quarter-to-eight, so she took out the remainder of the previous day's bread and crumbled it into small pieces for the birds. Smokey Joe sat and watched her intently as she put the bread on the bird table.

'Now, off you go. Leave the poor birds in peace for a while,' she told him, as she chased him back into the house.

She had made a chicken pie for their supper, and it was browning nicely in the oven. The cat could smell it; he curled up on the chair and kept a watchful eye on the oven door. The weather was still quite warm, despite the fact they were now into September, so she'd made a green salad to accompany the pie. Ian liked salad. Not like her husband; he would have been most upset if she'd served him salad with chicken pie. She could imagine him saying, 'What's this Bridget? Where's the potatoes and gravy?' He liked potatoes and gravy with everything; it wasn't a proper dinner otherwise. Her husband had been dead almost four years and she still missed him as much as ever. She felt her loss even more keenly today; if only he could be here to see Jimmy again.

'Hi, Gran,' Ian said, putting his head round the back door. 'It's only me.'

'Ian. I didn't hear you arrive. You look tired; have you had a hard day?'

'No, not really. I suppose it's seeing Mum; it always makes me feel a bit down.'

'How does she look? Any change?'

'No, nothing. Michelle was sitting with her when I arrived. I think she'd been there all afternoon.'

'Michelle? I haven't seen her in ages. How is she?'

'She seems fine. She says Dad is going to move in with her.' He looked at his grandmother to see her reaction, but she was checking to see if the pie was ready.

'Oh, I thought that might happen. Poor Teresa.'

Ian helped himself to a beer from the refrigerator and sat down at the table. 'Did you know about them then, Gran?'

'Well it's hard not to notice. Your Dad hasn't actually said anything to me, but I'm not completely senile you know. I've still got eyes and ears.'

She passed Ian a glass and nodded towards the can that he was about to drink from. Ian sighed and dutifully poured the beer into the glass.

'And you don't mind?'

'Of course I mind. I don't want my son-in-law living with someone else, but what can I do about it. I want things to be as they were before this awful accident, but that isn't going to happen.'

'Maybe Dad will be a bit happier now. He's been quite depressed lately.'

'Maybe. We'll see. I don't begrudge him some happiness, as long as he doesn't abandon my daughter. She needs him; she needs all of us.'

'Do you think seeing Jimmy will make any difference to her, Gran?'

'I don't know. It's been a long time. If she won't rouse herself for us, her family who have been visiting her every day, why should she for Jimmy, who abandoned us?'

Ian looked deflated at her words.

'Now don't worry Ian, I'm sure it will do some good,' she said, trying to reassure him, but not sounding very convincing. 'Anyway, tell me the whole story now. How did you find him?'

So while Bridget served the chicken pie, Ian told her how he'd tracked down her errant nephew.

'Do you think he will really come?' she asked.

'Yes, I'm sure of it. He wants to see Mum, and he wants to see you too, Gran,' he added.

She thought back to the last time she'd seen Jimmy; he'd been sixteen. Each summer she had gone to Ireland on her own, to visit him. The first time he'd cried and begged her to take him home with her, but she'd refused. After that whenever she went over he made a point of always going out with his friends; he stopped speaking to her. She knew he blamed her for his exile, but what else could she have done? What would he say to her now?

'Oh, by the way, Gran, I'm going to see Dad tonight. I won't be late.'

'Alright. Make sure you take a key, and don't let that Smokey Joe in when you get back. Last time he woke me up at three-thirty to go out again.'

'Okay Gran.'

'Maybe your Dad will take him back now he's moving in with Michelle. That would be good.'

'Who? Smokey Joe? I'll ask him.'

*

Michelle was in the kitchen washing up when Ian arrived, and his father was watching a football match on the television.

'Hi Ian, grab yourself a drink. This is nearly over, just another ten minutes and a bit of injury time.'

'Hi Dad. Who are playing?'

'Man United and Arsenal. Arsenal are one up.'

Ian flopped onto the sofa next to his father. It felt strange to be in Michelle's house; he hadn't been there since he was a kid. He looked around; it was tastefully furnished but not as homely as his Mum's house, more chic and less warm, lots of hard, shiny surfaces and modern paintings. Still his Dad seemed well at home here, shoes off, feet on the sofa, smoking a cigarette. He'd never smoked in the house before. He wondered if this was a concession that Michelle made or if she really didn't mind.

The game was uninteresting; the winning side seemed content to keep control of the ball until the whistle blew, passing it from one to another as though it were a practice session. There was no need for any more goals, one was all they required.

'Pathetic,' his Dad said, switching off the television. 'So, how are you Ian? Tell me what you've been up to then.'

'I've tracked down Mum's cousin, brother, Jimmy.'

'You have? That's fantastic. How on earth did you find him?'

Ian explained to his father how, with the help of a few well placed friends he had managed to trace Jimmy O'Sullivan and that he was arriving the next day to visit Mum.

'Well that's good news. If you're right and your Mum is fond of this brother or cousin, whatever he is, then it might be just what she needs to buck her up.'

'That's what I'm hoping.'

'She asked me to help her to die, you know.' He said it in such a matter-of-fact way that Ian looked at his father in amazement. He knew his mother talked about wanting to die, but he just thought that was her rage talking. Saying you wanted to die was not the same as asking someone to help you kill yourself.

'Suicide?'

'Sort of, euthanasia she likes to call it.'

'I can't believe it. What did you say?'

'At first, I said no. I couldn't do it.'

'At first? What does that mean? At first?'

His father explained what he'd found out about the legal position. 'So you see, even if I was in agreement with her committing suicide, it isn't easy to arrange. Anyway I've told her that I will help her but not yet.'

'Not yet?' Ian was bewildered.

'It's too soon. I've been thinking about it and I think she needs more time to come to terms with her situation.

Who knows, in a couple of years she might have made enough improvement to be able to cope with her life.'

'That's what I hope will happen,' Ian added. 'I don't want her to give up. I don't know how you could even consider it, Dad.' He was furious with his father.

'It's what she wants, Ian.'

'It's what she says she wants. Nobody really wants to die. I can't believe you'd even consider it. Murdering your own wife? God Dad, what's happened to you?'

'Maybe you're right. Anyway, as I said, I've told her we'll wait and see how things go.' It was as if he wasn't listening to him. He seemed so calm Ian thought he could be talking about the purchase of a new car or an expensive holiday that they wanted.

'I'm sorry. I've got to go. Here. It's a copy of Alex's email.' Ian tossed the email on the table and stormed out. He'd planned to break the news gently about Alex's homosexuality, but he couldn't stay there a moment longer. Let him read it for himself. He couldn't sit there, looking at his Dad, all cosy in his new home with his mistress and at the same time, planning to get rid of Mum. Euthanasia. Wouldn't that be convenient for him. That's why it was illegal, so people like his father couldn't use it just to make life more comfortable for themselves.

Thank God he'd found Jimmy; it could be just what Mum needed to make her realise that life was worth living after all. Then there would be no more talk of ending it all.

*

After Ian left, Mark went up to the bedroom. He could hear the clatter of dishes as Michelle cleared away the dinner things and the droning of the television. Why had Ian flown off the handle like that? Maybe he shouldn't have told him he was considering helping Teresa die. He'd only meant, if it was a last resort. Surely Ian wouldn't want to see his mother suffer forever, if there was no future for her? Well maybe, now he'd tracked down that cousin, things would be different. He felt almost euphoric; he wouldn't need to go through with it after all. If this Jimmy was as special to Teresa as everyone thought, then she would drop the idea of assisted suicide. She'd regain the will to live and he wouldn't be obliged to do something that he knew would haunt him for the rest of his life, even if he managed to get away with it. And it was Ian he had to thank. Quick-tempered Ian who wouldn't give up; who kept worrying away until he found a way back into his mother's heart.

He opened the email Ian had tossed at him in anger. What was that about?

CHAPTER 32

Jimmy left his small cottage just after six; the sun was just beginning to show above the horizon and the sky was stained with a wash of pink. A flock of hungry gulls filled the air with their cries as they wheeled and turned, following the fishing boats back into harbour, hoping for scraps. He could make out the guttural call of the Great black-backed gulls, newly arrived for the winter and spotted a gannet, its dry, crackling voice almost lost among the other raucous screams. The air smelt clean and crisp and salty, with a hint of the rain to come. He put his small suitcase into the boot and folded his jacket carefully on the back seat. Within a few minutes he was heading in the direction of the motorway. There wasn't usually a lot of traffic on a Saturday, but he wanted to get on his way as early as possible. In fact he'd considered driving through the night and arriving at Bridget's for breakfast, but common sense had prevailed. As he drove inland, leaving the glassy, grey sea behind him, a feeling of excitement gripped him. He was filled with such a longing to see Teresa and Bridget again, that he couldn't stop himself from smiling at the prospect. He'd followed their lives over the years, albeit from a distance, until the pain of being excluded became too great to bear. He should have got in touch with them as soon as he came back to England but he'd hesitated and then, the longer he left it, the harder it was to just walk back into their lives. He could see now that Bridget and Patrick had only been thinking of his well being; they wanted to protect Teresa and Jimmy from themselves. They'd realised where their friendship was leading, long before Jimmy knew. It was not until he was separated from Teresa, alone in a hostile world, that it dawned on him how much he loved her. Maybe that was their mistake; maybe their parents should have left them as they were and the teenage infatuation would have burned itself out. Instead it had burned slowly and matured into a passion that nothing could quench. He'd had plenty of women in his life, but none of them could compare to Teresa. As soon as they wanted to talk about going steady or marriage or worse still, having children, he carefully extricated himself from the relationship and moved on. If only he'd known that Teresa had felt the same about him. He remembered what Ian told him about the letters she'd sent and he felt angry with his grandmother for destroying them. How different his life could have been if he'd received even one of those letters, if he'd known that she hadn't abandoned him.

*

Bridget peered from behind the bedroom curtain; she wanted to look at him first, to make sure it was really him. She'd been waiting in her bedroom all morning, jumping up every time she heard a car. This time it was a dark blue BMW. It stopped outside her gate. She watched as a tall man, with a slight stoop, got out of the car. He wore dark trousers and a cream shirt, but no jacket. Ian had been right, he was bald, but not completely: even from her lookout point she could make out the remaining dark red hair. He locked his car and turned round to look at the house. It was definitely Jimmy; despite the years she would have recognised him anywhere. He looked worried: a slight frown creased his brow, pulling his reddish eyebrows down over his eyes and his mouth was set in a thin line. His face was much thinner than she remembered, but he was just as handsome as ever. He appeared to hesitate for a moment, then walked resolutely up to the door and rang the bell. The sound startled her as if were completely unconnected with what she had just been watching. She sat down quickly on the bed.

'I'll get it Gran,' Ian called up to her.

She heard him open the door, and the sound of voices, but still she couldn't move. She seemed to have no strength in her legs.

'Gran. It's Jimmy. Aren't you coming down?'

She could hear them talking, and then footsteps: someone was coming up the stairs. She sat and stared at the bedroom door, mesmerised. There was a soft knock and Ian came in. 'Are you alright Gran? What's the matter? You look awful.' He came over to her and felt her forehead. 'What is it? Are you ill? You don't have to see him if you don't want to, you know.' Her grandson was becoming concerned.

'I'm alright, Ian. Really. It's just such a shock after all these years. Just give me a few minutes and I'll be down. Why don't you make him a cup of tea.'

'Okay Gran. You're sure you're alright now?' he asked again.

'Yes, go on with you. I'll be right down.'

Once Ian had left, she went into the bathroom and splashed some water on her face and neck. She combed her hair for the tenth time that morning and dabbed her nose with some powder. Now she felt ready to face him.

As she went down the stairs she could see them; they were sitting in the back garden, chatting like old friends and enjoying the autumn sunshine. She said nothing, just looked at the two of them for a moment.

'Gran. There you are.' Both men stood up. How tall Jimmy had grown. He was smiling at her in his old mischievous way.

'Hello Mam,' he said, holding out his arms.

She went towards him and hugged him. There was no anger now, just pleasure at having him home again. 'Oh, Jimmy, I've missed you so,' she sobbed against his chest.

He held her and stroked her head gently, murmuring that he was sorry, that he'd missed her too. After a few moments, he gently pulled her away from him and sat her in the chair he'd vacated. Her tears had washed the make-up from her face, but she didn't care. It was such a relief to cry.

'Shall I make you some tea, Gran?' Ian asked. He looked worried.

'That'd be nice, Ian. Thank you.' She felt more composed now.

Jimmy picked up her hand and held it. 'You look just grand, Mam, just grand.'

She smiled. 'You've still got a touch of the Blarney, I see, James O'Sullivan,' she said.

'Well, maybe. Some things never change, you know, Mam.'

CHAPTER 33

Ian led the way along the endless corridors. Teresa was allowed visitors any time after ten o'clock, and neither he nor Jimmy were inclined to wait any longer.

'I hope you're going to show me the way out of this rabbit warren,' Jimmy said, as they turned yet another corner into a passage identical to the last.

'It's easier getting out. You just follow the exit signs.' Ian was feeling nervous; he'd tried so many things to encourage his mother to communicate with them and now this seemed to him the only one left. What if it didn't work? What would he do then? He wasn't a man to be easily discouraged, but even he couldn't face the possibility that his mother would continue like this forever. And the alternative that she was proposing for herself was too awful to contemplate.

'Are you sure we won't be too early?' Jimmy asked. He too seemed nervous.

'No. It's Saturday; she doesn't go down to the gym on a Saturday. And there're no doctors' rounds. Besides I thought it was better to come early before anyone else came to visit her.'

'Yes, I'd like to see her alone for a few minutes,' Jimmy said.

'Here we are.' They stopped outside the door to the Neuro Rehab ward. 'Do you want me to go in first?' Ian asked.

'No, I think it would be better if I went in alone and surprised her.'

Ian was doubtful of the wisdom of this plan—his mother didn't respond well to surprises—but nevertheless nodded his agreement. He opened the door quietly and pointed. 'That's Mum's bed. There, the one with the vase of white chrysanthemums by the side.'

Jimmy followed his gaze. 'Is that Tess, with the blue tracksuit?' he whispered.

'Yes.'

'Give me ten minutes, then you can come in. Okay?'

'Okay. I'll wait in the corridor.' Ian watched his uncle go towards the bed and sit down beside his mother, then he closed the door and went to wait.

He hadn't told him that Teresa had asked his father to help her die; he couldn't bear to break the spell that Jimmy's reappearance had woven over everything. He'd never seen his grandmother so animated in a long time. She too felt that this was a turning point, that things could only improve from now on. She hadn't said much when he told her that Alex was in love with a man, just smiled and said she was happy for them. The night before, as soon as they'd eaten, she had hurried off to church to give thanks to God, she told them, leaving Jimmy and Ian, chatting over a bottle of Jameson's and getting to know each other.

*

Jimmy couldn't stem the tears that rose to his eyes when he saw her; Ian had told him that Teresa had changed, but he hadn't expected this. She lay, propped up on her cushions, her eyes closed as though she was sleeping; her mouth was partially open and a dribble of spittle ran down her cheek and onto the bib that had been tied around her neck. There was a slightly sour odour coming from somewhere. The long, black hair that he remembered so well, was dank and lifeless now, more grey than black and in need of cutting, and her skin, always pale, had the additional pallor that comes from never being outside. She'd lost a lot of weight; her skin hung loosely around her neck and her beautiful cheek bones were more prominent than ever.

He pulled out a handkerchief and blew his nose. She seemed to be oblivious of his presence. He wondered if she were sleeping. Gently he took a corner of the bib and wiped her mouth; she made no movement. He picked up her hand and held it in his.

'Tess. It's Jimmy. I've come back for you. I said I would and now I'm here.'

*

Her husband has telephoned to say he is on his way; his flight is early, so he is taking a taxi. Teresa is relieved; her head hasn't stopped thumping all day. She knows Petie will be disappointed—he loves seeing the aeroplanes—but Teresa was dreading the drive. Maybe she is getting flu; her legs feel heavy and she has no energy. At least now she will have plenty of time to prepare their evening meal.

She covers a loin of pork in salt; it is rough sea salt and she can press it around the meat like a jacket; and that's just what it is: a thermal jacket to protect the meat from burning. Once it is in the oven on a low heat, she starts to prepare the vegetables: small, waxy potatoes and a salad. The elderly woman next door had sent her son round earlier with a basket of vegetables from their garden: a head of lettuce, a few carrots, an endive, some beetroots and a bag of potatoes, the dark earth still clinging to them.

She hears the taxi pull up outside and Petie's high-pitched voice telling his father about the up-coming County Fair. She hears Tommy run down the stairs to join them. Even Foxy is out there, barking his greeting to the man of the house, while upstairs, Jack remains oblivious to it all, cocooned by his music. She wants to run out to greet her husband; she wants to bound up the stairs and remove Jack's headphones so he can hear that his father is home. She wants to be with her family, to throw her arms around her husband and tell him what a long week it has been without him, but she can't move. She is rooted to the spot.

The kitchen door opens and Jimmy is standing there, a wide smile on his face. He is answering his sons' barrage of questions but his eyes are on her alone.

*

But something was interrupting her; somebody was there, by her bed. What was happening? Was she still dreaming? Someone was holding her hand and talking to her softly; he was saying he was sorry; he was telling her he would make it up to her; he said he loved her. She knew that voice. It was a voice from her past. She opened her eyes and looked at him. It was her Jimmy. He had come for her at last.

*

When Jimmy saw her open her eyes, he knew that despite her appearance, Teresa hadn't really changed at all. He looked into their green depths and saw his own reflection as if she had held it there all those years, protecting their love against the passage of time. He knew that he, like Ian, could never abandon her now.

'Tess, my love,' he began. 'My own sweet love,' but he couldn't continue. He laid his head on her chest and cried the tears of his childhood.

*

Ian looked at his watch. Ten minutes had passed and still Jimmy hadn't called him. He folded up his newspaper and walked over to the door and looked into the ward. Jimmy was sitting next to Teresa, holding her hand; he'd moved her head slightly to one side, so she could look straight at him. He could hear the murmur of Jimmy's voice. Ian felt a tightening in his stomach; his plan was working. He hesitated, unsure whether he should disturb them, but then Jimmy looked round and beckoned him across.

'Your clever son made this possible. We've a lot to thank him for,' he said to Teresa. 'Come on Ian, pull up a chair. Your Mum has promised me she's going to try to get well.'

'Hi, Mum. I told you I'd bring you a surprise, didn't I?' He couldn't believe it; there was his mother, her eyes were wide open and they were twinkling.

'She's had a bit of a cry; well we both have actually, but she's alright now,' Jimmy told him as he carefully wiped her eyes for her. 'Later on, you'll have to tell me how this alphabet board works. Your Mum and I have lots to talk about.'

Ian felt a twinge of jealousy; his mother hadn't wanted to talk to him, or Alex. She hadn't wanted to talk to anyone unless she had to.

He took her hand and stroked it. 'That's wonderful Mum,' he said, trying to hold back his own tears. 'That's wonderful.' He looked down at her hand, nestling in his own broad one with its stubby fingers covered in fine red hair; it was like an injured bird in a nest. He squeezed it gently and there it was, an almost imperceptible response.

'Jimmy, she tried to squeeze my hand. I'm sure she did. Look, there it is again.' This time he was sure his mother's hand had moved. 'Oh my God, I think she's going to improve after all,' he said, his voice breaking with excitement.

CHAPTER 34

Ian left Jimmy sitting by his mother's bedside and went to telephone his father. After a couple of rings, Michelle answered.

'Hi Ian. Your Dad's not home right now. Everything alright?' There was the usual hint of anxiety in her voice; they were all the same, always ready for the bad news that they felt would inevitably arrive.

'Everything's fine actually. I'm sorry about storming out yesterday. Alright if I come round?'

'Of course. Your Dad will be back in about half-an-hour; he's just gone to the garage to wash the car.'

'Right, see you then.'

Next he telephoned his grandmother and told her the news. Such small occurrences but with such mighty potential: an imperceptible squeeze of the hand, a pair of open eyes but what promise they held for the future. A small inner voice told him not to get carried away, not to let reason desert him. 'This could be all there is,' it said, but his heart believed otherwise and he wouldn't let the voice of reason deprive him of the joy that he felt at that moment. If he was to be disappointed, so be it. For now he was happy to cling to the hope that Jimmy's appearance would make a difference to all their lives.

*

His father's car was outside when he arrived at Michelle's house. He rang the bell and almost instantly the door opened.

'Ian, is everything alright?' His father's face was lined with anxiety, as usual expecting the worst.

'Yes, everything's fine Dad. Can I come in?'

'Of course. So what's this all about?' he asked following his son into the living room.

'Hi Michelle.'

'Hello Ian. Can I get you something? A beer?'

'Please.' He was beginning to feel a bit foolish; his news didn't seem so earth-shattering any more.

'It's about Mum.'

'Yes?'

He explained about Jimmy and how his mother had reacted to him.

'Well that sounds like very good news to me,' Michelle said, handing him a cold beer.

'So where has this guy been all these years?' Mark asked.

'Not very far away, actually. Maidenhead.'

'Maidenhead? But that's just down the road. Why on earth didn't he get in touch with her before?'

'He loves her Dad. Not like a brother; he really loves her. He didn't want to mess up her life by turning up again after all these years.'

'But you found him?'

'Yes.'

'You were never going to give up on her were you?' Mark reached over and gave his son an embarrassed hug. There were tears in his eyes. 'This could be the turning point you know.'

'Yes but we still have to keep on with the therapy, Mark. She isn't going to get better just because she now wants to. It's not as simple as that,' said Michelle.

'I know but the one thing that's been missing all this time has been Teresa's will to live. Now maybe she'll make some progress.'

'Let's drink to that,' Ian said, downing his beer.

As soon as Michelle went into the kitchen to prepare some food, Mark turned to Ian and said, 'You don't know how pleased I am with that news. I know you were upset yesterday when I told you about the euthanasia, but your mother's been on and on at me about helping her to end it all. I've been at my wits' end.'

'I know. You told me.'

'But what I didn't tell you was that I'd ordered the morphine. It arrived this morning.'

'What?' Ian couldn't believe his ears. 'You'd actually gone as far as buying morphine? Isn't it illegal? How the hell did you get hold of it anyway?'

'It's not that hard, you know. It seems you can get anything on the internet if you know where to look.'

'So, are you planning to go through with it?' Ian could feel his anger returning. 'It would make life easier for you, wouldn't it?'

'Of course not. I wouldn't be telling you if I was going to do it. And it's nothing to do with making life easier for me. It was what your mother wanted.'

'So what's changed your mind?'

'You did. Finding Jimmy. Giving her something to live for.'

'Where is it?' Ian asked. He was furious that his father could be so callous. To actually plan to poison their mother. To go as far as to actually buy the morphine. 'Give it to me.'

'The morphine? Here.' Mark went over to the sideboard and took out an opened jiffy bag. 'Take it, if you want to. I'm not going to use it.'

'So, you won't need it then,' Ian said, snatching it out of his father's hand. 'I'll get rid of it, before you change your mind.'

'Don't be like that, Ian. I was only thinking of your mother.'

'What if I hadn't found Jimmy? What if I'd found him in a month's time? Or six months' time? Would it have been too late? Would my mother already be dead?' He was beginning to realise how close he'd come to losing his mother for good and it frightened him..

'I told you, Ian. I wanted her to wait a while longer, to give the hospital a chance.'

'Well, good job you did.'

'Everything okay?' asked Michelle, coming in with a plate of sandwiches in one hand and a bottle of wine in the other.

'Yes, darling. Everything's fine,' said Mark.

'I have to be going,' Ian said, tucking the jiffy bag under his arm. 'Thanks for the beer, Michelle.' He stared at his father for a moment then said, 'I really don't recognise you, Dad.'

*

When Michelle went to visit Teresa on Monday she saw an instant change in her. The first thing she noticed was the writing on the message board.

'Hello Teresa. I hear you've had a visitor. Do you want to tell me about him?'

Her friend blinked her eyelids once and Michelle took up the board. 'Look don't bother to spell all the words correctly. Pretend you're texting a message to someone on your mobile. That'll make it quicker and less tiring for you.'

There was a sparkle in Teresa's eyes as she blinked once to denote her agreement. Nevertheless by the time she'd composed her short text Michelle could see that she was exhausted.

'So he was your first love was he? Why did you never mention him to me? All those years we were friends and you never once said anything.'

A tear formed in Teresa's eye and rolled down her cheek. Michelle leant across and wiped it away gently. 'Never mind. I understand. Now I was wondering if you'd like me to do something about all those grey hairs that are starting to show. They have a peripatetic hairdresser here who will cut and colour your hair at a very reasonable price. Would you like me to make you an appointment?'

She looked at Teresa. At first there was no response, then she blinked once.

'Good. I'll arrange it for later this week. Then you'll be looking lovely for when Jimmy comes again at the weekend.'

She picked up Teresa's hand and started to work the muscles. 'Time to get down to some work my girl; let's get those muscles moving again.'

*

Teresa had long since given up feeling resentful of Michelle. She'd grown to tolerate her friend's daily visits and although they inevitably interrupted her day dreams she often managed to block out Michelle's casual chatter. Now she listened to her with renewed interest. If Jimmy still loved her and he'd said so over and over again then she must at least try to get well. They'd said there was no cure but they'd also said that she could make progress if she tried. Well she would try. She would start with that damned message board. She had to master it in order to tell Jimmy that she still loved him.

It was strange, since he'd come to see her she'd been unable to conjure up her dream life; she could remember all the details but she couldn't bring it to life. She knew what her darling Petie looked like but she could no longer see his face, and Tommy and Jack, they were just blurs. It made her sad. She'd always known they weren't her real children but for a while they'd been real to her. She'd escaped into their world and claimed it as her own. Now they'd rejected her. What if Jimmy tired of her? What if he was just feeling sorry for her? Gradually he would weary of her inability to communicate with him and his visits would become fewer. Then what would she do? Locked out of her dream world and locked into a nightmare. She felt the panic clutch at her heart and was once again spiralling down a tunnel of hopelessness.

'Okay, now let's give those legs a turn.'

Teresa opened her eyes; Michelle was smiling at her as she vigorously bent her left leg to and fro.

'Mark will be in later. He's been to see if he can get you a better television, one with a larger screen and more channels.'

As Michelle continued to chatter away to her uncommunicative friend, Teresa began to accept that she was not alone in this; she had friends and family to help her and the feeling of panic gradually subsided.

*

It was almost lunchtime by the time Ian arrived at the hospital. He'd intended to leave early, before it got light, but Jenny had pulled him back to bed and before he knew it the alarm clock had showed eight o'clock. He'd abandoned the idea of driving down and instead took a taxi to the airport and caught the first available flight.

As he approached Teresa's room he could see through the glass partition that she was propped up in bed, watching the television.

'Hi Mum. My, you look well. What have they been doing to you?' He was genuinely surprised. Her hair had been cut into a stylish bob that framed her face, removing the gauntness from her cheeks but emphasising their delicate bone structure. There were traces of make-up on her eyes and even a touch of lipstick on her lips. 'Gosh, you're all dolled up. Is this in my honour?'

She blinked at him twice. He thought he could see a twinkle in her eyes. 'No, I thought not.' He bent over and kissed her forehead.

'You do look lovely Mum. Just like the old days,' he added then instantly wished he hadn't said it.

'Hi Mr Rushton.'

'Oh hello Julie. I was just telling my mother how well she's looking.'

The nurse unclipped the empty food sachet from the stand and attached a full one.

'There you go, Teresa. Roast beef and Yorkshire pudding. Yes, your mother's starting to make a little progress at long last. Something seems to have motivated her. I think it must be that handsome guy who keeps visiting her.' She winked at Teresa. 'She's running us ragged now with that new telly she's got. Won't watch just any old channel, oh no. It's got to be a drama or something educational. Loves the Discovery Channel and can't abide the adverts.'

'No she never could stand the adverts. Well I hope it lasts.'

'The doctor has ordered extra physio for her and she has the speech therapist twice a week now. I reckon he thinks we should try and make up for lost time.'

'Does it work like that?'

'Can't hurt, can it? And that nice healing woman still comes in every week; she was delighted to see such a change in your Mum's attitude. And it's nice for us to see more of those lovely green eyes of yours, my dear.' She patted Teresa's hand and moved on to her next patient.

'So has Jimmy come to see you again, Mum?' Before she could blink in answer a voice behind him spoke, 'Yes he has.'

'Hi Jimmy. Didn't realise you were here.'

'I just popped out to get a coffee. Your Mum and I are getting along just fine. I was telling her that I've heard that there may be a job going at my old golf club in Maidenhead. The pro there is due for retirement and I've let them know that I'm interested. I know they want shot of him; he's a bit too fond of the hard stuff and some of the members have been complaining.'

'That would be great. But where would you live?'

'Well I expect Bridget will put me up for a while. She says she could do with the company.'

Ian could hardly believe it; everything seemed to be working out so well. And his mother, well when he looked at her he could almost believe that she would recover. He stayed chatting to Jimmy and his mother for almost an hour then announced he would go and see how Bridget was doing.

'Tell her I'll be home about eight, will you Ian. They start getting Tess ready for bed around seven-thirty.'

'Okay. Well I'll probably see you there then. I'm staying at Gran's tonight and I thought I'd visit Mum first thing tomorrow before I set off back to Edinburgh.'

'Fine. Look Ian, I'll be coming down every weekend to see your Mum. If you want to take the odd weekend off and spend some time with that girlfriend of yours, it'll be fine because I'll be here. It's a hell of a long way to come for a few hours. And you don't want her slipping through your fingers because you're never around.'

At first Ian wasn't sure how to respond to his offer; he felt as though he was being usurped. He hesitated then said, 'Okay. I'll think about it.'

Jimmy was right. It wasn't really necessary for him to come down every weekend now. He even felt in the way; he was sure his mother wanted to be alone with Jimmy. A small part of him felt rejected, even annoyed by the suggestion that his presence was no longer needed but Ian was a practical man, if nothing else. It would be good to have more time at home. Jenny would like it for a start. Their relationship was beginning to flower at last and now was not the time to keep disappearing down south. Maybe he would take Jimmy's suggestion in the spirit it was given and start living his own life.

As he was walking out to the carpark, his mobile rang. 'Hi Jenny.'

'Ian, I just had to ring you. I've seen this article about a woman with Locked-In Syndrome, just like your Mum. She's an American and she's had it for eight years. Now she can talk to her daughters; they were just little when she became paralysed. It was from a stroke.'

'Slow down a bit, Jen. Start from the beginning.'

'Ach, sorry. It's like I said, this woman had a stroke when she was in her forties, and at first they thought she was brain dead, but then they discovered that what she had was the same as your Mum, Locked-In Syndrome.' Jenny sounded excited.

'Yes?'

'Well, she's recovered. Not completely, you understand, but she's made fantastic improvements.'

'She can speak?'

'Not only that, she can walk and move around with the aid of crutches. It's a miracle.'

'But what happened?'

'She had a stroke.'

'No, I mean, what happened to make her recover?'

'It doesn't say, just that after eight years of physio and the usual treatment she gradually improved. It wasn't anything sudden. Just small improvements every day.'

'That's fantastic news. I knew there was a way out of this. Wait until I tell Mum.'

'It'll give her some hope.'

'It'll give us all hope. Look I'll be home in time for lunch tomorrow. I'll come straight to your place, okay?'

'Yes, I'll be waiting, hen.'

The warmth in her voice made him smile. Yes, Jimmy was right; it was time to start living his own life. He suddenly realised how important Jenny was to him; he didn't want to lose her.

CHAPTER 35

The weather was definitely getting colder. Ian turned up the central heating and went into the lounge. It was only four-thirty, but Andrew had suggested that everyone go home early; there'd been talk of blizzards that evening. He poured himself a small whisky and took it into the bedroom. This was a good opportunity to write to Alex and tell him their news. He switched on the computer by his bed and sipped the whisky while he thought where to begin.

Hi Alex,

Sorry its taken me so long to answer your last email; it's been pretty hectic here. I'm really pleased you can make it for Christmas; we all are, and we're looking forward to meeting your new friend Baruti. The reaction to your news was very positive. Nobody cares that you're gay. I think they were more excited about the fact that you said you were in love. Even Dad seems okay with it. As for me, I don't care what you get up to but I'm a tad disappointed that you didn't tell me before. Surely you didn't think I'd disapprove? Not your reprobate younger brother?

You wouldn't believe the changes in Mum since Jimmy arrived; I don't know if it's his influence or just an accumulation of things, but things have really improved. The Rehab team were so surprised when they arrived one morning and found her with her eyes wide open, demanding her message board.

Jimmy is a grand guy; he visits her every weekend and spends both days with her. That means Dad and Michelle get a bit of time to themselves and I only go down once a month now which is helping my finances recover a little.

Dad is much more positive than he was and between him and Michelle they spend quite a bit of time with Mum. I had a bit of a falling out with him—I won't go into details—but I'm over it now. He's been just as confused as the rest of us about what is best for Mum. Now Jimmy's here and taken over the role of decision maker and, to be honest, we're all secretly relieved.

I can understand your reaction to the fact that Dad and Michelle are living together, but honestly if you were here you'd see it wasn't so bad. We've all become used to it now, and Mum seems okay with it. Like you said, we've all got to get on with our lives.

He didn't mention anything about the morphine; he remembered how stunned he'd been when he saw that jiffy bag in Dad's hand. It had made the danger so real. No, there was no point sharing that information with anyone, not Alex and certainly not Jimmy. It had been a close call but it was over now and his mother wouldn't thank him for telling everyone. He resumed typing.

Mum has a wheelchair now. It's a pretty fancy piece of work; she's well strapped in and her head is held in a clamp so it can't roll about. She was a bit reluctant to try it at first, but then I think the temptation of having some fresh air was too much. Mostly we push her around the hospital grounds, but Jimmy has taken her down to the river a few times. He sold his BMW and bought an old 4 x 4; he had the back converted so that Mum's wheelchair could go in, with her still sitting in it, a bit like in that old TV series we used to watch when we were kids: Ironside I think it was called. I think the mods to Jimmy's car probably cost more than the car is worth, but he doesn't seem to care. He's besotted with her..

We've all been given our orders for Christmas: Michelle is cooking the turkey, I'm in charge of the tree and Gran is doing the Christmas pud and the cake. Dad has opened up our old house and you and I'll sleep there, Baruti too, of course. Jimmy will stay with Gran, and Dad and Michelle will go back to their place. Mum will have to go back to hospital afterwards, unfortunately; it's too soon for her to live away from the Rehab unit. She still depends on them for so much, like her food pump for example. The doctors say that sometime in the future, possibly in the new year, it will be possible for her to spend some time at home, but they're very reticent about her long term prognosis. The trouble is, if she did come home, she would need full-time care. I don't think any of us have thought that far ahead yet, we are just happy to have some of our old Mum back again.

I wouldn't say Mum is happy; I still catch her crying at times, but she is definitely happier than she was. She wants to live now, in any way she can.

Well Bro, send me the details of your flight and I or Dad will come and pick you up. Can't wait to see you. A year's a long time; we've got a lot to catch up on,

Ian.

He pressed the send button and switched off. He was looking forward to seeing his brother; he wondered if he'd changed. He drank down the last dregs of his whisky and checked his watch. It was five-thirty; he would have a shower and get ready to see Jenny. They were going to a carol concert. He smiled to himself as he thought of her. She'd agreed to spend Christmas with him and his family, but only on condition he got her back in time for New Year's Eve. He hadn't told Alex about Jenny yet; he wanted to keep it a surprise.

He thought back to their previous Christmas together; the future couldn't have looked bleaker. Now he felt full of optimism, for himself, for his mother and for the rest of his family. He started to hum quietly to himself.

CHAPTER 36

Jimmy left the estate agents in good spirits; the flat was just what he wanted: on the ground floor, with two bedrooms, a large lounge and an open plan kitchen and dining room. Besides that, it had two en-suite bathrooms and a patio garden. All he would have to do was get someone in to widen the doorways, put a ramp up to the front door and make a few changes in the bathroom. He'd paid a deposit on it, now all that was left was to convince the bank manager that he should lend him the money.

He strode to the car, whistling to himself. Teresa would be so pleased. He was sure that once she was out of the hospital and back in a normal home environment she'd feel happier. He'd talked to the doctors about it and they'd all agreed that provided she kept up the physiotherapy and checked into the hospital on a regular basis, there was no reason why she shouldn't live at home. It was going to be hard work and they would need a carer. He would never have considered it if it hadn't been for Michelle and Bridget. They both pledged their time to helping to look after her. Even the husband, Mark—who Jimmy didn't really have much time for—had promised to take his turn in caring for Teresa. He was sure he'd covered everything. It would work. It had to work.

Teresa had been so much more animated since they'd talked about the flat; he could see that it meant a lot to her. Thank goodness he'd got the job at Maidenhead Golf Club; it meant long hours but they were flexible. He could decide which days he gave lessons and which he didn't. He'd employed someone to run the golf shop for him, which meant more expenses of course, but gave him more free time. Yes, he thought it could work. Nevertheless, he was glad he had some savings to fall back on.

*

The doctor was just ending his rounds when Jimmy arrived.

'Hello Mr O'Sullivan. I've just finished with her. I must say she's a lot brighter these days and we're starting to notice a definite improvement in her condition.'

Jimmy took off his coat and sat down by the bed. He was impatient to speak to Teresa but what the doctor said intrigued him. 'What sort of improvements?'

'Haven't you noticed? There is certainly some movement in the left forefinger now. Look.'

He took Teresa's hand in his own and squeezed it gently. Teresa's finger attempted to pull away.

'You see, that was a conscious effort, not a random spasm. Teresa can you hear me?' Teresa gave her customary blink for 'yes'. 'Good. Now I want you to move your finger once for yes and twice for no. Is that understood?'

Teresa's finger moved slightly. It was not much of a movement but it was there and it was deliberate.

'Would you like me to ask Mr O'Sullivan to leave?' he asked with a smile. Again the finger moved, this time with more definition and it moved twice. 'No, I don't think she does want you to leave.' The doctor beamed at her. 'Excellent progress, Teresa.'

Yes, it was encouraging, but Jimmy wouldn't have called two tiny movements after almost two years, excellent progress. Still, it was important to remain positive and he had to remind himself that he hadn't seen her at her worst.

'It is indeed. Great going, Tess. We'll soon have you up on the dance floor again,' he said, stroking her hand gently. He could see by the shine in her eyes that she was pleased.

'I'll be off then. See you tomorrow, Teresa,' the doctor said, picking up his charts and moving off to the next patient.

'And I've got something else that will please you,' Jimmy said, holding his mobile up in front of Teresa's eyes and showing her the photos of the flat.

*

It was about six weeks later that Jimmy received a call from the hospital. It was Dr Stevens' secretary, asking if Jimmy could call in to see the doctor that morning.

Jimmy was apprehensive. It sounded very formal the way the secretary had put it and left him with that nervous feeling in his stomach that was always induced when he was called before someone in authority, a headmaster, the police and, in this case, the doctor. What was it that could not wait until his usual visit?

He'd been very busy lately, what with the purchase of the flat, getting a grant from the council for the alterations and most of all trying to supervise the cowboys that they had sent to do them. Still it was progressing well and he hoped that he and Teresa could move in at the end of May.

He looked at his watch; it was nine-thirty. The doctor wanted to see him at eleven, plenty of time to give Mrs Jennings her lesson and be there with time to spare. He swung his clubs over his shoulder and headed out to the practice ground, where he knew his pupil would be waiting.

*

As he'd calculated, he arrived at the hospital just before eleven and went straight to the Neurology department.

'Good morning, Dr Stevens. You wanted to see me?' he asked, putting his head around the door.

'Yes, come in Mr O'Sullivan. I just wanted a quick word. I'm off on holiday tomorrow and I wanted to speak to you before I went.'

Jimmy sat down opposite the doctor's desk. He was used to this tiny office by now, with its clutter of papers and files all over the place. He wondered why the doctor's secretary didn't keep it tidier. Maybe she'd get a chance to clear it up while her boss was away.

'Has something happened? With Tess?'

'No, no, nothing like that. I was going to ring Teresa's husband, but then I thought it might be better speaking to you as you seem to be Teresa's chief carer these days.'

Jimmy nodded and waited. God, this chap rambled on a bit. When would he get to the point?

'It's something we received the other day. It made me think of Teresa.' He handed him a glossy brochure.

'What is it?'

'It's a Virtual Reality device. The sort of thing that's used in video games.'

Jimmy read the blurb: 'Relief for thousands of stroke sufferers. New virtual reality device will give patients freedom of speech.'

'What does that mean?'

'It's more or less what it says. The patient wears a head band that is linked to a computer. It monitors the eye movements and the wearer can use the computer to point to letters and words which are then fed through a voice synthesiser. It's in the early stages yet which is why the company that produce the machine want to know if we'd like to help with some trials.'

'You mean Tess could speak through a voice synthesiser? Like that scientist chap?'

'Steven Hawkins? Yes. It's not complicated; I'm sure she'd pick it up in no time. Basically it's a more sophisticated version of her old message board; she will still be using her eyes to communicate as before.'

'How long would the trials go on?'

'It says here, six months,' he replied, reading from the letter that had obviously accompanied the brochure. 'It's up to her, and you. There're a couple of others who might benefit from it, but I thought that, as Teresa is making such an effort at the moment, she might be a good guinea pig for them.'

Jimmy wasn't certain he liked the thought of Teresa being a guinea pig for anyone, but the idea was intriguing.

'Look, take that bumph with you and talk it over with her. If she's interested, let me know and I'll set it up.'

'Okay. I'll do that.'

'It's amazing what they're developing now. The latest thing, although it's still very much in its infancy, is a brain-computer interface, where a person's thoughts can be recorded and translated into actions.'

'What, you think something, so it happens?'

'Yes, more or less. For example if Teresa wanted to change the TV channel, she would just think BBC1 and it would go over to BBC1.'

'Instead of pestering the nurse all the time, or me.'

'Just so.'

'Sounds a bit like science fiction to me.'

Dr Stevens smiled. 'Well I've got a lot to get through today, so I'll leave it with you. If Teresa wants to go ahead with the trial, just let my secretary know and we'll set it up.' He paused and then added, 'You know I'm so pleased that son of hers tracked you down. Teresa had given up hope, you know; all she wanted was to die. You've given her back that hope.'

Jimmy looked at the doctor in surprise. He hadn't realised that Teresa had become so low that she wanted to end it all.

'Thanks Doctor. I'll tell her about the trial. Enjoy your holiday. You deserve it.' Dr Stevens certainly deserved a holiday; what a job, working with people whose prospects of recovery were so slight.

Jimmy walked along the corridor, just in time to see Michelle leaving. She stopped and waited for him.

'Hi Jimmy. How're things?'

'Okay. Another couple of weeks and the flat should be finished.'

'That's wonderful.'

'And Tess? What's she like, today?' He nodded towards Teresa's room.

'She's fine. We've gone through all the usual exercises this morning. I'm sure she's getting stronger all the time. Check out her face. I think the muscles in her face are starting to respond. I was telling her about a funny incident that happened at work yesterday and I'll swear she almost smiled. There was certainly some movement there.'

'Well I've got some good news for her, so I'll watch carefully and see if there's any reaction.'

'What good news?'

Jimmy showed her the brochure and explained what the doctor had said.

'That's brilliant, but what about afterwards? When the trial is over, will she still get to use the machine?'

'Damn. I never asked. I can't imagine they would give it to someone for six months then take it away again. Especially if it was working for them.'

'Well check anyway.' She gave him a peck on the cheek. 'I have to go. Mark's waiting for me. See you tomorrow.'

'Yes, I'll be here, as usual.'

CHAPTER 37

Teresa was sitting in her wheelchair on the patio. The early autumn sunshine was warm on her arms. It was hard to believe that less than a year ago she'd been begging Mark to help her end her life. Thank goodness he'd made her wait. She would never have believed that things could have improved so much. True, she was confined to her wheelchair and dependent on Angelina—the Central American woman who came in every morning to care for her—but, thanks to the efforts of her family, her world had opened up. The new technology had made such a difference; she could email her sons, she could surf the internet and she could look through the album of family photos, which Michelle had uploaded onto her computer. Admittedly it was still a slow process, but so what, she wasn't going anywhere.

She must remember to answer Alex's email today. She felt sad when she thought of her son, so far away. What a surprise his news had been; he and Baruti were to be married. She found it hard to imagine her son married, and to a man as well. Selfishly her first thought had been about grandchildren; there wouldn't be any grandchildren. Well, what did it matter as long as Alex was happy? Maybe Ian would get married and have children; that would be something to look forward to.

Alex's wedding was to take place in Johannesburg. They'd invited all the family to the wedding but only

Ian and Jenny, and Mark and Michelle were going. The doctor had advised against Teresa making such a long trip and to be honest she couldn't imagine how she'd cope on an aeroplane for twelve hours, even with Jimmy by her side. Her mother had said something similar; she'd used her arthritis as an excuse for not going.

Alex loved living out there; he said he could never return to the grey skies of England after Africa. The country had got into his blood. It was a long way but she'd have made the trip regardless, if she thought it was her only chance to see her son. But, the good news was that they were coming back to England for their honeymoon, just as soon as Baruti could get a visa. She would see him then. She was excited at the prospect of his visit. What would he think of her new house? And all the latest technology? Some days she felt like the bionic woman there were so many cables and switches attached to her and her wheelchair. It was wonderful. The movement had come back into three fingers now and last week, for the first time, she had been able to move her right arm. Of course it was the wheelchair that made so much difference—she no longer had to lie on her back looking at dead flies on the ceiling—she could sit up and she could move about the house. She could even go into the garden when the weather was nice.

She looked at the shafts of sunlight falling through the silver birch trees that bordered their patio, dappling the paving stones with a myriad of tiny lights. Already the leaves were beginning to change colour. Soon they would fall. How could Alex leave England for good? There was nowhere so lovely when the sun shone. Last weekend Jimmy had taken her to the south coast for the day; they'd parked on the cliffs and looked at the waves crashing below them. A brilliant sun had hung in the sky, turning the sea golden and fulmars screamed and swooped above their heads. She hadn't felt so happy in a long time.

Her sons had grown up. Even Ian had a steady girl-friend now. He'd brought her down to spend Christmas with them and surprised all the family. Teresa liked Jenny; she didn't stare at her as some people did when they first encountered her and she didn't speak to her as though she were deaf, or worse, an idiot. Teresa hoped she made Ian happy. She felt a wave of gratitude to her younger son; he'd never given up on her. He'd been determined to make her want to live and he'd succeeded.

The plump, homely figure of her carer moved into her line of sight, closely followed by the cat.

'HAVE YOU FED SMOKEY JOE?' Teresa typed.

'Of course, I've fed the cat. Can't you see how fat he's getting.' She picked up Smokey Joe and put him on Teresa's lap.

Angelina was a middle-aged woman from Venezuela, whose husband had disappeared in mysterious circumstances. She and her son had fled the country in 2006 and found refuge in England. Back in Caracas, she'd trained as a nurse, so she soon found work in the National Health Service. She was ideal for Teresa, who still needed daily care beyond that which Jimmy could give her: there were still medicines to administer and the food pump to operate. Although a physiotherapist came three times a week, Angelina was also there to monitor her exercises. Teresa knew she could never manage without her; if it were not for Angelina, Jimmy would have to give up work and stay with her full time. Teresa didn't want that, even if they'd had enough money; she wanted Jimmy to have a life away from her. From time to time she was still seized with the grim fear that he would tire of her and leave, despite the fact that he constantly told her how much he loved her and that he was going to make sure she got better. She didn't really believe that she'd ever be as she was before. Progress she could make, but she wasn't stupid, a complete recovery didn't seem feasible after all that the doctor had told them about her condition. She was content to make small improvements and to live here in this lovely flat with Jimmy; she didn't want anything more.

Teresa's answer came up on the screen: 'HE'S NOT FAT. HE'S JUST GOT THICK FUR. I'D LIKE TO SPEAK TO MARK. CAN YOU RING HIM, PLEASE, ANGELINA,' and a computerised voice read out her words. She hated the sound of that artificial voice; it made her realise what an automaton she had become, totally dependent on machines for any quality of life. Even Smokey Joe didn't like the automated voice and jumped down from her lap, with a loud meow.

'He'll be at work now, Teresa. I'll call him and ask him to come in when he's finished. Alright?'

'THANKS. A CUP OF TEA WOULD BE NICE.'

Angelina smiled. 'Mañana,' she said, as she did every time Teresa made the same request. 'For now, you'll have to make do with this.' She connected the food pump and regulated the amount that Teresa should receive. 'Rachel will be here this afternoon,' she added. 'You'll enjoy that.'

Angelina was right. She looked forward to Rachel Hammond's weekly visits. She had been very dismissive of the healer at first, but now she had to admit that whatever it was Rachel was doing to her, it did help her. By the time each session was over, Teresa felt so relaxed and pain free that she could almost imagine that there was nothing wrong with her. She knew it wasn't repairing the damage to her body but it made her feel less hopeless. Jimmy said that he always knew when Rachel had been to see her because Teresa glowed.

At first the electronic headband was not very comfortable, but she'd soon got used to it and the freedom it gave her was astounding. She could even watch television programmes on the computer without having to ask someone to take her into the lounge. It was amazing. The trial had gone well, so well in fact, that when the six months were up, they'd left her with the headband and the computer; they'd even promised to use her in further trials when they made any refinements.

There were developments in this field all the time. Ian had emailed her an article only last week, that explained how some scientists in Israel were working on a system whereby people, such as her, could learn to communicate by sniffing. She had smiled at that, a lopsided smile she knew, but Jimmy had been so happy the first time she'd managed it. It seemed that even the paralysed were still able to sniff because the soft palate, which regulated sniffing, was not controlled by nerves that passed through the spinal cord. So the damage that she'd suffered hadn't impaired that ability. She sniffed loudly, just to reassure herself. Unless the patient had suffered brain damage to the one, small part of the brain that controlled it, then sniffing remained possible. With that premise in mind, the young scientists invented a system whereby a patient with Locked-In Syndrome could dictate words onto a computer screen, much in the same way she did now, but by sniffing through a tube. A sensor would detect the changes in air pressure and translate it into words. They said the system could even be adapted to propel a wheelchair: two inward sniffs would propel it forward and two outward ones, back. But for now she'd have to be content with her electronic headband.

'Señora,' Angelina said, coming back into the room. 'I spoke to Mr Rushton. He doesn't start his shift until two o'clock, so he'll call in this morning.'

'THANK YOU, ANGELINA.'

That was good news. She'd been thinking about this for some time. She had to speak to him. She couldn't let this hang between them any longer. It wasn't fair. She knew Peter's death was a terrible accident but she'd treated Mark as though he was the culprit, as though he was solely to blame for the demise of their son. Her grief had engulfed her and left no room for anyone else. She realised now how wrong she'd been and she had to tell him. They had all been devastated when Peter died but she had been too angry to care about what others felt. Now she had to make amends. Slowly and patiently she composed what she wanted to say. The beauty of this new way of communicating was that she could prepare it beforehand, instead of leaving him to sit and wait while she torturously spelled it out letter by letter.

*

Her message was just finished when the doorbell rang. She knew it must be Mark. Ian was in Edinburgh, Michelle was at work, Jimmy was teaching and her mother always came round after lunch.

'Teresa. How are you? Angelina said you wanted to see me. I hope everything is alright,' her ex-husband said as he collapsed into the chair opposite her. He was wearing a tracksuit and from the beads of sweat on his rather flushed forehead, it looked as though he'd been running.

'EXERCISE?!!' she typed.

'Yes, don't look so surprised. I've decided I'm going to get fit. A five-mile run every morning. I've lost six pounds already,' he said, patting his stomach, with a look of self-satisfaction.

She gave him her lop-sided smile.

'So what do you want? Is something wrong?'

'NO. I WANTED TO APOLOGISE TO YOU.'

'Apologise? Whatever for?' If anyone should be apologising, it's me.'

She moved her finger and brought her message up onto the screen.

'What's this?' Mark asked, leaning forward so that he could read it more easily.

'DEAR MARK, I AM SO SORRY FOR THE WAY I TREATED YOU WHEN PETER DIED. I KNEW IT WASN'T YOUR FAULT. YOU WOULD NEVER HAVE DONE ANYTHING TO HURT OUR BEAUTI-FUL SON. BUT I WAS JUST SO ANGRY AND UN-HAPPY I HAD TO HIT OUT AT SOMEONE AND THAT SOMEONE WAS YOU. I WANTED YOU TO BE AS UNHAPPY AS I WAS.

I COULDN'T BELIEVE THAT YOU WERE THERE AND HE HAD DROWNED. I TOLD MY-SELF IT HAD TO BE YOUR FAULT. THAT YOU SHOULD HAVE SAVED HIM. BUT I KNOW THAT'S NOT THE CASE. IT NEVER WAS. THESE THINGS HAPPEN AND THERE IS NOTHING WE CAN DO ABOUT THEM.

I LOVED PETER SO MUCH, BUT I ALSO LOVED THE REST OF MY FAMILY AND I SHUT THEM OUT.

I HAVE HAD LOTS OF TIME TO THINK ABOUT MY LIFE SINCE THEN AND THAT'S WHY I HAVE TO TELL YOU THAT I DON'T BLAME YOU—I NEVER DID.

I'M SORRY MARK. PLEASE FORGIVE ME.

'Oh, Teresa, there is nothing to forgive.' He reached across and touched her hand. 'There is not a day goes by when I don't ask myself if I could have done anything differently, that day. And the truth is that I don't know. It all happened so quickly that I was stunned. I jumped in after him, but I was too late; I couldn't reach him. If a man, out walking his dog, hadn't leaned over and grabbed me, I'd have been swept away as well. There was nothing I could do. Nothing anybody could do.'

'I KNOW,' she typed. 'I'M SORRY TOO FOR ASK-ING YOU TO HELP ME END MY LIFE. I WAS WRONG TO DO THAT. I WAS WRONG TO PUT YOU UNDER SUCH PRESSURE. FORGIVE ME.'

'I told you things would get better. Aren't you glad we waited a bit?'

Teresa smiled at him and blinked once. Then typed, 'YOU'RE A GOOD MAN, MARK.'

'Would you like a cup of tea, Mr Rushton?' Angelina asked.

'No, thank you. I really should go home and get cleaned up before I go to work.' He bent over Teresa and kissed her forehead. 'Thank you,' he whispered.

*

She was impatient to get started on her novel. Jimmy had left at seven o'clock that morning; he had a full teaching schedule and wouldn't be home until five. She usually managed an hour's writing before it was time for her exercises then, when that was over, she did another hour. After that her day was interrupted by visits from her mother, Michelle, her neighbour—a young woman with a new baby—and sometimes even Mark. By the time it was evening she was tired and eager for Jimmy to come home.

It had been Michelle's idea that she start writing; she'd suggested she write about her experiences, let people know what it was like to be locked inside your own body. Teresa had made a start but then gave up. It was too depressing. It was bad enough having to live this half-life without going over it in minute details. She felt so bad that she couldn't continue. Someone else could tell that story; she was going to write about her other life, her other family, the ones that had saved her sanity in those early days.

Angelina carefully removed the food pump. 'I suppose you want the computer?' she asked, pushing it back into position, so that Teresa could see it. She adjusted the back rest and made sure Teresa's headband was firmly in place.

'Okay?'

Teresa blinked once. She waited until Angelina had gone into the kitchen then called up the file she'd been working on. She began to spell out her story:

"She pulled open the shutters and looked out over the lawn. Childish screams and cries of excitement were coming from the garden What were they up to now? She stepped outside. Tommy had the garden hose and, every time Petie came round the corner, he turned the hose on him and soaked him. The dog thought this was a great game and ran madly up and down, barking wildly..."

AUTHOR'S NOTE

The characters and events in this story are wholly ficti-tious, however I wouldn't have been able to write it without the help of a number of articles about Locked-In Syndrome on the internet and Jean-Dominque's moving account of his own experiences as a locked-in patient. I have also taken the liberty to describe new technological developments, which at the time of writing were not widely available and some still at the prototype stage.

*

Thank you for taking the time to read LOVE IS ALL. If you enjoyed it, please consider telling your friends or posting a short review on Amazon. Word of mouth is an author's best friend and much appreciated.

Thank you, Joan Fallon

BIBLIOGRAPHY

Marie-Aurélie Bruno, Jan L Bernheim, Didier Ledoux, Frédéric Pellas, Athena Demertzi, Steven Laureys. "A Survey on Self-Assessed Well-Being in a Cohort of Chronic Locked-In Syndrome Patients: Happy Majority, Miserable Minority." BMJ Open, 23 February 2011 DOI:10.1136/bmjopen-2010-000039

Jean-Dominique Bauby "The Diving Bell and the Butterfly" Harper Perennial 2004

"Not to be Sniffed At" Technology article on the research of Dr Noam Sobel, in the Economist, December 11th, 2010